EMP AFTERMATH

Broken World

Chaotic World

Dangerous World

Divided World

Collapsed World

Lawless World

This is a work of fiction. Names, characters, places and incidents either are the product of imagination or are used fictitiously. Any resemblance to actual persons, living or dead, events or locales, is entirely coincidental.

RELAY PUBLISHING EDITION, MAY 2023
Copyright © 2023 Relay Publishing Ltd.

All rights reserved. Published in the United Kingdom by Relay Publishing. This book or any portion thereof may not be reproduced or used in any manner whatsoever without the express written permission of the publisher except for the use of brief quotations in a book review.

Grace Hamilton is a pen name created by Relay Publishing for co-authored Post-Apocalyptic projects. Relay Publishing works with incredible teams of writers and editors to collaboratively create the very best stories for our readers.

www.relaypub.com

EMP AFTERMATH BOOK FOUR

DIVIDED WORLD

GRACE HAMILTON

BLURB

They went looking for their daughter. They found a civil war…

Laurel and her husband Bear are finally reunited. But South Minneha Hospital is no longer the haven it once was. Together, they take on a new quest: leaving the hospital behind, and setting off to find their daughter, Mae.

Accompanied by Trent and Jess, Laurel and Bear leave the safety of Minneha and begin their search, knowing only that Sergeant Mae Petersen was serving in the US Army when the EMP hit. The Internet is just a memory, and phones are now quaint relics. Finding out where one soldier was stationed—and where she might be now—will take a miracle.

Laurel is up for the challenge, but the world changed while she was fighting to save South Minneha. Roving bands of gunmen have given way to organized paramilitary groups. The land she and her companions must cross is contested by two factions, the Militia and the Freemen. Tensions are rising, lines are being drawn, and one fact is painfully clear…

If Laurel and Bear are to reunite their family, they're going to have to fight.

CONTENTS

1. Laurel — 1
2. Bear — 9
3. Laurel — 15
4. Mae — 24
5. Laurel — 31
6. Mae — 36
7. Laurel — 41
8. Mae — 51
9. Bear — 56
10. Mae — 67
11. Laurel — 75
12. Mae — 82
13. Laurel — 90
14. Bear — 99
15. Laurel — 111
16. Bear — 118
17. Laurel — 127
18. Mae — 135
19. Bear — 143
20. Trent — 151
21. Mae — 160
22. Laurel — 170
23. Laurel — 183
24. Laurel — 191
25. Bear — 199
26. Laurel — 204
27. Mae — 210
28. Bear & Laurel — 217
29. Trent — 227
30. Mae — 234
31. Bear — 243
32. Laurel — 253
33. Mae — 260
34. Bear — 267
35. Cornell — 274

36. Laurel	278
37. Bear	285
38. Laurel	291
End of Divided World	301
Thank you	303
About Grace Hamilton	305
Sneak Peek: Collapsed World	307
Sneak Peek: Burned World	317
Also By Grace Hamilton	319
Want more?	333

1

LAUREL

"All set?" Laurel crouched down and tucked the blanket a little closer around her mom's legs.

"Stop fussing, darling." Her mom smiled and tweaked her index finger beneath Laurel's chin. She was wearing her customary bright red lipstick and a splash of mascara, but her complexion was paler than normal.

"It wouldn't hurt to wait until it's a little warmer out." Laurel glanced at the large glass windows that enclosed the hospital foyer. Still only March, and while it was sunny outside, it was also bitterly cold. Especially when the wind blew.

For a long moment, Laurel's mother looked at her. Her eyes softened, as if she was feeling sorry about something. But then she said, "Nonsense, come on. I need some air. I've been stuck inside for weeks."

Standing up, Laurel moved to the back of her mom's wheelchair and flexed her fingers on the handles. Since her return to South Minneha, no one had ventured outside unless it was for hunting, scavenging, or one of their weekly trips to look for townsfolk who might need medical help; it had been too cold for leisurely walks. But the last snow fell more than a week ago now, and the ground was starting to thaw. So Laurel had promised her mother a short outing. Looking at her mom's diminutive frame, however, she was beginning to wonder whether it was a good idea.

That morning, once the sun was up, and the snow a little softer, Bear and Henry had cleared something of a path around the building using Henry's special salt mixture and two large shovels. Laurel intended to start at the front, exiting from the foyer, and loop around until they were back where they'd started. She had packed a thermos of coffee and some cookies for them to enjoy when they reached the bench that looked out at the forest. *If* her mom was doing okay.

Over the past few weeks, she'd been quieter than normal. When she caught Laurel watching her, she made an effort to smile and pretend to be upbeat. But Laurel knew she was hiding the true extent of her discomfort. As Bear pulled open the doors for them, she made a mental note to discuss her mother's meds with Hannah later. The new combination they'd started her on was never going to have the same effect as the trial meds had, but Laurel would have expected to see at least *some* improvement.

"See you soon." Laurel allowed her hand to graze Bear's as she walked past him. He smiled at her and nodded.

Once he was out of earshot, Laurel's mom reached up and patted Laurel's hand. "Things seem to be going well between the two of you?"

Pulling her scarf tighter around her neck, Laurel laughed. "Well, that took all of thirty seconds."

"What did?" Her mom folded her arms around her middle.

"Asking about me and Bear. We've been out of the building less than a minute."

"Well," her mom chuckled, "I don't get any other chance to ask you. Lately, it seems that wherever you are, he's only a few steps behind you." She looked over her shoulder and gave Laurel a knowing glance. "So…?"

"So, nothing." Laurel pushed the chair over a difficult patch of ground and winced at the twinge in her ankle. Although the injury had healed, she was still experiencing discomfort and it was starting to irritate her. She was *not* used to being unable to shake something when she wanted to. Several times, Bear had offered to give her some PT, but she'd refused, telling him it would sort itself out soon. Now, however, she was beginning to wonder whether she should give in and allow him to help.

"Not nothing." Her mom's tone had become sharper, the way it was when she was about to tell Laurel off about something. "Laurel, the world crumbled around our ears. Bear came all the way here from Thunder Bay to find you. You were the first thing he thought of. *You.* That has to mean something."

Laurel pressed her lips together and pushed her glasses up the bridge of her nose; the cold was making them slip. "Maybe, but do we need to figure it out right now?"

She expected her mom to answer right away, but instead there was a long pause. She watched her mother's shoulders gently rise and fall as she took several deep breaths. "I'd like you to figure it out before—"

"Coffee," Laurel interrupted. She knew what her mother was about to say and, not for the first time, stopped her from saying it. She couldn't hear talk like that. Not now. Not ever. Not after such a long, hard journey to get back here. "I brought coffee and cookies. We're nearly at the bench. Do you feel up to stopping for a snack break?"

After a short, sharp sigh, her mom replied, "When have I ever turned down cookies?" then laced her gloved fingers together in her lap and remained quiet while they made their way around the side of the hospital building toward the picturesque lawn and forest out back.

"I have to say," Laurel spoke up—feeling the need to fill the silence with words. "You know I'm not Robert Sullivan's biggest fan, but it was a good idea to keep this area open. Part of the hospital grounds. It's good for the soul to be close to nature."

"Is that a scientific opinion?" her mom asked, slightly sharp.

"Yes, actually." They were almost at the bench. Bear and Henry had cleared a path directly to it. On the brow of the dip that led down toward the trees, it gave a perfect view of the forest and the sky beyond. "There was a study. I remember reading about it—"

Mid-sentence, Laurel stopped.

"Did you hear that?" She stepped sideways, so she was standing next to her mom, and strained her ears. "I swear I heard something." She looked down at her mother. She too was listening intently, but shook her head.

"No, dear. I can't hear anything."

"I'm sure…." Laurel peered down the slope at the trees. The spaces between them were dark and uninviting. She'd ventured in there a couple of times with Bear and Trent on their hunting expeditions, but on the whole, had left food gathering to them; they were better at it and Trent seemed to revel in the alone time with Bear. He hadn't said anything, he was too sweet a kid for that, but Laurel could tell he was finding it hard to adjust to sharing Bear's attention with someone else.

She was shaking her head, about to take out the coffee, when something moved in the periphery of her vision. She stepped forward, watching the tree line.

"Is someone there?" her mother asked, following Laurel's gaze.

"I'm not sure." She turned and flicked the brakes on her mom's chair. "Mom, can you wait here a moment?"

"I can't exactly make a run for it," her mother quipped.

Striding away from the path Bear cleared for her, Laurel inched through the thinning snow until she was a few feet away from the bench. There. Something was definitely moving.

Reaching for her gun with one hand, she waved the other and called, "Hello? If there's somebody there, I'm a doctor. This is a hospital. Do you need help?"

For a moment, nothing moved. A cold breeze whipped across Laurel's face. Then a voice carried forward on the wind. "Help! Help! My sister-in-law. She needs help!"

As Laurel took another step forward, a figure emerged from the trees. A woman. Waving frantically, she called again, "My sister-in-law needs help. Please!"

"Mom," Laurel turned to her mother. "I'll be right back. Wait there."

Then she charged down the slope in the direction of the trees.

By the time Laurel reached her, the woman was no longer alone. She'd been joined by another, who was clutching her stomach and seemed barely able to stand. When she looked up and moved her arm, Laurel realized why.

"You're pregnant...." Laurel rushed forward and took the woman's other arm. In answer, she simply groaned and clutched her stomach harder.

"Her name's Tory. She's thirty-six weeks. I'm Kate. She's my brother's wife." The woman who'd shouted at Laurel from the trees adjusted her friend's weight on her shoulder and winced.

"Okay, Kate. We're not far from the hospital. Let's get Tory inside. Is your brother—" Laurel glanced back at the trees, but Kate replied with a solemn shake of the head. Laurel nodded in understanding, then motioned for them to start moving. Slowly, they began to help Tory up the slope.

"Tory, I'm a doctor. Can you tell me what happened? When did you start experiencing pain?"

Tory breathed in hard, gritted her teeth, then replied, "This morning. It just started this morning."

"Are you having contractions?"

"I don't know." Tory gripped Laurel's arm a little harder. "How do I know?"

"Does the pain come in waves? Or is it constant?"

"Constant. All the time. No waves." Tory winced and wobbled, but Kate steadied her. Then, stopping, she looked up at Laurel. "This is a hospital, so you can help me? Right?" Her voice wavered and moisture sprang to her eyes. "I can't lose my baby."

"We can help you, Tory." Laurel nodded firmly. "We just need to get you inside."

As they drew closer to the bench, and Laurel's mom realized what was happening, Laurel saw her push herself gingerly out of her chair and shuffle to the bench itself. "Mom," she called, "sit back in your chair!"

But when they reached her, her mother simply said, "This young woman needs it more than I do. Take her inside and send someone back for me. I'll be fine for a few minutes."

Laurel bit her lower lip. Her mom had already been outside for almost half an hour. But there was no way Tory would make it to the foyer without the chair.

"All right," she said, lowering Tory into the wheelchair. "But I'll send someone right away." She grabbed the blanket and wrapped it firmly around her mom's shoulders. "Just hang tight, okay?"

Her mother's answer was drowned out by another pained cry from Tory. "It hurts," she moaned. "Please. Help me. It hurts."

"Help her!" Kate grabbed Laurel's elbow.

"Okay, Tory. Here we go." Laurel looked briefly at her mom. "I'll send Henry right back." Then she nodded, and began pushing.

As they approached the foyer doors, Laurel began to shout. By the time they reached them, Bulldog—who'd been waiting for their return—had heaved the doors open and was calling for backup.

"Bulldog, this woman's in labor. I need Bear's side room. Is the fire lit?"

Bulldog nodded firmly. "He's been keeping it lit for emergencies."

"Good." The chair was moving easier and faster now that it was on the shiny hospital floor. Laurel was already halfway across the room. Looking back over her shoulder, she yelled, "Bulldog, please go get my mom! She's out there alone. I had to take her chair."

Bulldog wavered for a moment. "You don't need help?"

"I'll fetch help. You fetch my mom." She turned around and backed into the double doors, wheelchair in front of her, pulling Tory through them. As they swung closed, she saw Bulldog stride off into the snow. He didn't have a chair with him, which meant he was planning on *carrying* her mom back inside. *Mom will love that!*

In the hallway, Laurel stopped and pointed at a closed door. "Kate, take Tory in there and sit her by the fire. I'm going to get some nurses to help us. I'll be right with you."

Kate's eyes widened, but Laurel placed her hand on the woman's arm. "I'll be *right* with you. But we can't do this single-handed. We need help. Okay?"

"Kate, I'm okay. Let her go," Tory panted.

Looking at her friend, Kate nodded. "All right. But hurry, doctor. Please."

Laurel waited barely a second before sprinting for the dorms. As she burst into the room, a few dozen faces looked up at her. Some were playing cards, some reading. Her eyes landed on Chris Jenkins. "Chris, where are Hannah and Janet?"

Chris slowly stood up, worry creasing his face. "Cataloging medication, I think. Is everything—"

"I need them." Laurel had already turned and was heading back to the door. Over her shoulder, she called, "Tell them I have a mother in premature labor and that we're going to need to deliver a baby." She paused at the door and fixed her eyes on Chris.

"Tell them to hurry!"

2
BEAR

"It starts here." Henry pushed open the door to the second-floor corridor and instantly wrinkled his nose.

Bracing himself, Bear sniffed the air and slammed a hand over his mouth. "That's foul."

"Oh my god," Trent groaned, stepping behind Bear as if it might shield him from the smell. "What *is* that?"

"My guess would be skunks." Henry had taken a rag from his pocket and was holding it to his face.

"Skunks? In here?" Trent looked from Henry to Bear.

"It's possible," Bear replied. "They usually mate when the snow starts to thaw. Could have come here looking for somewhere warm and cozy to do their business."

"Like a stinky skunk love pad?" Trent chuckled at himself and then began to cough when the smell reached his nose again.

"Something like that." Bear pulled his fleece up to cover his nose and tried to breathe only through his mouth. "We need to find their den, and figure out how they're getting into the building."

"Do we?" Trent looked as if he was ready to run back the way they'd come. "Can't we just seal off this floor?"

Shaking his head, Henry answered, "Don't want them finding their way into other spaces." He jerked his thumb, indicating that Bear and Trent should follow him, and stepped farther into the ward.

"Which ward is this?" Bear asked, tugging Trent's elbow to make the young teenager follow him.

"Oncology." Henry had stopped in front of a slightly open door. "This was Deb's room." He pushed it and watched it swing open, then walked in and checked under the bed. When he stood up again, he looked toward the window. "Most nights while you and Laurel were gone, she watched for you from this window. When she couldn't make it upstairs to the roof."

Leaving the room, Bear indicated that Trent should go check the nurses' station opposite while he and Henry continued to check patients' old rooms.

"How's she doing?" he asked after a few minutes of silent searching. "Deb? How is she?"

Without turning to look at Bear, Henry's shoulders tensed. "Not good." He released a small sigh. "But she doesn't want Laurel to know."

Pressing his lips together, Bear swept his fingers through his hair. It needed a good trim, as did his beard. During the winter months, they had been keeping him warm. But now the cold snap was starting to break, he might be brave enough to go for a more clean-shaven look.

"She's tired, Bear." Henry turned to face him and looked up to meet his eyes. "She thinks she has to keep going for Laurel, but she's tired."

Noticing Trent was back at his side, Bear patted the boy's shoulder; he'd grown very fond of Deb and, although he was aware she wasn't well, this might have been the first time he heard anyone talk about her like this.

To Bear's surprise, Trent said quietly, "My nan got tired toward the end." His usually broad grin had dropped into something sadder and smaller. "She had cancer too. One day, she said she'd had enough and didn't want the drugs anymore. She stopped taking them. She was happier after that, but she didn't stay long."

Closing his eyes, Henry nodded and turned his face away.

Bear gripped Trent's shoulder. As they continued their way down the ward, he took a deep breath and said to Henry, "I'll talk to Laurel."

Henry didn't stop walking, just nodded again. Slowly. "Thank you."

Bear swallowed hard. He knew he had to do it: talk to Laurel. But he had no idea *how* he was going to do it. Usually, she was one of the few people he could count on to be ferociously honest. Frank. Upfront. She'd always believed in being honest and open with her patients. And in return, she encouraged them to be open with her too. With her mom, however, she was different. She wasn't behaving like a doctor, she was behaving like a daughter. And Bear needed to find a way to help her bridge that gap.

Changing the subject slightly, as they neared the double doors at the back of the ward, Henry said, "Aren't you two supposed to be heading off soon? To look for your daughter?"

Bear pressed his lips together. Henry was right; they were supposed to be leaving soon. When they returned to South Minneha, they had talked about it. They decided; as soon as the snow began to melt, they'd leave. But for the past few weeks, Laurel had refused to talk about it. Whenever Bear broached the subject of looking at a map and deciding their plan of action, she found an excuse to be somewhere else or to talk about something else.

It was because she didn't want to think about leaving her mom, he knew that. But he also knew that if Mae was camped out somewhere, she too could be planning to start moving with the turn of the season. And that would make their task of finding her a million times more difficult.

"What's through here?" Trent asked as they pushed the doors.

"The sky corridor." Henry waved an arm at the space they found themselves in — a large, wide corridor with glass walls on either side. On one side, the front lawn, the fountain, and the parking lot. On the other, the courtyard space in the center of the square hospital building. Bear walked to the glass and peered down. A slightly woozy sensation gripped his stomach but he pushed it aside. Down below, the snow was thinning, and for the first time in weeks, the sky was pale blue instead of white or gray. He could just about make out the path they'd cleared for Laurel and Deb's walk.

"Where does it go?" Trent asked. "And how come it doesn't smell in here?"

Bear looked up and down the corridor. Good question. They'd found no trace of the skunks on the oncology ward, but they had to have come from somewhere.

"Let's check down here, then we'll circle back." Henry had reached the end of the hall and another set of doors. This time, they opened onto a carpeted space that looked like it would be more at home in a movie theater than a hospital.

"VIP offices." Henry rolled his eyes and walked over to one, sticking his head in, then shaking it.

Trent wrinkled his nose. "Smells here too."

Ahead, Bear's eyes settled on a gold plaque bearing a name he recognized: Robert Sullivan. He'd never met the man, but had heard all about what he did to Laurel and her mom. Gritting his teeth, he strode over and knocked the door with his elbow to open it.

Instantly, the smell intensified.

"There." Trent's eyes had widened at the stench, but he was pointing at the desk in the middle of the room. He ducked down and pointed again. "There, look. Underneath. A heap of papers all shredded up."

Bear stooped to look too. Trent was right. The skunks were nesting in Robert Sullivan's office. Coughing, Bear straightened up and turned to find Henry standing next to him. "Well, well, well," Henry said, almost smiling. "How appropriate. Couldn't think of a nicer man to host a bunch of skunks."

"How'd they get in?" Bear mused, stepping forward, concentrating hard on not letting any air past his nostrils.

"There…." Trent's voice had gone up an octave, the way it always did when he had an idea he was pleased with. "Is that an AC vent?" He was looking up at the ceiling.

Bear moved over and raised his eyes.

"Sure is." Henry folded his arms. A tall bookcase was positioned beneath the vent, and the grate that should seal it off was lying on the ground.

"So they're in the ventilation system?" Bear groaned and turned to march back out, because his eyes were starting to water.

"How the heck do we get them out?" Trent asked, following Bear and Henry as they walked quickly back toward the glass-walled corridor.

"Good question." Henry folded his arms. They were both staring at Bear, waiting for an answer.

His mind ticking slower than normal, because he was thinking of Deb and Laurel at the same time, Bear reeled through their options. "We need to seal off exits to all the wards, offices, rooms…. Henry, do you have a blueprint showing all the vents?"

Henry nodded in response.

"Good. Right, so we'll seal off the exits and that should force them back outside."

"Seal them off *how*?" Trent asked, raising his eyebrows.

"I haven't quite figured that out yet." Bear rubbed his beard and chewed on the side of his cheek. "But I'll think of something."

"You mean *skunk*thing?" Trent hesitated barely a second before his lips spread into a huge grin and he started laughing at himself.

Shaking his head, Bear laughed too. "Yeah, kid. *Skunk*thing ingenious."

3

LAUREL

When Laurel entered the room, she found Tory by the fire, still in the wheelchair. She looked up, eyes wide. But before she could say anything, she let out a wall-rattling cry and clutched her stomach. Reaching for Kate's hand, she struggled to catch her breath. Her cheeks were flushed, her hair sticky against her face. She shook her head. "I can't do this, Kate. Not here. Not like this. Not without Will."

Laurel waited a moment, watching the two friends as Kate looked into Tory's eyes and placed her hands firmly on her shoulders. "Yes, you can. You have to. Will would want you to."

As Tory pressed her lips together, clearly trying not to cry, Kate spun around and fixed her gaze on Laurel. "Can you help her? Please?"

Nodding, Laurel tugged off her coat, hat, and scarf, and tossed them onto a nearby chair. The private ward Bear had created, and her mom had been using, was warm and dimly lit. Under other circumstances, it would have been a lovely place to give birth. Quiet. Lit by the flicker of the fire. Especially with a birthing pool and some whale music. But, scanning the room, a knot formed in Laurel's chest. It had been a long time since she'd delivered a baby. They were massively underequipped, without ultrasound or fetal heart rate monitors to rely on, and she had a strong feeling that this wasn't just a case of premature labor.

"Kate, help Tory out of her outdoor clothes, let's get her comfortable on the bed and I'll examine her." Laurel pointed to the bed, which was close enough to the fire to ensure Tory wouldn't be chilled without her layers of outdoor clothing.

Quickly, Kate followed Laurel's instructions, helping Tory stand up and easing her out of her coat.

"We'll need to lose the bottom half too," Laurel said gently, gesturing to Tory's thick winter pants. "But you can cover up with the sheet while I wash up."

Heading for the sink in the corner of the room, Laurel hurriedly sanitized her hands with the alcohol rub they—thankfully—hadn't run out of yet. Tory was letting out another fierce groan when the door swung open and Janet entered, closely followed by Hannah.

"We brought supplies," Janet said, handing Laurel a surgical gown, then fastening her own. "Henry's bringing hot water."

Behind Janet, Hannah was pushing a metal instrument cart. She took the stethoscope from her neck and handed it to Laurel.

"Tory, I'm going to examine you first, then I'll try and listen to the baby. Is that all right?"

Tory nodded, pressing her lips together as pain continued to roll through her.

"All right, I'm sorry if my hands are cold." Laurel smiled and began to feel Tory's stomach. "Did you have any of your prenatal checks before the power went out?"

Tory gripped the sheet below her and breathed out hard. "Just two."

"But she's been taking her vitamins," Kate interjected quickly. "And the baby's been kicking and moving this whole time. So, that's a good thing. Right?"

Laurel smiled. "Absolutely."

"Is thirty-six weeks too early?" Tory looked from Laurel to Janet, who was standing at Laurel's side.

"*Technically* thirty-six weeks is premature," Janet answered. "But did you know that in some countries, like France, they give mothers a due *month* instead of a due *date*?"

Tory's eyes narrowed, as if she didn't quite understand the implication.

"So, if we were in Europe, this would be completely normal." She smiled, but Tory didn't look any more at ease.

As she'd listened to Janet, Laurel had been trying to assess the baby's position. "Tory, I'm going to have a listen now, okay?" As the room hushed, Laurel listened hard. She waited. Moved the stethoscope. Her chest tightened.

When she stood up, she smiled and made sure her face showed nothing but calm. "Tory, I can hear your baby's heartbeat. It's strong and regular."

Tory let out a whoosh of a sigh, reaching to grip Kate's hand. "Good. Thank God. Good."

"However, I believe baby is currently in what we call a breech position."

There was a moment's silence, then Kate said loudly, "That means they're the wrong way up. Right?"

"It does." Laurel opened her mouth to continue but Tory interrupted.

"Doesn't that mean I need a c-section? Can you do that here?" She looked around the room, clearly horrified by the idea. "You can't do that here. You can't cut me open...."

"Tory...." Janet stepped in and reached for Tory's other hand. "You need to stay calm for the baby. Take a deep breath, that's it, one-two-three...."

As Janet tried to calm Tory's breathing, there was a knock on the door. Hannah ran to answer it, and Laurel saw Henry's arms appear, presenting a large metal container of water.

"It's already warm. It won't take long to boil." Hannah hurried to the fireplace and positioned the container carefully so it was hugged by the flames.

A little calmer, Tory wiped her forehead with the back of her hand and looked at Laurel. "What do we do?"

"I can try to turn the baby naturally. It will be uncomfortable, but baby coming out head first really is the safest way. So, we'll give it a go. Yes?"

"And if you can't turn them?" Kate asked quietly.

Not allowing her smile to waver, Laurel straightened her shoulders and tried to look like a midwife who'd done this a thousand times before. "Then we'll come up with a Plan B."

Stepping away from the bed, Laurel gestured for Janet to follow her.

"Have you done ECV before?" Janet asked, folding her arms in front of her chest; she was wearing her concerned face.

Laurel shook her head. "I volunteered at a women's clinic in the Middle East, but it was mostly prenatal. I haven't dealt with a birthing mother since my residency rotation in obstetrics. Even then I think I did one, maybe two, ECVs. And not while the mother was in labor."

"I've seen it done several times. I was a temp nurse on an obstetrics ward a few years back. But I haven't done it myself."

"Okay." Laurel breathed out slowly. "Hannah?"

Hannah shook her head. "I've only read about it."

"Then we better hope my muscle memory is up to scratch." Laurel shook her hands at her sides, then took off her glasses. She didn't need her eyes for this; she needed to feel, not see.

"Tory, you're only a few centimeters dilated, so it's a good time to do this. It's going to feel very uncomfortable. If the pain gets too much, you tell me. Okay?" Laurel placed her hands on Tory's stomach. Tory nodded. "Okay, here we go."

As Laurel began to press down on Tory's stomach, Tory began to groan. The greater Laurel's pressure, the louder Tory's discomfort. She reached for Kate and gripped her hand. Laurel tried to tune out everything but the feel of the baby. Janet's calm words, Hannah's sorting of meds and towels, Kate telling Tory to be brave.

Laurel's heart thumped in her chest. It wasn't working. It wasn't going to work. Then, suddenly, it did. "Here we go!" she cried, unable to hide her own relief. "Almost there, Tory. Hold on…. There!"

Laurel stood back from the bed, her arms aching with the effort of having to physically encourage the baby to move its position.

When she looked at Tory, tears were streaming down her cheeks, but she was smiling. "You did it?"

"No." Laurel put her hand firmly on Tory's shoulder. "*We* did it."

Chuckling a little, her face finally brighter, Janet leaned in and, offering Tory a bottle of water, said, "And now, the hard part… are you ready?"

Tory took a long sip, then nodded. "Ready as I'll ever be."

For over an hour, Tory made little progress. Laurel had only just asked Hannah to go and find out how her mom was doing, because she anticipated the baby taking at least the rest of the day to make an appearance, when Tory's contractions worsened.

Within minutes, she was fully dilated. And before Laurel had a chance to be anything other than calm, a tiny, crying baby was in Tory's arms.

Smiling, laughing, and crying all at the same time, Laurel put her arm around Janet and hugged her as they watched the new mother kiss her baby daughter's head. After her initial lung-testing cry, the baby settled and became quiet. Tory stroked her face. "She looks like Will," she breathed.

Kate, who was crying so much Laurel was surprised she could even see the baby, replied, "She sure does. But let's hope she doesn't get his nose, huh?"

Laughing, the two women pressed their heads together as Kate climbed onto the bed and sat next to her sister-in-law.

Pulling gently away from Laurel, Janet said softly, "I just need to take baby and clean her up. All right? I'll be over here. You'll see her the whole time."

Hesitantly, Tory held out her arms and allowed Janet to take her daughter from them.

"Have you thought of a name?" Laurel wet a damp cloth and passed it to Kate so she could wipe Tory's sticky brow.

"Will said if the baby was a girl, he wanted to call her Beatrix." Tory smiled and shook her head. "I hated it when he suggested it, but now…." She looked over toward Janet.

"I think it's perfect." Laurel hugged her arms around her own waist. "Baby Beatrix."

From over by the fire, Janet called, "Well, Miss Beatrix is small but perfectly formed." Swaddling the baby in a clean blanket, she brought her back to Tory. "Congratulations, Mom. You did great."

Watching Tory cuddle Beatrix, Laurel was suddenly very aware of how warm the room was. Important for baby, but almost stifling now she'd come down from the adrenaline of the labor.

"I'll be right back. I just need some air." She nodded at Janet, who'd taken an empty chart and was writing down Beatrix's measurements.

"I'll help Mom try a feed," Janet replied.

Laurel smiled gratefully and ducked out of the room. In the corridor, she leaned against the cool wall and a chill went through her. So many things could have gone wrong. In her head, her mother's voice told her: *Laurel, women have been having babies for generations without any fancy equipment,* but even so… while she'd had to improvise in plenty of hairy situations as a field medic, she'd never had to do so with mothers and babies. It was something she couldn't bear the thought of: breaking bad news to a new mother. And she was incredibly thankful she hadn't had to do so today.

"Laurel? Are you okay?" Hannah rounded the corner and hurried over, clearly worried something had happened.

"Everything's fine." Laurel smiled. "Baby's here, and she's perfect."

Hannah's eyes widened. "Well, that took an unexpected turn. I thought we'd be here all night."

"Me too." Laurel squeezed Hannah's arm. "But she's okay."

Breathing out a loud breath, Hannah leaned on the wall too and the pair of them slid down so they were sitting with their legs outstretched. Rubbing her upper arms, Hannah said, "I saw your mom, she's fine. She wasn't too happy with Bulldog for carrying her back to the building." She smiled and bit back a laugh. "But she's playing cards with the boys. And she's insisting Tory and the baby keep her room."

Laurel tilted her head to the side and rubbed her neck. Of course, her mother would sacrifice her own comfort for others.

"She'll be all right in the main dorm. We'll make sure she gets a bed close to the fire." Hannah met Laurel's eyes. She'd been looking after Laurel's mom since the two of them first met on the oncology ward, and continued to be the one her mom trusted the most with her care. Even more than she trusted Laurel sometimes.

"Laurel...." Hannah breathed in sharply and turned, angling herself so she was facing Laurel. There was a determined glint in her eyes, as if she was about to say something she'd been meaning to say for a long time. "Your mom—"

"We better check on Tory." Laurel sprang to her feet. Hannah probably wanted to talk about her mom's meds. As her doctor, she definitely needed to catch up about them, but as her daughter, it was a subject she didn't want to discuss right now. "If you want to get back to the dorm, Janet and I can handle things here."

Hannah clambered to her feet. Her eyes traced Laurel's face. She wrinkled her nose and smiled thinly. "All right," she said. "If you're sure?"

"Absolutely." Laurel turned toward the door. "We'll shout if we need you."

She was pushing the door open when Hannah said, "Laurel? Maybe later we can talk about your mom? About her meds? It's been a while since we've had a proper conversation about them. About her."

Laurel paused, palm flat on the door. "Yes. Of course. Later."

She waited a beat, for Hannah's footsteps to head away from her, back down the corridor, then sighed. A knot had formed in her throat. Telling herself it was the result of nothing but the emotion of watching Tory give birth, Laurel straightened her shoulders, put her glasses back on, and returned to baby Beatrix.

4

MAE

"Captain, we've been on the road for three days. Are you able to share where we're going?" Mae asked as she jogged up to Cornell's elbow. She watched his face carefully as she waited for his reply.

Pausing, making what Mae thought was a pretty deliberate show of tucking his hands into his belt so that his jacket exposed his gun, Cornell narrowed his eyes at her.

Trying not to show any flicker of nervousness, Mae stood up straight and put her arms by her sides. "Sir, forgive my directness, but the rest of the troops are beginning to feel uneasy."

"You don't like my style of leadership, Sergeant Peterson?" Cornell's jaw twitched. He had a large, square head, closely shaved hair and beard, and unnervingly blue eyes.

Mae opened her mouth then closed it again; there was no good way to answer that question. Cornell had never liked her and, although Mae was certain he didn't know for sure about her relationship with Neil, he *suspected* something had happened between the two of them. And Cornell was not the kind of captain who'd take that lightly.

Thinking of Captain Neil Mackenzie, Mae swallowed hard; she still couldn't believe he'd simply walked away without saying a word to her. Everyone was sticking to the story, of course—that he'd gone to find his wife and kids—but she *knew* him. He wouldn't leave without saying goodbye to her.

"Well?" Cornell was waiting for an answer.

"I just think it's prudent for more than one person to know our planned course of action." She spoke slowly and firmly, meeting his eyes but ensuring her tone remained measured enough that she couldn't be accused of being disrespectful.

Raising his voice, looking over her head at the others, Cornell barked, "You will be told what you need to know when you need to know it. And that's the last I have to say on the matter." Gesturing to the carts containing the gear they'd brought from the barracks, he signaled for the group to keep moving.

Stepping back into line, Mae clenched her teeth and concentrated on quickening her pace. Noticing someone close to her elbow, she turned her head to find Gideon — the only soldier from her original squad — next to her. "What's he up to?" Gideon asked through thin lips.

"I don't know, but I don't like it. Neil would never have simply handed over the reins to Cornell. Never." Mae glanced at Gideon. He knew about her relationship with their previous captain, but he'd never said anything to anyone. She knew that. She trusted him.

"Rumor is they had a disagreement about what Cornell wanted to do with the unit, so Mackenzie split, using his family as an excuse for leaving."

Mae shook her head. A lump had formed in her throat but she pushed it aside. "I don't believe it." She shook her head.

"So, what are you going to do?" Gideon adjusted his pack on his shoulders, staring in front of them at the back of Cornell's head.

"What can I do?" Mae asked. "Cornell's in charge now."

"Stop!" Captain Cornell's deep, gravelly voice broke through the low chatter of the group. Once again, the carts stopped, horses scraping their hooves frustratedly at the stop-start motion.

"Gas station. There. On the left." Cornell signaled ahead with his arm. The road they'd been traveling on was wide but hemmed in by trees. It was an unlikely place to find a gas station, and it looked in better condition than any they'd come across so far.

"Peterson, Garber, James, with me." Cornell looked at Mae, Gideon, and the female sergeant behind them — Claire. "The rest of you, wait here."

Nodding, Mae and the other two soldiers jogged over to join Cornell. As if his giant pack weighed nothing, he hurried to the edge of the road and weaved through the trees until they reached the small, seemingly deserted building.

"Gather anything useful. Meet back here." He pointed to the tree they were standing under.

"Sir, we don't have spare packs." Claire looked around as if she might find a pile of shopping bags or a wagon.

Repeating himself tightly, Cornell replied, "Gather anything useful. It can be loaded into the carts."

Claire nodded, her cheeks flushing, but Mae was already scanning the building. Windows intact. Door too. "Doesn't look like this one's been looted yet, sir," she said as they made their way forward.

"Precisely." Cornell took his gun from its holster and flexed his fingers on the grip. "We're looking for food, water, medical supplies. Got it?"

Mae nodded. They were running dangerously low on painkillers. If they could replenish their stash, it would make the journey to wherever they were going much less risky.

Reaching the door, the captain stopped. Quietly, he tried the door. When it didn't open, he took a step back and nodded at Mae. "Door, Peterson."

Turning her rifle the wrong way around, Mae pulled her arm back and then smashed its heel into the glass panel. The first time, nothing happened. The second time, a small fracture appeared. The third time, it splintered into a spider's web of cracks.

Before Mae could give it one last push, Cornell moved in front of her and used his elbow to push the glass free of the frame. Reaching inside to turn the lock, he said, "Stay alert." Then he pushed the door open and stepped inside.

Entering behind the captain, Mae and Gideon checked their blind spots. "Looks empty." Gideon lowered his gun slightly. Behind him, Claire had already slotted hers back into her belt to free up her hands.

Gideon was right; the place did look empty. In front of them, aisles of candy bars, chips, moldy bread, and warm soda bottles sat untouched.

"You do food, I'll do meds." Mae headed straight for the counter and the large set of shelves behind it that contained glorious unopened boxes of Tylenol, Sudafed, and Advil.

"Claire, help me with the water." Captain Cornell gestured to the aisle containing large two-liter bottles of drinking water.

Grabbing a plastic bag from behind the counter, Mae began pulling meds from the shelf. In no particular order, she threw them in. Pausing, she almost tucked a box of Tylenol into her pocket to keep as her own emergency supply. But then she shook her head and shoved it into the bag with the rest.

She'd almost finished when a gasp from Claire made her look up. "Captain!" Claire yelled. There was a note of panic in her voice. Mae walked out from behind the counter, hand on her gun. Cornell strode over from the door. By the time the drinks aisle was in sight, Cornell a few steps ahead of her, Mae could make out a figure that wasn't part of their group. A woman. Scrawny, with long, matted hair. She was standing in the middle of the aisle and she was holding a shotgun.

"This is my place," she said, voice shaking. "My place. You should leave."

"Ma'am, please put down the gun." Claire spoke gently, but the woman's eyes narrowed.

"I have the right to defend my property. And this is *my* property. You need to go now."

Claire glanced over her shoulder at Cornell, who was approaching slowly, his hands in the air. No gun. "Ma'am, we're with the US Armed Forces. We need supplies for our unit. We've been traveling for many days, and we're tired and hungry."

Mae looked to her right. Gideon had emerged from the food aisle, arms full of candy. Tipping her head toward the captain, she inched forward. Slowly, he put the food down and followed her.

"Captain…." Mae approached Cornell's shoulder. Through gritted teeth, she said, "Perhaps we should—"

But before she could finish, he took a stride forward. "Ma'am, by order of the President of these United States and the US military, we have jurisdiction here. If we need to commandeer supplies, we can. But we'd like to do that with your cooperation."

Blinking at them, the woman looked past Cornell to Claire and Mae, as if because they were women they might be a little softer. "This store is all I have. I can't travel for more supplies. My husband's sick and—"

To Mae's surprise, Claire raised her palm to stop the woman from talking. "I'm going to stop you right there." Her eyes flitted to the captain and Mae watched her push back her shoulders. "Are you refusing to give us what we need?"

Mae opened her mouth to speak, but Cornell spoke first. "Ma'am? My sergeant needs an answer."

Holding her breath, Mae willed the woman to back down. *Just put down the gun and I'll make sure they don't take everything.* For a brief moment, she thought it was going to happen. But then the woman's eyes widened, and her hands moved, and before Mae could react, a shot rang out.

"What the…?" Next to Mae, Gideon aimed his own gun. But then the woman clutched her chest, wavered, and fell.

Barely taking a breath, Cornell holstered his gun, then strode over to pick up the shotgun from where it had landed. When he turned back around, he nodded approvingly at Claire. She hadn't fired her weapon, he had, but she'd backed him up and he was clearly impressed.

"Good, James. Good. Let's get this water to the carts, shall we?"

Nodding, Claire put her weapon away, picked up a four-pack of bottled water, and hurried past Mae without meeting her eyes.

At the door, Cornell paused. As if he knew what she'd been intending to do, he snapped, "Peterson. Leave the body. Focus on the supplies."

Mae screwed her eyes shut. She was breathing fast and heavy. When Cornell was out of sight and earshot, Gideon put his hand on her arm. "What was that?" Mae muttered. "We're killing civilians now?"

"She was armed," Gideon replied weakly.

"We were trying to *rob* her," Mae hissed in reply, turning to fix her eyes on Gideon's.

Looking away, Gideon pressed his lips together, then slowly walked back to the pile of food he'd left on the floor. "It's done now." He stooped to pick it up, glancing over his shoulder at Mae. "There's nothing we can do for her."

"What about her husband? She said her husband was sick." Mae swallowed down a lump of nausea.

But Gideon simply shook his head. "Cornell's on his way back. He's bringing the carts over. We better get moving."

For a long moment, Mae lingered at the top of the aisle. A pool of blood was now spreading out beneath the woman's back. Mae allowed herself one last look, counted to ten, then turned away.

5
LAUREL

TWO DAYS LATER

Laurel looked up at the sound of footsteps behind her. She'd know them anywhere, and smiled when she saw Bear's large frame approaching. He had a cup of steaming coffee in each hand, and a small white dog at his heel.

After giving Laurel's hand a brief lick, Jessamine hurtled off down the slope toward the trees. Off to hunt rabbits, most likely.

Laurel watched her with a smile on her face. She'd recovered remarkably well, and Laurel couldn't help feeling relieved every time she saw the small dog running or playing; she didn't know what Bear would have done if the worst had happened. Or Trent. The pair of them were ga-ga over Jessamine. From what they'd told her, Jess deserved a medal for her heroism on the journey from Thunder Bay. Not to mention the fact she was Bear's ears when he needed her to be. There was no doubt about it; Jessamine was irreplaceable.

"How's Tory doing?" Bear asked, sitting down beside her on the bench she now thought of as her mom's bench — because she knew she liked it so much.

"She's good." Laurel accepted the coffee and blew across the top of it. Stifling a yawn, she took a sip. It was hot and black, no sugar. But it was coffee, and after a night with Tory, Kate and the baby, she needed all the caffeine she could get.

"And the baby?"

"Beatrix's good too."

"She has a name." Bear sat down and leaned forward onto his thighs, looking down at the trees. "That's great." Glancing back at Laurel, he smiled.

Laurel smiled back. Little Bea was the most adorable baby. Quiet, like preemies often were, with a shock of dark hair that reminded Laurel of Mae when she was born.

"You're doing a good thing. Helping her."

"I'm a doctor. It's my job." Laurel sat back and crossed one leg over the other, wishing she had a donut to dunk in her drink.

"I know, but you're going beyond your job with this one, aren't you?" Bear chuckled, nudging her knowingly with his elbow. "She's got her sister-in-law with her. You don't need to be there all night helping with the feeds."

Laurel shrugged a little. "I know," she replied softly. "But there's something about Bea. She reminds me of Mae."

Nodding, Bear tapped his gloveless fingers on his cup, then looked back at the trees. It was late afternoon, the sun glowing softly in the sky, the days slowly creeping out a little longer now that spring was on the way.

"Speaking of Mae...." Bear breathed in heavily and rubbed his knees. "I was hoping we could talk about when we're going to start looking for her."

Laurel bit her lower lip and pushed her glasses up the bridge of her nose. Her long hair was hanging loose, pinned down by a knitted black hat that her mom had made. She moved her head so her hair fell over her shoulder, shielding her face from Bear's view. She'd been expecting this conversation for days, if not weeks. Now, here it was. He was asking her outright and she couldn't avoid it any longer.

"Did you get rid of those skunks?" She brightened her tone and turned to look at him. *Please, Bear, can't you see I don't want to talk about it now?*

"Laurel...."

"Putting bleach in the vents was genius. Ammonia. Recreating the smell of urine. Really clever."

His jaw tensing, Bear said tightly, "Trent wanted to physically pee in each vent. I told him that was both unhygienic and time consuming."

Laurel laughed, too loudly. Nerves were bubbling in her chest. She'd never been shy of difficult conversations, but this one was different.

"Laurel...." Bear angled himself toward her and took the coffee from her. Placing it on the ground, he reached for her hands and pressed them between his own. "We need to talk about this. If you've changed your mind about looking for Mae, I can go alone."

"No." Laurel's heart thumped in her chest. "No. I haven't changed my mind. And I don't want you to go alone."

"Then we *need* to talk about leaving."

"Bear...."

"There are practically no patients here anymore. Liam's doing great."

"He's still grieving."

"*Physically* he's doing great," Bear corrected. "And he's got Peter and Chris to take care of him."

Laurel nodded. Chris was doing a great job with Liam, and he and Peter were like brothers.

"So, apart from Tory, you're out of people to help."

Closing her eyes, Laurel inhaled slowly. When she opened them, she took her hands back and looked down at her fingernails. "Except my mom."

Bear didn't move, just sat silently next to her.

"I can't leave my mom again, Bear. She needs me."

Although she was trying not to look at him, Bear dipped his head and caught her gaze. "Laurel, I'd never ask you to leave your mom. You know that. But she isn't getting better. She's in pain and she's tired. She's ready for this to be over. So we should plan for what happens when—"

"Ready? What do you mean *ready*?" Laurel stood up as if a hot poker had been placed beneath her.

Bear winced a little. His hair was shaggy, falling across his face in a way that made him look a little like a sheepdog. His beard was thicker than normal, too. Rubbing it with his thumb and forefinger, he said steadily, "Laurel. She's told Henry. She's tired. The new meds you brought from Lone Oak aren't working like the trial meds did. She's tried to talk to you, but—"

"Tried to talk to me? No. She hasn't." Laurel turned and hugged her waist. She'd know if her mom felt that way. She'd know if it was really that close to the end. Wouldn't she?

She sensed Bear standing up and almost pulled away, but when his warm hand landed on her shoulder, she found herself leaning into it instead.

"I would never make you leave your mom, Laurel. I just think we should have a conversation about what happens when she's gone. And I think you need to talk to her about what *she* wants. What she *really* wants. Because, right now, she's hanging on for you, not for her. And I know you don't want that."

For a moment, Laurel allowed Bear's words to settle over her. But then an indignant fire gripped her belly and she found herself spinning around to face him. "You want her to go, don't you?"

Bear sighed heavily and shook his head. He could tell what was coming, she could see it in his eyes. It used to infuriate her when they were together; the way he simply refused to argue with her. The way he'd just stand there and wait as if by doing nothing he could make her anger subside.

"You want her to hurry up and die so we can get out of here? Because you're bored? Because this isn't exciting enough for you? Hunting skunks and—"

"Laurel…."

"No. Let me finish!" Clenching her fists, she took a step forward, ready to keep yelling. But Bear was looking at something. Not her. Past her. Turning slowly, she followed his gaze. "Hannah?"

The blonde nurse was running toward them, jacket flapping in the wind, stumbling on the snow. "Laurel, it's your mom. Come quickly."

6

MAE

"Listen up, everyone!" Cornell signaled the drivers to stop the carts and drew their small procession to a stop. "We'll soon be arriving at our new home."

Mae looked up at the sky. It was almost sunset. They'd been traveling for two weeks with no idea where they were heading. The past two days, they'd barely stopped during the day, just at night. Everyone was exhausted, but so far Mae had been the only one with the guts to ask what was going on.

Looking around as if he expected someone else to speak up, but was pleased no one had, Cornell smiled at them. "You've been very patient. You've trusted me to bring you this far. I appreciate that." He put his hands in his pockets and paced into the middle of the road so he was standing in front of them. They were, it seemed to Mae, in the middle of nowhere. She'd tried to keep track of their location in her head, but without a map, or any road signs, which were oddly missing the last dozen miles, all she knew was that they'd traveled about three hundred miles north and were nearing Iowa.

"In a short while, we will be meeting with a group of civilian soldiers. We will join forces with them and take joint control of the area's Army Ammunition Depot. When we have the depot, we will be able to fight back against the growing threat of the Freemen."

Mae exchanged a glance with Gideon. She thought part of the reason they left their last location was to avoid groups like the Freemen. Not to seek out more.

Cornell took a compass from his pocket, checked it, then looked at the sun. Taking a map from his pocket, he motioned for his second-in-command Gray, then pointed at something on the map. "This is the rendezvous point."

Gray nodded. Looking up, he waved at the rest of the unit. "Move out. Two miles to rendezvous."

As they began to walk, Claire stepped in line with Mae. "Fighting the Freemen? That's our mission?"

Mae's jaw tensed. "I thought you were on board with Cornell's way of doing things?" she snapped, tucking a strand of blonde hair back under her cap.

Silently, Claire hung back, leaving Mae and Gideon to walk side by side.

After what Mae calculated was at least forty minutes of walking, they reached a bend in the road. Nestled in the trees was a small building. It looked like it had been constructed from old highway signs, which explained what happened to them. A handmade plaque on the door read: CHURCH.

Mae watched as Cornell nodded at Gray and two others to follow him. Slowly, they approached. With one soldier behind him and one on either side, Cornell rapped his knuckles three times on the door and shouted, "Cornell. Five, six, two, one."

No reply.

Cornell repeated the motion. "Cornell. Five, six, two, one." Then after a pause, he added, "Banks, are you in there?"

When there was still no reply, he raised his gun and nodded at the other three to back him up. With one hand, he tugged the door open. Then the four of them disappeared inside.

Out on the road, the rest of the unit — twenty-five soldiers, four horses, and two carts full of supplies — waited on high alert. Cornell still hadn't returned when Mae spotted something moving in the trees. A shadow. Just the smallest flicker.

"Gideon. Two o'clock." She signaled to the undergrowth. In unison, she and Gideon turned. At the same moment, the shadow moved urgently forward.

"Stop right there," Mae called, causing the rest of the unit to turn and look in her direction. "Come out slowly with your hands up."

A figure emerged. A man, in camouflage fatigues with a thick, dark beard. He raised his arms. Mae narrowed her eyes. And then he fell.

Lowering her gun, she raced forward.

"Peterson, don't!" Gideon yelled after her but she ignored him.

Dropping to her knees, she looked down into a younger face than she'd expected to find. "Are you injured?" she asked, scanning his clothes for signs of an injury.

Nodding, he turned his head slightly and Mae winced. Blood. Lots of blood. "Cornell," he coughed. "Are you Cornell?"

Shaking her head, Mae looked up. "Get the Captain. Now!" she yelled over her shoulder. A flurry of movement told her someone was fetching him.

"I have a message for Cornell." He breathed in a deep, rasping breath, his eyes rolling a little in his head.

"He's coming. What is it?"

"The Freemen. They... took over the depot. They said...." He groaned and closed his eyes.

Pressing her hands on either side of his face, Mae turned him toward her. "What? What did they say?"

"They said join them or run. Art King said join them... or... run."

Sitting back on her heels, a heavy knot of dread settled in Mae's stomach. "The captain said we were meeting civilian soldiers. Where are they?" Mae gently shook the man's shoulder. His breathing had become shallow.

"Gone." He opened his mouth and licked his lower lip as if his mouth was suddenly dry. "They're gone. Art King killed them."

"Art King?" Mae leaned down, lowering her ear closer to the dying man's mouth. "Who's Art King?"

"Thank you, soldier." Captain Cornell's heavy hand on her shoulder caused Mae to look up. Tucking his hand under her elbow, he tugged her to her feet and took her place at the man's side. But he was too late.

"He's gone." Mae closed her eyes and allowed her shoulders to drop. When the captain stood up, she fixed her eyes on his, refusing to look away from that icy blue. "He said a man called Art King killed the civilian soldiers we were supposed to be meeting."

Cornell's eyebrow twitched, but the rest of his expression remained still.

"He said the Freemen have the depot."

At that, Cornell's jaw twitched. "Then we'll have to take it back. Won't we?"

Deliberately raising her voice so the rest of the unit could hear her, Mae stood as tall as she could and replied, "He said Art King had a message for us: join him or run." As she snapped out the words, she watched Cornell's face.

His eyes narrowed a little. Then a smile spread across his face. "Join or run? I think there's a third option, don't you?"

"A third option?" Mae straightened her jacket against the breeze.

"Yes, Peterson. We fight."

7
LAUREL

"What happened?" Laurel's feet weren't carrying her fast enough. Reaching the foyer, melting snow clinging to her boots, she slipped. At her elbow, Bear steadied her but didn't tell her to be careful.

Her pace slowing, Hannah met Laurel's eyes. "She lost consciousness. Only for a few minutes. She's awake now, but she wants to see you."

"Where is she?"

"In the dorm." Hannah pushed open the doors that separated the foyer from the corridor.

"Can't we put her somewhere more private?" Laurel shrugged her coat off and Bear seamlessly took it from her.

"She didn't want to take the private room from Tory and the baby." Hannah paused at the door to the communal area. "Laurel, before we go in…." Hannah sucked in her breath and wrapped her arms around her waist. "You should ask your mom about her meds." She fixed her eyes on Laurel's.

"Her meds?" Laurel's mouth was suddenly dry.

Not looking away, Hannah nodded. "Ask her."

As Hannah entered the room, Laurel found herself unable to move. Swallowing hard, she turned to Bear. "What does she mean? Ask about my mom's meds?"

A look crossed Bear's face that softened his features. "I don't know, but I think now's the time to listen to her, Laurel. Listen to what she has to say to you."

A tight knot formed in Laurel's chest. "She's been doing okay, hasn't she?" Laurel scraped her fingers through her hair. "I mean, we ran out of her trial meds but she's been stable on the new ones. We've been keeping her stable."

A hot, prickling sensation was creeping down her arms. Moisture sprang to her eyes, but she swiped it away.

Bear placed a large, firm hand on her shoulder. Part of her wanted to reach up and put her hand on his. Another part wanted to push him away. Closing her eyes, she took two deep breaths.

"Laurel, you're a doctor. Right now, that's what your mom needs. She needs you to treat her like any other patient."

"But she's not another patient, she's my mom." Laurel shook her hands at her sides. It didn't release any of the tension in her body.

"Okay, let me put it another way." Bear's voice grew sterner. His piercingly blue eyes traveled her face. "I know you, Laurel. I know you feel guilty for leaving your mom and going with Arlo. I know you feel guilty because you couldn't make her cancer go away. But it's time to put that aside and focus on making the most of the time you have left together."

Folding and unfolding her arms, Laurel nodded slowly.

"Let the doctor inside you take control of your mom's illness. Treat her body the way you'd treat any other patient's body. But let this…." He pressed his palm to her chest, above her heart. "Listen to what her soul needs. What she needs from her *daughter*."

Trying to center herself, Laurel smiled and tilted her head. "Her soul? Did you find religion in the woods, Bjorn?"

Bear scoffed at that. "We both know the soul exists. I don't need a god to tell me that."

Straightening her shoulders, Laurel took another deep breath and counted to ten. When she looked back at Bear, she nodded at him. "Thank you, Bear. I'm ready."

Entering the dorm room, Laurel steeled herself and headed for her mother's bed. A curtain had been set up, shielding the bed from the rest of the room, which was humming with the usual pre-dinner activity. When the weather got warmer, they'd be able to spread out and use other spaces in the hospital. Some had already been talking about choosing a room of their own, then using the summer to prepare for next winter; making fireplaces the way Bear had, "nesting" her mother would call it.

When she heard people talking that way, it warmed Laurel's heart. She was proud that they'd created a safe space for the people who'd chosen to stay, and proud of what Bear had done to help everyone while she was gone.

"Mom?" Laurel pulled her hat off and smiled as she stepped around the curtain.

Her mother's eyes were closed, her face pale, but her lips still customarily red. Henry was sitting next to her, hands on his knees, rubbing them anxiously as if he wasn't sure whether he wanted to stand up or sit down.

"What happened?" Laurel slid into the chair next to Henry's.

"We were walking. She passed out." Henry sucked in a deep breath then added, "She said she didn't need the chair. I should have insisted."

Putting her hand firmly on Henry's shoulder, Laurel smiled at him. "Mom doesn't take no for an answer very often, does she?"

Smiling thinly, Henry replied, "Sure doesn't."

Turning away from him, Laurel scanned her mother's fragile frame. She'd lost weight recently, but how much? Laurel instinctively looked at the end of the bed for a chart, but there wasn't one.

"Henry…." She cleared her throat and folded her arms in front of her stomach, hugging her waist. "Hannah told me to ask about my mom's meds." She looked sideways at him. "Is there something I should know?"

As Henry opened his mouth to speak, Laurel felt movement on the bed.

"Leave him be, Laurel." Her mother's voice was croaky, but as determined as always.

When Laurel looked at her mother, she found her attempting to push herself up on her elbows. "Here, Mom, careful." Laurel leaned forward and adjusted the pillow behind her mom's head, gently helping her up.

"I'll give you two some space." Henry stood up, patted Laurel's mom's hand, and stepped back around the curtain.

For a moment, Laurel waited, expecting Bear to appear. When he didn't, she moved into Henry's chair and took her mom's hands.

Somehow, the hum of those around them cheerfully gathering for dinner was putting her at ease.

"What have you been up to, Mom?" Laurel kissed her mom's knuckles, grasping her hand tightly.

"I'm sorry, Laurel."

"Don't be sorry." Laurel used her free hand to brush her mom's hair from her face, then picked up the cup of water from the bedside table and held the straw to her mom's lips. "You didn't tell me you were feeling bad." Laurel set the cup back down, careful to keep her voice measured and soft. "You should have told me, Mom. I could have tweaked your meds."

Wincing a little, her mom turned her head and reached out to stroke Laurel's cheek. "Darling girl," she said quietly. "You know I stopped taking them." She moved her hand to Laurel's chest and tapped it, just above her heart. "In here, you know."

Laurel's heart started to beat faster in her chest. Did she know? Had she suspected and chosen to ignore it? "No," she said, pressing her lips together. "I didn't."

As indignation started to bubble in her chest, Laurel breathed in slowly through her nose and tried to remember Bear's words. If this was another patient, a patient who was terminally ill, and who no longer had access to the trial drugs that had been keeping her alive, what would she say?

"You spoke to Hannah about it?" she asked quietly.

Her mom nodded.

"She explained what would happen if you stopped taking them?"

This time, her mom closed her eyes. "Yes, Laurel, she explained."

"And this is…" Laurel's words caught in her throat. She cleared it and then continued. "This is what you want?"

Turning her head to meet Laurel's eyes, her mom blinked as a tear fell down her cheek. "I'm tired, Laurel. I stayed until I knew you were safe. But now it's time for me to go."

A loud unexpected breath escaped Laurel's lips, as if she'd been physically punched in the chest.

Her mom's fingers tightened around hers.

"I'm sorry, Mom. I should have asked you sooner." Wiping tears from her cheeks, Laurel sniffed loudly and tried to smile. "I should have—"

"Laurel Magdalena Rivera, you know I don't believe in 'should have' or 'could have'." Her mom's familiar fiery tone eased the tightness in Laurel's chest. "All I want now…" she seemed brighter as she sat up, "is to spend what time I've got left with my daughter. Is that all right?"

"Of course." Laurel leaned forward and rested her head on her mom's chest. "Of course it's all right."

Back behind the curtain, Laurel shook her hands at her sides and breathed out a long, heavy breath. Across the room, the dining tables were filling up and Mrs. Johnson was dishing out something that usually would have smelled delicious, but today made Laurel feel nauseated.

Scanning the room, she found Bear and Henry standing over by the doors. When she reached them, Bear moved as if he was going to put his arm around her but then changed his mind and let it hang loose at his side instead.

"She says she's ready to…." Laurel looked at Henry and saw instantly that this was not new information. Was she the only one who hadn't known that her mom was too tired to continue her fight?

"Yes." Henry nodded solemnly and cleared his throat. "How long do you think…." He faltered and swiped a shaky hand through his hair.

"I need to speak to Hannah." Laurel slotted her fingers together and squeezed. Her knuckles whitened with the pressure.

"She's with Tory. She said she'd be right back." Bear nodded in the direction of the private room where Tory, Beatrix, and Kate were staying.

Brushing down her pants, Laurel was about to stride forward and find Hannah for a debrief when her mom's words rang in her ears. Pressing her lips together, she paused, then turned to Henry and Bear. "Mom loves watching the sun set. Would you take her up to the roof for me? I'm going to ask Mrs. Johnson for some of that red wine I know she's been hiding."

"What about Hannah?" Bear asked.

"It can wait." Laurel met his eyes, hoping he could see that she was taking on board what he'd told her. "Right now, I owe my mom a drink and a sunset."

A short while later, Laurel pulled her jacket back on and took the stairs up to the roof two at a time. On her shoulder was a bag containing a bottle of red wine, two wine glasses wrapped in a towel, her mom's manicure kit, and a box of chocolates Bulldog had been saving for Hannah's birthday.

When she reached the roof, Bear and Henry were tucking a blanket around her mom's knees and another around her shoulders. As Henry kissed her mom's forehead, Laurel looked away. When she looked back, Bear was leaning down to hug her and she was whispering something in his ear.

And then the two of them were gone, and it was just mother and daughter.

"Here we go, Mom." Laurel handed her mother a wine glass, unscrewed the cap on the wine bottle, and poured.

A little disapprovingly, her mom peered into the glass and frowned. "Come on, Laurel. I can still handle my drink."

Adding a splash more, Laurel laughed and then filled her own glass. Settling onto the bench next to her mom's chair, she squeezed her hand. Silently, as the sun began to dip in the sky, they sipped their drinks.

"Almost like we're back in Texas." Her mom was smiling at the sky. It was turning from pale blue to a dusky orange.

"It was a little warmer on the porch," Laurel said, pulling her scarf tighter around her neck. "It feels like a lifetime ago. Me and you, rattling around your big old house together."

Her mom smiled and sighed.

"You didn't like living with me?" Laurel angled herself toward her mother and raised a playful eyebrow.

"You know I did." Her mom tsked. "But I was sad for you and Bjorn."

Wrinkling her nose, Laurel nodded. "I know. Sometimes I thought you were more fond of him than I was."

A broad grin spread over her mother's face. "You have to admit, he's a dish."

"A dish?" Laurel laughed loudly. "Is that really the word?"

"Oh, I'd say so." Her mother took a shaky sip from her wine glass and closed her eyes. When she opened them again, they were moist and Laurel couldn't tell if it was the breeze making them water or if her mom was crying. "Laurel…."

"Mom… let's just—"

"No. I need to say this." Her mother turned sideways a little and reached for Laurel's hand. Laurel took it, tucking her arm through her mom's. "Bjorn is your family. He cares for you, and you care for him. Don't take that for granted."

"Okay, Mom. I won't." Laurel nodded sincerely.

"And when you find Mae—"

"Mom—"

"When you find Mae… tell her Nanna says she's a good girl, and to be nice to her parents." As her mom smiled, the smile turned into a cough and Laurel reached over to rub her back.

"Okay, Mom. I promise."

"I'm proud of you, Laurel. And your father would have been too."

Laurel leaned her head down onto her mom's shoulder and breathed in her scent. Perfume and something else. Something warm and homey. "I'm proud of you too, Mom."

For a long few minutes, they sat together in silence, watching the sun creep lower in the sky. Finally, Laurel sat up and turned to find the manicure bag. "Okay, we better do this while it's still light. Are we thinking red to match the lips or something a little different? Hannah gave me a turquoise that might work." She'd opened the bag and was rifling through it. "Mom? Red or blue?" She looked up briefly, then back down at the bag.

Suddenly unable to look away from the red nail varnish she was holding, Laurel's grip tightened on the bottle. "Mom?" Her voice was small. "Mommy?"

She took her eyes from the bottle at the same moment the glass slipped from her mother's hand.

8
MAE

"Captain? It's nearly dark. We should find somewhere to camp." Mae approached Cornell and stood straight, hands behind her back, at his side.

He was crouching in the cover of the trees, peering at a map spread out on the ground. To her surprise, he looked up at her and nodded in affirmation. "Yes, Peterson, we should."

Standing up, he clapped his hands to draw the attention of the soldiers waiting nearby. Four were guarding each cart, four guarding the tree line, the rest taking the chance to drink some water and give their legs a break after a long journey.

As Cornell spoke up, everyone straightened themselves up and paid attention.

"I've located a warehouse nearby. Me and two volunteers will go and see if it's empty." He said the word "volunteers" pointedly, as if he was expecting an immediate show of hands. "If it is, it'll make a good base while we plan how to take back ground from the Freemen." As two soldiers stepped forward, Claire and an older guy called Duke, Cornell nodded approvingly. Then he turned to Mae. "Peterson, take Garber. Get as close as you can to the depot's perimeter. I want you on recon until sunrise, and I want a full report when you're done."

Mae fought the urge to look at Gideon and simply nodded.

"Meet back here at sunrise. If we've relocated to the warehouse, someone will be here to collect you. If the warehouse isn't suitable...." Cornell narrowed his eyes as he scanned their surroundings. "We'll be here planning our next move."

Mae nodded and straightened her shoulders. "Yes, Captain."

Gideon echoed her. "Yes, Captain."

There was a pause, in which he looked like he was about to say something else. But then Cornell turned to the map and indicated the outline of a large building, surrounded by trees. "That's where you're heading. Got it?"

Mae tilted her head, plotted the coordinates in her mind, then said, "Yes, Captain."

"What is it?" Gideon's question was innocent enough, but it made Cornell huff unappreciatively.

Cornell offered Gideon a withering glare, and his jaw twitched. "That information is above your paygrade, soldier." He opened his mouth, as if he was going to continue telling Gideon precisely why he shouldn't be asking questions about things that didn't concern him. But before Cornell could say anything further, someone yelled for his attention. There was movement in the trees. Suddenly, twenty soldiers had their eyes on the same spot.

Mae reached for her gun and narrowed her eyes, body tense, squinting into the gloomy half-light.

"Captain Cornell!" A woman's voice. "Is Captain Cornell here? We were with the militia group at the depot. We were supposed to meet you."

Cornell stepped forward, gesturing for Duke and Claire to flank him. "Hands in the air. Show me your weapon."

"I'm not armed." The woman moved into the light. Then Mae realized she wasn't alone. "None of us are."

Behind her, Mae counted one, two, three, four, five others. Then a sixth. Soon, ten more people were in the clearing, all with their arms in the air.

"The password is Heracles," the woman said, voice a little shaky. "You can search us. We're not armed."

Nodding, Cornell indicated for the newcomers to be searched. When they'd been sufficiently patted down, he nodded again for the woman to come closer.

Extending her hand, she shook his and said, "Felicia Myers. You knew Rick? I'm his wife." She swallowed hard. "He *was* my husband."

Shivering a little, the woman pulled her knitted hat down farther over her ears. She was wearing large black boots, weatherproof pants, and a padded jacket. Mae could just make out a series of symbols tattooed on her knuckles, and a silver stud in her nose.

Was. So her husband was dead. Mae pressed her lips together and bit back a sigh.

"He told me to give you the password and also to remind you of what happened in Fallujah. With the insurgents. He said you'd know what that meant."

Felicia fixed her gaze on Cornell's. He wasn't giving anything away, just studied her for a moment before putting a heavy hand on her shoulder and turning to the others. "These people are part of the militia group we were due to meet. They are our friends, equally committed to making sure the so-called Freemen don't take over this state." Cornell looked at Felicia and she nodded, determination settling in her eyes.

With his hand still on her shoulder, he said, "Do you know anything about the warehouse situated three blocks from here?"

Felicia was about to respond when Cornell turned to Mae and snapped, "Peterson? What are you still doing here? Are you confused about what I asked you to do?"

"No, sir." Mae adjusted her pack on her shoulder. "Not at all, sir. Rendezvous here at sunrise." Then she gestured for Gideon to follow her and jogged off into the trees.

Once they were out of earshot, they slowed to a walk and Gideon shook his head firmly. "What's going on? Who was Cornell meeting? This guy? Rick? Civilians, who think they're soldiers? Since when do we need—"

Mae stopped and breathed in sharply. "Look," she said, hands at her sides. "I don't understand it any more than you do, but it's not our job to understand. Right now, it's our job to figure out who and what is at that depot, so we can plan how we're going to take it back from the Freemen."

Gideon frowned at her. She knew what he was thinking; that she could usually be counted on to question what was happening. That she was usually the first to feel frustrated by a lack of answers or an unclear motivation for something—a habit she knew she got from her mother.

But where had that gotten her? Perhaps, this time, she'd learn more by shutting up and doing as she was told.

Gideon opened his mouth to speak but then closed it again. "All right," he said tightly. "Lead the way."

9
BEAR

The mood in the dorm room was unusually somber. Bright light was streaming through the windows, and yet it didn't permeate the sadness hovering in the air. Although Deb was Laurel's mother, she'd been like a mom to everyone at South Minneha over the past few months, and there wasn't a single person who wasn't feeling the effects of her loss already.

When Bear and Henry had carried Deb downstairs to the morgue, it had nearly broken Bear's heart. He'd done things like that before — many times. Heck, he'd moved how many bodies from the hallway after the incident with Murph and his men? But carrying someone you've known and loved for several decades was very different from carrying a stranger. Someone who died in a fight they caused through their own vicious actions, not someone who died because they lost a very different kind of fight.

Bear had offered to stay and help, but Henry insisted that he could handle things on his own. So Bear had returned to the roof where he sat beside Laurel for a long time. They didn't speak, simply sat next to each other watching the last of the sunset. Laurel hadn't been crying, just blinking slowly. Eventually, as the sun dipped behind the horizon, she'd reached out and taken his hand. "Thank you," she'd said.

He turned to her but she wasn't looking at him.

"If you hadn't told me what you did, my mom and I would've had a very different goodbye. Thanks to you, it's one I don't have any regrets over." She sniffed a little and looked down at her fingernails. "Except maybe that she didn't get to try the turquoise nail polish."

Dipping his head, Bear looked down at Laurel's fingers too. Entwined with his, the way they had been so many times before.

"You could still…." He trailed off but Laurel smiled a little.

"Yes, I think I will."

"And we can have a ceremony." Bear nudged closer and put his arm around Laurel's shoulders. "A funeral."

"Yes," Laurel replied. "A good one. A proper send-off." She looked at her mom's empty chair, then stood, picked up the blanket which lay on the seat, and folded it neatly over her arm. On the floor, broken shards of glass crunched underneath Laurel's boots. A sinister red wine stain marked the ground near the chair's front caster.

As Laurel bent to start picking up the glass, Bear took her elbow. "I can do that."

"It's okay." She nudged her arm free. "I can do it."

"Laurel."

"I can do it." Her voice lifted a few octaves but became sharper. She wobbled on her haunches, steadied herself on Bear's arm, then her shoulders started to shake.

When the tears came, Bear sank to the ground behind her and wrapped his arms around her. They stayed like that for a long time, until it was dark and cold and he had to wrap the blanket around them because Laurel was starting to shiver.

They didn't move until Henry came to find them.

"Do you want to see her?" he'd asked.

Laurel had looked up at Bear. In that moment, she was his wife. They might not have truly reconciled. They might have been separated for almost three years. But then, right then, she was his wife and he'd do anything to help her through the tsunami of grief he knew was coming.

As Bear met Laurel's gaze, she nodded slowly. "Yes, thank you, Henry."

He helped her to her feet. Henry had put his hands on the chair, ready to wheel it away, but Laurel shook her head. "No, leave it." She pulled the blanket from her shoulders and folded it once again, setting it neatly on the seat. Then she turned to the makeup bag that was still sitting on the bench, and rifled inside it. It was barely light enough to see one another, let alone the contents of the bag, but when Laurel took out a small cylindrical object, Bear knew what it was; Deb's red lipstick.

Laurel placed it gently on top of the blanket, then touched the back of the chair, closed her eyes, and said, "I'm ready. Let's go."

Now, remembering, Bear shuddered. In front of him, his morning oatmeal was untouched and his coffee lukewarm.

"You okay, PB?" Trent's voice nudged him back into the room. He'd slid onto the bench next to Bear and was nursing his own coffee, staring at it as if he wasn't sure whether he really wanted it or not.

"Yeah, kid. I'm okay." Bear patted Trent's back, then shoved his breakfast bowl away from him. "Just not all that hungry."

"When is the…." Trent trailed off, clasping his hands tightly in front of him. "You said Laurel wants to have the funeral today?"

Bear nodded. He didn't need to go into the reasons why it was better to have the burial sooner. Trent was growing up fast, but sometimes Bear thought he was growing up *too* fast. This was one of those times.

"I'll go find Laurel." Bear stood up, leaving his coffee. "See if someone wants that. I'll let you know when we've figured out what's happening."

Bear didn't have to search long before he found Laurel. She was exactly where he'd expected her to be; with Tory and the baby. In the corner of the room, Kate was dozing. Tory was asleep too. Curled up in bed, she was clutching what looked like a dark blue piece of fabric.

Catching Bear staring at it, Laurel stood up from her chair by the fireplace and walked over. In a hushed voice, she said, "It's her husband's shirt. She doesn't have any pictures of him. Their house caught fire after the EMP. He didn't make it out, and she doesn't have a single memento."

Bear's jaw twitched. He glanced at Kate. "She's his sister. She doesn't…?"

"When the snow thaws, Tory wants to try and make it to Kate's place in New York. She was on vacation here when the power went out."

"New York?" Bear shuddered; things were cut-throat enough in a small town like South Minneha, let alone a big city. He sure as heck wouldn't want to take a newborn on that journey.

"Kate's trying to persuade her otherwise." As Laurel continued to whisper, Beatrix made a small mewling sound.

"Mae used to make that sound." Bear leaned in and looked at the baby's round, pink cheeks, her pudgy fingers. Somehow, she was small but still plump. The way babies were supposed to be.

Laurel offered Beatrix her little finger and the baby wrapped her own tiny ones around it. When she looked up, Bear put a hand on her shoulder and said, "Laurel, can we talk?"

Sucking in a deep breath, Laurel turned and placed Beatrix back into the crib they'd taken from the maternity ward. Before leaving the room, she nudged Kate and told her she was stepping out. Yawning, putting her hand over her mouth, Kate sat up in her chair. "Mm hmm, okay. Sure, Doc."

Both women were exhausted, perhaps more from their arduous journey than the birth itself. In the hall, Laurel headed for a row of light blue visitors' seats and sat down. "I hope they don't try to leave too soon." She rubbed her arms. The change in temperature from the warm and toasty private room to the corridor made her shiver. "In fact, I hope they decide to stay. Certainly while she's so small, it'd be better for Beatrix to be somewhere she can have help if she needs it."

Bear let Laurel talk for a moment. He knew this tone—slightly urgent, slightly high-pitched. She adjusted her glasses on her nose twice before removing them and cleaning them on the hem of her sweater. Finally, when she took a breath, he said, "Laurel. Do you still want to have a service for your mom today?"

Laurel blinked slowly. She didn't look at him. Putting her glasses back on, she closed her eyes. Bear waited a moment, not speaking. When she opened her eyes, she fixed her gaze on the wall opposite them, on a skyline photograph of South Minneha at night, taken from the roof of the parking lot.

"Yes." Her voice was quiet but firm. "We should do it today. I don't want her...." She trailed off, but Bear knew what she intended to say; she didn't want her mom to remain unburied for too long.

"The ground's pretty cold, but Henry and I think we can—" Before Bear could finish, Laurel shook her head.

"No. She didn't want to be buried. She always said she wanted to be cremated."

Bear pressed his lips together. He was struggling to be tactful, and his hearing aid was playing up, which was severely affecting his volume control. "Laurel, are you sure you want to–"

"The Vikings did it. They sent people off into lakes on burning rafts."

"They did, but we don't have a lake or a raft, Laurel."

"No, but Mom was adamant she didn't want to be buried."

Bear wanted to ask whether Laurel had confirmed this was still her mother's wish by talking with Henry or Hannah. But the thought that either of them might know her mother better than she had—toward the end—would have been too much for Laurel. At least right now. So, Bear said, "Okay. I'll talk to Henry and Bulldog. We'll figure it out."

"Sunset." Laurel finally turned and met his eyes. Hers were watery and wide. He wanted to pull her into his arms and sit with her while she cried, but he knew her well enough to know that this would have been to make himself feel better. Not her.

Laurel's entire demeanor told him she was working hard to keep herself together, and when she was doing that, any show of affection was *not* okay. It had been the same when they'd been on tour together. Despite being husband and wife, she'd made it clear he was *not* to comfort her in public. Rarely in private, either.

Laurel coped with the hard stuff by putting up walls. What worried him now was that the walls wouldn't be strong enough, and that if she tried to get through her grief alone, it would overwhelm her.

Breaking away from his gaze, Laurel reached into her jeans pocket and took out a small notepad. "I wrote down some ideas."

Bear took the list and read through the bullet points. "I remember that song," he said, grinning. "Don't think a day went by when she didn't play it. You remember? The summer she broke her ankle and had to live with us. Mae must have been five or six?"

A smile fluttered across Laurel's lips, but it disappeared as she swallowed hard and scraped her fingers through her hair. "She loved it. If Mae was here, I'd have asked her to sing it."

"She has a great singing voice, that kid."

"Mom loved it." Laurel rubbed her palms on her thighs. She looked like she was ready to get up and head back to the baby.

"I'll sort this." Bear held the list tightly. "As much of it as I can."

"You don't have to—" Laurel started to shake her head, but Bear dipped his head to meet her eyes.

"I need to keep busy. It'll help." He wasn't lying; he did need to keep busy. He wasn't all that comfortable with addressing his own feelings right now, either. But he also knew that the only way Laurel would allow him to help was in a practical sense. So if organizing was all he was allowed to do for her, organizing it would have to be. "Trent too. He's feeling it. He'll enjoy sourcing the food and drink. Sweet-talking Mrs. Johnson."

Laurel smiled again. It stayed a little longer this time. Then finally she stood up. "Thank you, Bear. I'll…." She gestured to Tory's room.

"Take care of your patient. I'll take care of the arrangements."

Just before the sun started to dip in the sky outside, everyone who was able gathered in the snow outside. Down by the tree line, Henry, Bear, and Bulldog had constructed a funeral pyre. It gave Bear chills thinking about it, but Henry had reiterated what Laurel said; Deb did not want to be buried. And he was determined that she get her final wish.

Thankfully, Laurel hadn't had to witness them moving Deb's body from the morgue to the pyre. She'd said her goodbyes and spent the rest of the day blocking out what was about to happen by helping Tory and Kate look after Beatrix.

As Laurel emerged from the building with Hannah on one arm and Janet on the other, she met Bear's eyes and remained focused on him until she reached him. Everyone remained silent.

"Before we start our final goodbye to Deb...." Henry's voice surprised him and he looked around to find the ex-janitor stepping into the middle of the semi-circle. Uncomfortable being the center of attention, he cleared his throat and then reached for a large plastic bag. Bear had assumed it contained fire-lighting equipment, but Henry picked it up and held it close to his chest. "She has a final request for you all."

Bear exchanged a glance with Laurel, who clearly had no idea what Henry was talking about.

"Deb was a woman who loved to be bright, and bold, and noticed. And she would have *hated* to see us all standing here looking so glum." He dipped a hand into the bag and pulled out something that looked like a knitted hat, bright yellow with a pom-pom on top. "Deb knitted one for everyone. She wanted to make sure there was color at her funeral." Henry handed the yellow hat to Bear and gestured for him to swap it for the dark khaki one he was wearing.

Grimacing a little, because yellow had never been his color, Bear quickly made the exchange and looked at Trent. Previously holding back tears, Trent now grinned. "Suits you," he said.

"This one's for you." Henry handed Trent a bright green hat in the same style, then went around the group. Peter got blue, Chris got purple, Hannah bright Barbie pink, Bulldog black and white stripes. At his side, Jess watched everyone keenly, tilting her head as if she wasn't quite sure what was going on but somehow knew it wasn't playtime.

Finally, Henry came to Laurel. The hat he gave her was a bright crimson color. It reminded Bear of Deb's lipstick. "And one more." Henry reached into the bag and then leaned down to Jess. "This one's for you, little lady."

It was a new red coat, the same shade as Laurel's hat.

Chuckling, Bear helped her out of her pink one and into the red. Jess wagged her tail, pleased with her new look.

For a moment, there was silence. His task finished, Henry shuffled from one foot to the other, awkward now that he was standing in front of everyone without a purpose.

Finally, Laurel cleared her throat and stepped up beside him. "Thank you for coming, everyone. Mom was so happy and grateful for you all." Her voice faltered, but she inhaled slowly and kept going. "As Henry said, my mom was the kind of woman who did everything loud and proud. She loved being the center of attention, and she was never afraid to say what was on her mind."

At that, Bear chuckled and said, "And didn't we know it…."

Laurel smiled at him. "I could stand here all evening and tell you all the things I loved about her. I could tell you her life story. All the amazing things she achieved. But none of it would sum up just how wonderful she was." Again, Laurel's voice caught in her throat.

Bear wanted so badly to reach over and grab her hand, but he didn't.

"So, I'll just say this—she was the best mom in the world. She was brave, and fierce, and I have her to thank for everything I have and everything I am." Blinking up at the sky, Laurel added in a whisper, "I love you, Mom."

As everyone hung their heads, a hushed sadness swept through the group.

For several long moments, no one spoke. Then Laurel sniffed, wiped her eyes, and said, "If anyone else would like to say something, please feel free."

To Bear's surprise, Henry was the first to step forward. In his faltering, deep voice he told everyone the story of his and Deb's first proper date, the day they admitted they had feelings for one another. It was surprising, but heartwarming to hear. Then Trent told everyone about the time Deb tried to cheat because he was getting too good at cards. Hannah described the varied relationship advice Deb had given her. Bulldog told how, despite the fact he was a six-foot-something ex-con, Deb had no qualms about standing up to him and letting him know that if he hurt Hannah, she would hurt him back.

Finally, it was Bear's turn. As everyone else spoke, memories flitted through his head. He'd known Deb Rivera for so long that it seemed almost impossible to pick just one memory. Wondering what Mae would have said if she were there, Bear began to smile.

With no preface, no explanation, and no warning, he launched into song, as loudly as he possibly could.

For a moment, he was greeted by blank stares. Laurel's eyes widened, then she started to laugh; he had a terrible singing voice. Truly terrible. But it was Deb's favorite song, the one Laurel had written on her list.

When she joined in, the others did too.

Together, they belted out all five verses of the crooning Dean Martin number.

When they finished, they applauded themselves and Laurel tucked herself under Bear's arm. "Thank you," she said. "Thank you, Bear."

"Your mother is the only woman I'd risk making a fool of myself for." He kissed Laurel's head. *Well, maybe not the only woman.*

10

MAE

"Where are you going?" Gideon's hand on Mae's arm made her spin around.

Stepping back into the shadow of the warehouse, she pulled him with her and put her finger to her lips, "*Shhhhhh*."

"Seriously, Mae. What are you doing? Are you running?"

Mae scoffed and shook her head. "No. Of course not." Movement over by the fence made her move around the corner and tug Gideon with her. "I'm going to go get proof that attacking the depot is a bad idea."

"Proof? What kind of proof?"

"I don't know yet." Mae pinched the bridge of her nose. "But I have to do something. Cornell's going to walk everyone into a disaster. We'll all end up like Felicia's husband. And the rest."

"Mae, come on. It's not like you've got a camera to document what you find. How are you going to convince people to go against

Cornell?" Gideon pressed his lips together and straightened his shoulders a little. Lowering his voice, he added, "Plus, what you're suggesting… it's *mutiny*."

Mae's mouth dropped open a little. Her heart was thumping in her chest. "I don't want to convince people to go against him." She frowned. She might not like Cornell, but she wasn't insubordinate. She still respected the chain of command. "I want to convince Cornell that this isn't a good idea. How could you even suggest that I'd—"

Before Gideon could answer, Mae adjusted her pack on her shoulder and fixed him with her most purposeful stare. "I'm not asking you to come with me. Just cover for me if they ask where I am."

"Cover for you how?"

"Tell them I saw someone on the boundary and went to investigate." Mae nodded toward the trees beyond the wire fence that encircled the warehouse. "All right?"

Gideon was uneasy. He was a good soldier, and had been her best friend ever since they met in basic training, but that meant she knew him well enough to know he did not like thinking for himself. Mae respected the chain of command, but couldn't shake the fact that she needed to *believe* she was taking the right course of action before fully getting behind it. Gideon was different; his opinion was the opinion of whoever was in charge, and that was that. Up to now, he'd backed Mae. But she could tell he was wavering; she was sailing too close to being insubordinate and that wasn't something Gideon could ever support.

"Gideon. Just don't say anything. Tell them you don't know if you're not willing to lie."

He paused for a long moment, then nodded. "Okay."

Before he could change his mind, Mae peered back around the corner, checked that the coast was clear, then jogged to the fence and hurled herself up and over it. Luckily, whoever owned the warehouse hadn't been so worried about security that they'd put barbed wire around the top.

When she reached the woods, she stopped and strained her ears. Everything was quiet. Nothing to suggest that Gideon had raised an alarm or that anyone had spotted her leaving.

If Cornell found out she'd left without permission, she wasn't sure what he'd do. He was volatile and unpredictable, which was partly why she was struggling to get behind his leadership. That and the fact Neil had never liked him.

But she had to do something to stop him from charging into that depot.

Weaving through the trees, Mae cut back to the rendezvous point, and then across toward the depot. She was a few yards away when she heard something. Movement. Voices.

Gun in hand, she turned slowly, straining her ears to discern which direction it was coming from. Whatever it was had stopped. She narrowed her eyes, examining the shadows. Still nothing. So, quietly, she slipped behind a tree and waited.

For several long minutes, nothing happened. Then a bush opposite her hiding spot rustled and two small figures tumbled out.

Kids. They were just kids.

Mae watched for a moment as the boy, who looked slightly younger, indicated for the girl to sit down, then crouched in front of her and started examining her leg. "She's injured," Mae muttered. Slotting her gun back into its holster, Mae stepped out from behind her tree.

Her first few paces were almost silent, but then a twig snapped and the children looked up. No more than seven or eight years old, their eyes wide with fear, they scooted back on their butts toward the bush they'd come from.

"Wait. It's okay. I'm not going to hurt you." Mae raised both hands in surrender and smiled at them. They were staring at her army fatigues. She looked at herself and shook her head. "I'm a friend. Are you hurt?"

Looking nervously at the girl, the boy stood up and stepped in front of her. "My sister's hurt. You got any Band-Aids?"

Mae crouched down, slipping her pack from her shoulders. "I'm pretty sure I do. Let me take a look." Opening her pack, she glanced up at them. "What are your names? I'm Mae."

"I'm Bryan and this is Sue." The boy moved toward her, but his sister lurched forward and grabbed at his pants leg.

"Bryan, don't! She's with the Army. We can't trust her."

Taking out her first-aid kit, Mae smiled again and tilted her head. "My mom's a doctor. I picked up some tips. Do you think I can take a look at that leg, Sue?" She placed the first-aid kit on the ground and sat back on her heels, waiting.

The girl looked from the kit to her brother. "I...."

"Let her help you or we'll never get back to camp." The boy turned and nodded at Mae. "You can look. She'll let you."

"Great." Mae picked up the kit and scooched over to the children. Gently, she rolled Sue's pant leg up. "That's a nasty graze. How'd it happen?" She took an alcohol swab from the kit and added quickly, "I'm just going to clean it up. It might sting."

"We were attacked." The boy sat down next to his sister and put an arm around her. " "Soldiers."

"They weren't soldiers," the girl interrupted. "Mom called them *militia*. She said they're working with the Army. Do you know them?" She blinked at Mae. "Are you with them?"

Unsure how to answer, Mae concentrated on cleaning Sue's wound. "Are you with the Freemen?" she asked gently.

When she looked up, the girl was frowning. "Who are they?"

Trying again, Mae asked, "Where are you from? Where are you staying?"

"We're camping in the hills behind that Army place." Bryan answered first. So, they were Freemen. They just didn't call themselves that.

"Perhaps you could show me? I could take you back to your mom?" Mae asked, leaning down to examine the graze a little closer. It looked deeper than she'd first thought.

When neither Bryan nor Sue answered, she looked up. They were staring at one another. Sue gave a little shake of the head, then turned to Mae. "You're trying to trick us."

Mae frowned. "No, honey." She tried to copy her mom's doctor voice but it had been so long since she'd heard it, she wasn't getting it right. "I just want to help you."

"You're a liar!" Sue yelled loudly, scrambling to her feet, her pant leg still rolled up to her knee.

"Liar!" Bryan yelled too. "You want us to take you back and then you'll shoot us."

"I would *never* do that." Mae stood up slowly. She'd been in tougher situations than this, but two kids were proving almost impossible to read and react to in the right way. "I promise. I just want to—"

"HELP!" In unison, the siblings began to yell at the tops of their voices. "Help! Militia! Help!"

Mae wavered for a moment, glanced at her pack, lying several feet away, then abandoned it and ran. Hurtling into the trees, she reached for her gun. Sue and Bryan were still screaming. Yelling. Shouting. Doing all they could to draw attention to themselves. She looked back over her shoulder. Stupid decision. She should have left them where they were. Now the Freemen would know they were in the area and watching their camp.

"Stop and put your hands in the air." A deep, female voice from behind made Mae's footsteps falter. Immediately, she lifted her hands. "Drop the gun," the voice said. "Kick it away."

Mae did as she was told.

"Hands behind your head, turn around slowly."

She followed the instruction. When she turned, she was confronted by a tall woman. Wearing a baseball cap, her hair tucked neatly beneath it, brown pants, and a thick khaki jacket, the woman eyed Mae up and down. "Army?" she asked tightly.

Mae didn't answer.

"You hurt those kids?"

Again, Mae didn't answer.

"How many others are with you?"

"Just me, and I didn't hurt them." It probably wasn't what Cornell would have told her to do, but right now she was on her own and she needed this woman to know that she didn't do anything to Bryan and Sue. "The girl was injured when I found them. I was trying to administer first aid. They became frightened and yelled for help."

"Became frightened?" The woman's head ticked to the side. "And you did nothing to elicit that reaction?"

Mae narrowed her eyes and swallowed hard. "No," she said tightly. "I did not."

"All right." The woman looked over her shoulder as two others, a man and another woman, similarly dressed, emerged from the trees. "Kids okay?" she asked them.

"Fine." The man looked at Mae as he spoke, his eyes narrow with distrust. "We should take her back to camp. Reckon Art will have some questions for her."

"Art?" The question escaped Mae's lips before she could stop it. Art was the name the injured civilian soldier had given them at the rendezvous. "He's the one in charge? Good, I'd like to speak to him." Perhaps if she could make Art see sense, she could broker some kind of negotiation with Cornell and him.

The woman didn't reply. Then, as the man grabbed Mae's hands and pulled out a cable tie to fasten them, she put her hand in the air. "Stop."

The man paused, still holding the cable tie.

"Let her go."

There was a pause. Even Mae was frowning.

"Let her *go*? Lisa...."

The woman shook her head and marched over to scoop Mae's gun from the ground. Holding it out, she gestured to it. "We're not like you. Take it."

Mae reached gingerly for the gun. Lisa pressed it into her hand.

"Take it, and go back to wherever you came from and do not return. Tell them we're stronger than you and we'll take you down if we have to. But we'd prefer peace. We *always* prefer peace." She shifted her gaze from Mae to the man next to her. Slightly solemn, he nodded.

And then they left. Simply turned and walked away, leaving Mae alone with her gun and her pack.

11

LAUREL

"Tomorrow." Laurel was leaning on the edge of the building, looking down at the lawn and parking lot as the sunlight faded. She heard Bear behind her and didn't need to turn around to know it was him. "We should leave tomorrow."

"Are you sure?" Bear walked up next to her. Trent was with him. She smiled at him, and he nodded sweetly.

"Yes. There's nothing holding me here now." Laurel braced her hands on the wall and sighed. "Tory and the baby are fine, Liam's doing well on his meds, Peter too. There are no other patients." She smiled a little. "So we should probably leave before another one turns up."

Chuckling a little, Bear exchanged a knowing look with Trent. "All right. If you're certain."

"I am." Laurel turned and wrapped her arms around her waist. "We just need to know where we're going."

Before Bear could answer, Trent cleared his throat and, rubbing his neck, said, "Um. Laurel?"

"Yes?" He looked nervous.

"I wanted to ask... I know you're going to find Mae and she's your family. But...." He looked at Bear, then back at Laurel. "Can I come with you?"

Unexpectedly, tears bit the back of Laurel's eyes as she smiled. "Of course you're coming with us." She put her arm around him and pulled him in for a tight embrace. "*You're* our family now, Trent. We stick together. Right?"

As Trent hugged Laurel back, she caught him grinning at Bear, who'd raised his eyebrows as if to say, "I told you so."

At their feet, Jessamine yipped, and Bear scooped her up.

"Okay then," Laurel said. "This is it. We're off." She paused and, while ruffling Jess's ears, looked up at Bear. "But where are we actually off to?"

"You haven't figured that out yet?" Trent looked at her, then at Bear, eyebrows raised.

Laurel shrugged a little sheepishly. "I haven't exactly been cooperative when Bear's tried to talk to me about planning."

"Thankfully, I went ahead and put together a route anyway." Bear gestured to the stairwell. "I have it mapped out. Let's grab a coffee and I'll show you."

Downstairs, in the dorm rooms, everyone was settling in for the evening. Some had retired to their beds, others were playing cards or reading. While Laurel was on her vacation to Lone Oak, Chris Jenkins and Bulldog had headed to the South Minneha library and brought back several backpacks full of books. They intended to return them when the snow thawed and come back with a fresh selection.

As she looked around the room, a strange sensation settled in Laurel's stomach. Somehow, over the weeks and months since the EMP, and after everything they'd been through, the people in this hospital had become a family. A dysfunctional family, but a family, nonetheless.

What had started as more than a hundred patients and doctors had been slowly whittled down to just a handful. Bella and the three members of her original crew who'd stuck around, Bulldog and Hannah, Henry and Janet, Chris and the boys, Mrs. Johnson and her husband, plus Bear, Laurel and Trent.

"Here." Bear snapped her out of her thoughts by touching her elbow and gesturing for them to sit down at one of the tables nearby. "I'll grab coffee and the map."

As he headed across the room, he put Jess down on the floor. Immediately she sought out the boys, Liam and Peter. They were playing chess, a game Peter disliked but one Liam was incredibly good at. Laurel had caught Chris whispering in Peter's ear that he should let Liam teach him. "You remember what it's like to lose a parent," Chris had said, placing a firm hand on his son's small shoulder.

Since then, most nights, the boys had played a game. Slowly, Peter was getting better. But he insisted he'd still rather be playing pretty much *anything* else.

When Bear returned, Trent at his side, he was holding a folded map and a cup of coffee. Trent was holding two more.

"I didn't realize you drank coffee," Laurel said, eyebrow raised. She sure as heck wouldn't have allowed Mae to drink coffee at Trent's age, but then she supposed Trent had been forced to grow up a lot more quickly than Mae did.

"Only with sugar." Trent grinned and took a long slurp from the mug, smacking his lips together afterward in an exaggerated fashion.

"Okay." Bear spread the map in the center of the table and jabbed at it with his index finger. "This is us."

Laurel nodded, hands wrapped around her mug. Narrowing her eyes, she reached out and tapped a small red cross—about seventy miles south of South Minneha hospital. "What's this?"

"This is our best shot of finding Mae." Bear sat back and folded his arms, stretching his long legs out beneath the table and crossing them at the ankles. He looked pleased with himself. Laurel waited for him to explain. "We can't just go wandering around the country looking for her. It's worse than a needle in a haystack."

"Agreed," Laurel said emphatically. Her eyes widened a little. "So, you think she's here? Why?" She looked at the red cross again.

"No, I don't think she's here. But I know someone who might be able to help us locate her and *he* lives here." Bear scratched his nail across the red mark. "In Sollon Falls."

"Sounds like a nice vacation spot," Trent said, squinting at the map as if he was trying to work out how long it would take them to reach it.

"It is," Bear replied. "Remote. Picturesque."

"I'm sure it's lovely, but who is this person? Why would he know where Mae is?" Laurel put her mug down, a sudden nervous flutter in her belly.

"His name's Kermit."

"Kermit? Like the frog?" Trent chuckled.

"Like the frog," Bear replied. "He's a veteran, but PTSD left him a little... paranoid. Now, he lives off-grid and makes a hobby out of hacking into military records. If anyone knows where Mae was stationed, it'll be him."

"Hacking? Doesn't that require computers?" Laurel asked.

"Last time I visited, he had it all in hard copy." Bear sounded confident. Taking in her expression, he added, a little quieter, "It's a start. The best one I can think of."

Bear was right; what other option did they have, even if it did still sound like a needle in a haystack?

"Okay." Laurel squeezed his hand. "Sounds good to me. Do we have a route?"

Tracing his finger over a series of roads, Bear said, "We'll try the highway. Then when we get to South Cable it'll be cross-country. Kermit's deep in the forest on the outskirts of Sollon Falls. Hoping I remember exactly where."

"If we're heading south...." Laurel trailed off, checking the map to confirm she was right. "We'll pass Cai's farm." She looked up at Bear. "Dr. Vong. He was a doctor here. His father died the day we lost the power."

"You want to check up on him?"

Laurel again looked at the map. "Would you mind? I'd like to know if he's okay. Plus, if we need supplies, he might be able to help us out." Picking up her mug again, Laurel added, "It doesn't feel right to take too much from the hospital. Besides, we're on foot."

"Yeah," Bear grumbled. "Shame the truck is frozen solid."

"But we'll take *some* stuff, right?" Trent's eyes widened at the thought of traveling on the light side.

"Of course, you'll take some stuff." A deep voice made Laurel look up. Henry was standing next to her, arms folded. "You think we'd let you leave without supplies after all you've done? Laurel, you risked your life for us multiple times. And Bear? You shared everything with us. Your truck? You could have kept it to yourself, but you didn't." Pausing, Henry added, "If you really do have to leave...."

"Henry." Laurel stood up, fighting the urge to put her hand on Henry's shoulder. "I'm sorry. I was going to tell you when we'd figured out the details. You're welcome to come with us...." She swallowed hard. "Mom would have liked that."

Tilting his head to the side, Henry scratched his chin. "I appreciate the offer, Laurel, but my place is here." He looked around the room. "This is home now, so I'll stay."

Turning back to Bear, Laurel pushed her glasses up her nose. "Should we ask the others if they want to come? The three of us leaving might change people's minds about staying here."

Bear's lips thinned. She knew what he was thinking; it could be dangerous. More people meant a slower pace. But all the same, he said, "Yes, we should."

Without giving herself time to change her mind, Laurel walked into the middle of the room and cleared her throat. Raising her voice, she waved for everyone's attention. "Excuse me, everyone. Sorry to interrupt your evening. I have an announcement to make."

Immediately, a hush fell and eyes rested on her.

"Bear and I have decided it's time for us to leave South Minneha." She sucked in a breath. "With my mother's passing, it's time we go in search of our daughter. She's in the military and we desperately want her back with us."

A rumble of understanding noises passed through her audience.

"When we've found her, we'll be heading to Thunder Bay to make a new life. We don't know how long that journey will take or what obstacles we'll have to face, but we do want to offer you all the choice to come with us. If that's what you want. You're like family to us now, and we care for every one of you."

As she finished speaking, Laurel's eyes landed on Liam. He looked away from her, blinking hard.

"I've decided to stay." Henry addressed the room but didn't offer an explanation.

"We'll stay too." Mrs. Johnson said, squeezing her husband's hand as she spoke. "We're too old for a long journey. It's comfortable here. We have what we need."

"Us too." Hannah and Bulldog exchanged a nod. "I don't want to leave the hospital without medical staff. People might need us."

"Agreed." Janet, who'd been reading, placed her book in her lap and nodded firmly.

There was a pause. Bella was muttering to the three remaining members of her crew. Laurel held her breath. Finally, Bella looked at Bear and said, "We're staying too. This lot will need someone to look out for them."

As Bear nodded at her, the only person left to decide—Chris Jenkins—stood up. Looking at the boys, he smiled and patted their heads. "These two can't manage a trek across the country, and if they need medical care, there are resources here. So, we'll politely decline the invitation to join you, Laurel."

A pang of guilt tugged at Laurel's chest. She was leaving to reunite her family. But saving Mae meant abandoning the people she'd grown to love and care for, the people she'd pledged to help.

Standing up, Bear took her hand and squeezed it. Loudly, he said, "You'll be in good hands with Bella. And I'll make sure I leave instructions on how to keep the animals out of the vents."

12

MAE

TWO DAYS LATER

"Listen up." Cornell strode into the center of the room and clapped his hands, causing everyone to look up from their breakfast. At the two long trestle tables, which had been set up in the center of the warehouse, they had been enjoying a breakfast of cold oatmeal and warm water. Their supplies ran out days ago, and Cornell had not let anyone go out to replenish them; he had been focused solely on taking back the depot from the Freemen.

"Once it's ours, we will have all the supplies we need. For now, I want everyone here focused on the task at hand," he had said, fixing them all with his steely glare — the one that could turn the room to ice. At his side, Felicia nodded

Mae was still struggling to figure out Felicia; she had lost her husband, which made Mae feel sorry for her, but there was something edgy about her that made Mae very uncomfortable. She seemed to be enjoying the idea of attacking the depot. For her, it seemed more like revenge than a necessity, yet Mae hadn't managed to get a straight answer out of anyone as to a tactical reason why they needed it so badly.

Several times, in hushed voices, she'd heard others asking what the Freemen were actually doing wrong, why they needed the depot, why they needed to get rid of them instead of working together. But the questions were never answered, and no one was brave enough to ask them out loud. If they were answered, it was with vague accusations like "they're stealing from people" or "they're hurting people" or "they think they own the place... they want to run the state... they want to make up their own laws." In truth, Mae had yet to see very much evidence of this apart from the injured civilians they'd discovered when they arrived at the rendezvous point. In fact, the worst thing she'd seen was the incident with the woman in the convenience store, which had been entirely *Cornell's* doing.

Now, however, Cornell seemed to have concocted his plan. After two days of sending teams back and forth to the depot to observe their movements, weapons, and resources, he'd determined they were ready to take it back.

"It's not enough time, surely?" Mae muttered under her breath.

Next to her, Gideon — who'd forgiven her for her impromptu outing — whispered back, "Is there ever going to be a good time to try and seize a depot when all we have are handguns and exhausted soldiers?"

Mae nodded and reluctantly spooned some oatmeal into her mouth. It was cold and the texture made her feel a little nauseated, but she needed the energy. Sipping the lukewarm water, she pretended it was coffee. Unfortunately, she'd never had a particularly strong imagination and it did little to wake her up from the fitful night's sleep she'd had.

Stepping back a little, Cornell allowed Duke to take the floor. Behind him, Claire wheeled what looked like a notice board out in front.

Pinned to it was a hand-drawn map. Using a long, pointed stick, Duke indicated the layout of the depot.

"Now, unfortunately we haven't been able to get a man inside." Duke looked around the room, a little accusatory, as if it was somehow everyone else's fault that they didn't have the answers they needed. "However, Felicia has filled us in to the best of her knowledge, and we've spoken with others who spent a little bit of time inside the depot before it was taken over by the Freemen. So, this is what we know about the layout...."

He went on to point out the entrances and exits, and what each of the other buildings was used for. Then he stopped and folded his arms.

"From what we've seen, at around midnight every night, there is a change of guard at this location. Here." He tapped the board with his stick. "For five minutes, the post is left unguarded, which should give us enough time to get our men inside and take out the other guard posts from the inside."

As Duke continued to outline the plan, Mae sat back and folded her arms. She couldn't quite believe they thought it was going to be this easy. She wanted to speak up, but she knew that to do so in front of everybody would put Cornell's back up and make him even more unlikely to listen to her. So she waited until the room had been dismissed and, while everyone else went back to their cold oatmeal and imaginary coffee, she followed Cornell out into the hallway.

She called his name. With Duke on one side of him and Felicia on the other, he turned around. He was not pleased to see her.

"Sergeant Peterson, what is it?

"Sir, has anyone considered that the Freemen know we're watching them?" She had to be careful; no one knew about her encounter in the woods. If she revealed it now, Cornell could blame her for exposing them. But, at the same time, she needed him to consider the fact that if the Freemen did know they were watching, then this whole thing could be a trap.

"How would they know we're here?" he asked tightly.

Next to him, Felicia's eyes widened as if she was looking forward to Mae's answer.

"They knew we came to the rendezvous. Plus, we've been watching them, so it makes sense that they've been watching us too. Doesn't it?"

"Perhaps. But even if they have, so what?"

Mae wanted to fold her arms defensively in front of her chest, but made an effort to keep them at her sides as she said, "If they've been watching us, Captain, and they know that we're planning to attack, is it possible that they've staged this whole thing? Wanted it to look like the post is unmanned so that they can attack us when we're supposed to be attacking them?"

For a moment, Cornell's eyes narrowed, and she thought he might be about to take her seriously. But then he started to laugh. It was almost a cackle, and it sent a shiver down her spine. On either side of him, Duke and Felicia grinned too. When Cornell straightened himself up, his lips became thinner and there was a bite in his tone. "Well, yes, Sergeant, I suppose it *is* possible. But then it's also possible that they're here right now among us. That Felicia is one of them and she's just poisoned all of our breakfasts." His grin widened.

Mae was breathing slowly and silently, trying not to show the rise in her chest because it would give away the fact that she was sighing. "Captain, with all due respect, what I'm suggesting is a little more likely."

"Is it likely? Because I don't think it is. We've had men watching that place for three days."

Mae bit back the urge to correct him. It had been two days, and the first night — when she was watching — she hadn't seen anyone take a break. She certainly hadn't seen a post left unmanned for several minutes.

"The fact of the matter is, Peterson, that the Freemen aren't soldiers. They are men and women who *want* to be soldiers. They are playing at it. They're civilians, and they don't have the brain power to know that leaving a post unguarded for even thirty seconds is a bad idea, let alone several minutes, and even if...." He stepped closer, pushing his face within a few inches of Mae's so that she could smell his breath and the tobacco that laced it. "Even if it is a trap, we're ready for them. We're armed—"

Butting in, Felicia nodded. "We weren't armed like you are. When they attacked us, we were weak, we couldn't fight back. But like the captain said, they're not soldiers."

Mae pressed her lips together. Felicia and Cornell were *assuming* the militia were the only ones with experience, but this wasn't fact. The Freemen could quite easily have veterans fighting for them. They could have a whole heap of resources that no one knew about because they hadn't taken the time to properly find out. Mae bit back the urge to sigh. She could continue arguing until she was blue in the face, but Cornell clearly wasn't going to change his mind. She'd said her bit, and she would have to accept that whatever happened next was on him. "Very well, Captain." She met his gaze and pushed her shoulders back, her chin up.

Cornell watched her as if he was waiting for her to say something else. When she didn't, he stepped back, taking his face away from hers as he nodded. "Return to the hall, Peterson. You'll need your energy tonight." Then he turned and strode away.

It was pitch dark when they began the journey from the warehouse to the depot. There were twenty of them. A mixture of soldiers and the civilian soldiers who came with Felicia had been recruited for the attack. The rest were waiting at the warehouse, with several messengers running in between to update them and bring backup if needed.

Looking around as they moved silently through the moonlight, all Mae saw was tired faces. After a long journey to get to the rendezvous point, and then several days of meager rations, they were not fighting fit, and a heavy sense of dread had settled in her stomach.

Spreading out through the tree line, they watched the perimeter. They were on the western side, where the captain predicted there would soon be a five-minute gap in the patrol. Right now, Freemen armed with guns were still pacing up and down the wire fence.

Next to Mae, Gideon was breathing heavily. Mae wasn't sure he'd ever seen live combat before, even when they were stationed in Syria. He tended to stay away from the action, and he now looked practically petrified at the thought of having to fire his gun.

After what seemed like hours, but was probably more likely minutes, Mae saw movement farther down the line. A message was being passed.

"Peterson? Are you Peterson?" the civilian soldier on the other side of her whispered into her ear.

Mae turned and nodded.

"Captain wants you up ahead."

Mae exchanged a nervous look with Gideon. So, this was Cornell's punishment for her; she would be sent in first because she doubted him. She passed six others before she finally reached Duke and the captain. Felicia was nowhere in sight.

"Peterson, I want you in there first, with Duke." Cornell didn't look at her as he gave the instruction.

Mae bit the inside of her cheek. Duke was smiling at her. He was clearly the sort of person who didn't really care whether he lived or died as long as it was a good show when it went down.

"Yes, Captain," she said tightly. If she was going to do this, she wasn't going to waste valuable energy starting a pointless argument. Instead, she needed to ensure her wits were about her.

She had no idea what time it was, but after a few more minutes, exactly as the captain predicted, the guard changed.

The sentries who'd been walking the border on the western side turned and headed back to the main building. One of them shouted, "Next shift!" But no one else appeared.

Nodding at her, Duke motioned for them to move forward. They left the trees, ran across the gap between the undergrowth and the fence, and scaled it with ease. This time, there was barbed wire at the top. Allowing Mae to go first, Duke threw up a thick blanket, which she placed on top of the wire, then rolled over and descended to the other side.

Duke landed next to her with a quiet thud, then took wire cutters from his pocket. Mae took hers out too, and together they made a hole in the fence. As others started to move forward, Duke gestured for Mae to go right while he went left.

She knew what she had to do: take out the first soldier she came across, so that the other guard points were left unwatched.

When she reached the edge of the building, she stopped, raised her gun and peered around the corner. In daylight, she might have been able to use a mirror to look, but in this light, it would have been hopeless. She had to rely on her eyes.

One lone guard stood at what looked like an old entry point for vehicles into the depot. A flicker of orange told her they'd lit a cigarette. Slowly, she stepped out of the shadow. They'd moved and were now standing with their back toward her. If she was lucky, she could hit them over the head and knock them unconscious without having to fire her gun, which would mean two things; first that she wouldn't need to kill anyone, and second that they wouldn't be discovered because of the sound of a gunshot.

However, she was inches from the guard when another gunshot rang out. Duke must have fired. The guard spun around, cigarette hanging from his lips. Mae raised her gun but he was quicker, aiming his first.

Slowly, he grinned at her, then he lowered his gun and shot her in the leg.

As Mae fell backward, she dropped the weapon from her hand and the guard kicked it away. There was a flurry of movement. She could hear feet and voices and more shots ringing out, but she couldn't see what was happening. Pain ricocheted through her body, and she screwed her eyes shut. When she opened them again, someone was standing above her. It was too dark to make out their face. They leaned closer. She blinked, her eyes blurry with pain. The face drew closer, and then she realized who it was.

"Lisa?"

"Hello again. I thought I told you not to come back."

13

LAUREL

Laurel woke to the smell of coffee. She was getting used to the weaker, non-sugared version they consumed these days, but she dreaded the day they ran out completely.

Pulling open the front of her tent, she smiled at the sight of Trent sitting by the fire. He was prodding it with a stick, watching the pot suspended over it. When he saw her, he waved. So far, their journey had gone smoothly. They'd taken as many supplies as they could carry—to see them through the journey—and said tearful goodbyes to everyone at South Minneha just before sunrise. With one last look out toward the woods where her mother had been cremated, Laurel had touched the golden cross that now hung around her neck—the one her mother had worn for more than fifty years—and whispered, "Bye Mom. We're going to get Mae."

After a full day's trek, they'd camped out in a clearing not far from the side of the highway. With the thinning snow, they'd managed almost thirty miles, and all three of them were pleased to rest and eat.

Now, ducking out of her tent, pulling her coat tightly around her, Laurel yawned as she headed over. She could swear Trent had grown since she first met him. Only a few months had passed, yet he became more gangly by the day.

With the lake in the background, framed by pine trees, and the fire crackling, she could almost imagine they were on a family camping trip. As if he was reading her mind, Trent said, "Nice, this, isn't it?" He gestured to the lake, then shrugged as a cool breeze whipped across their small clearing.

"It is."

"Thunder Bay's a bit like this." Trent stood up and peered over the pot. "Have you been? To visit Bear?"

Laurel sat down cross-legged and leaned onto her knees, supporting her chin with her hands. "No. I haven't." She glanced sideways at Trent. She wasn't sure how much he knew about the two of them, and wasn't sure she wanted to share the fact that — until Bear came hurtling out of the woods that day — they hadn't seen or spoken to one another in two years.

"It's nice." Trent smiled a little, but then the smile drooped. "But that's where you'll go? After you've found your daughter?"

Reaching over and taking a protein bar from the pile at Trent's feet, Laurel raised her eyebrows at him. "It's where *we'll* go, yes." She nudged him gently with her elbow while tearing the packet open with her teeth. "I told you. We're together now. The three of us."

Trent smiled and nodded. "And your daughter. Mae."

Laurel breathed in slowly. "Yes. And Mae."

"And Jess," Trent said pointedly.

"Speaking of Jess… where is she?" Laurel looked over at the tent Bear and Trent had shared last night. Jess had slept with her, but as soon as she heard Bear moving at first light, she'd scratched at the entrance and run off to his tent instead.

"Bear took her for a walk down by the river. Think he was hoping to find something we can cook."

"Like fish?"

"Rabbit, probably." Trent looked off into the distance. "Jess is good with rabbits."

Laurel was about to ask if the coffee was ready when Trent pointed toward the lake. "Here they are."

Disappointingly, Bear was not carrying anything that looked edible. His hands were empty except for firewood. Scampering up to them, Jess licked Trent's face, then dove into Laurel's lap for a cuddle. She was wearing her new red jacket. It reminded Laurel of her mom's lipstick and matched her hat. She stroked it, picturing her mom's fragile fingers knitting it by the fire.

As her cheeks began to flush and emotion tugged at her gut, she cleared her throat and looked for Bear. "Morning," she said, nodding at him.

"Morning." He moved toward her as if he was going to stoop and give her a hug, then stopped, put down the firewood, and shoved his hands into his pockets. She was starting to get used to his beard. It suited him in a strange, bush-man kind of way. "That coffee ready, kid?" he asked Trent, crouching down and picking up a metal cup from the stack of three next to the fire.

"Should be." Trent examined Bear's lack of food. "No luck with the rabbits, then?"

"'Fraid not." Bear took off his hat and scraped his fingers through his hair. "We'll catch something on the road. Let's drink up and move out. Yeah?"

As Trent poured the coffee, Laurel returned to her tent, fetched her pack, and found the map they'd brought with them from the hospital.

"Show me again where this friend of yours lives." She spread it out on the ground between them. Sipping his coffee, Bear leaned over and jabbed his finger at a spot about fifty miles away.

"Couple of days' walk." Bear took another drink, wincing at the lack of sugar; he'd always taken his coffee far too sweet.

"You really think he might know where Mae is?" Laurel tilted her head to examine the map.

"If anyone will know, it'll be Kermit." Bear took a protein bar and bit into it, wrinkling his nose at the lack of taste.

"Kermit and Bear?" Trent chuckled. "You two must have been *cool* back in the day."

"Must have been?" Bear made an "Elvis" type face and scoffed. "I'll have you know, kid, I'm the epitome of cool."

Watching the two of them, Laurel laughed quietly. It had been so long since she'd seen Bear like this; funny, smiling, *in* the world instead of existing on the periphery of it. It seemed Trent had done what she'd spent years trying to do after Bear's injury; he'd brought him back to life. Laurel was pleased that Mae would see this version of her father when they found her.

Returning to the map, she followed the route Bear had plotted for them. They were a few hours' walk away from Cai's farm. They should make it by midday. Of course, when Cai first made this journey in his old but functioning truck, it would have taken just an hour or two.

"Are you sure about stopping at Cai's place?" Laurel asked, pulling her scarf a little tighter as a cold breeze whipped through their makeshift camp.

"Of course. It's on our way." Bear surprised her with his sincerity; he'd been anxious to leave for weeks, so she wouldn't have expected him to opt for any kind of delay.

Laurel pushed her glasses up the bridge of her nose. The thought of seeing another friendly face — a face from *before* — was comforting. It eased a little of the swirling tightness that had settled in her chest after her mom's funeral. "Really?"

"Of course." Bear nodded, looking at her as if he couldn't understand why she'd think he wouldn't want to. "If we set off now, we could make it by midday and — if your friend doesn't mind — break the journey there overnight. Then make the final push to Kermit's in the morning."

"Sounds like a plan." Laurel stood up, downed the last of her coffee, then headed for her tent and began to dismantle it. For some reason, the thought of seeing Cai made her want to hurry. Perhaps because, all this time, she'd been picturing his farm as an idyllic slice of peace among the chaos. When things had gotten particularly dark, she'd imagined him tending his crops and milking his cows. Living a normal life.

"You weren't tempted to go with him?" Bear appeared at her shoulder and helped her pack up the tent. "When your friend left. You weren't tempted to go with him?"

Was there a hint of something in the way Bear said friend?

"I was." Laurel met his eyes. "But I owed it to the hospital to stay." She looked away, bending to do up her pack. "I've wondered several times if it was the right choice. If I'd gone with Cai, Mom could have spent her final months watching the sunset on the porch. Instead of—"

"Instead of meeting Henry? Falling in love one last time? Becoming grandmother to a whole hospital?" Bear glanced at Jess and smiled. "Learning to knit some pretty amazing dog-wear?"

Laurel laughed and wiped a tear from her eye.

"I know which option Deb would have chosen." He put his hand on her shoulder. "You made the right choice. For everyone. Including your mom."

Inhaling deeply through her nose, Laurel pressed her lips together. "You really think so?"

"I really do."

She shook her head a little, her hair falling around her shoulders, then nodded. "Okay, then let's get going." She walked with him to his and Trent's tent and started helping to dismantle it. "You'll like Cai," she said, glancing at him. "He's your sort of guy."

"Good." Bear didn't look at her. In a past life, she might have teased him for being jealous, but not in this one. In this one, they weren't husband and wife. Yet, they weren't friends either. They were something else. *Family,* her mom would have said. *You're family.*

As it neared midday, and they drew closer to Cai's farm, Jess became braver and started darting off into the undergrowth at the side of the road.

"Hope she brings us back a rabbit," Trent said, rolling his eyes at the dog's small white tail as it disappeared with her into the bush.

"Right now, I'd take a sparrow," Bear grumbled. "Anything that tastes of *meat.*"

They were approaching a sharp bend in the road. An abandoned truck sat in the middle, angled sideways as if the driver had skidded to a stop.

Instinctively, Laurel headed for it and looked inside. "Nothing useful," she called over her shoulder. "Just sunglasses and some chewing gum."

"I'll take the gum!" Trent jogged over and stuck his head in the passenger side door.

"Here." Laurel tossed it to him, then picked up the sunglasses and looked at the sky. It was growing brighter by the day. Perhaps they would be useful after all.

"Don't suppose there are any hearing aid batteries in there?" Bear was fiddling with his ear.

Laurel examined his aid. It was an old-fashioned kind, not the right fit for him, but he'd been getting used to it. "Your battery's dead?" She spoke loudly and Bear frowned at her.

"Not yet, but it won't be long."

Smiling, Laurel tried to sound confident as she said, "Don't worry. We'll figure something out. Maybe Cai's dad had one."

"Maybe." Bear frowned again, but then looked at Trent. "If not, you'll have yourself a full-time job as my scribe."

"Scribe?" Trent asked, confused by the term.

Laurel was about to explain when the sound of Jess's short, sharp bark permeated the air. A moment later, she hurtled around the corner up ahead, running straight for Bear, barking.

Immediately, Bear reached for his gun. Laurel did too. And when she looked at Trent, she realized he'd copied them.

They watched the corner, unmoving.

For a while, nothing happened. Then three figures appeared, all holding shotguns. "Steady." Bear gestured for them to hold fire, then raised his voice and shouted to the strangers. "We mean you no harm. If you put down your weapons, we'll put down ours."

Laurel watched, her breath quickening in her chest. The strangers didn't reply, just walked closer. Jess was now behind Trent, whimpering. The thud in her chest intensified. A rushing sound came to her ears, and a feeling like fire bubbled up in her gut.

In a split second, everything that had happened since the world lost power flashed in front of Laurel's eyes. Robert, Arlo, Britt, Jim.

"Not again," she muttered.

Bear looked at her sideways.

"Not again." She strode forward. Bear told her not to, but she ignored him. The men in front of her lifted their shotguns. But she wasn't going to give them chance to fire. She was quicker than them, and a better shot.

In a split second, she aimed and fired. One. Two. Three. Purposefully barely missing their toes. "Take another step and next time I won't miss!"

"Laurel." Bear spoke to her through gritted teeth. "What are you doing?"

"I'm not taking it, Bear. Not anymore." She shot again.

The men opposite had stopped in their tracks. One lifted his gun. But before he could fire, Laurel had pulled the trigger. She hit his hand, exactly what she was aiming for. He dropped the gun, screaming, and clasped his hand to his chest.

"I said, don't take another step!" Laurel was still moving forward. Bear was next to her, but only because he felt he had to be; she'd given him no choice.

"Man, she's crazy! Run!"

As she drew closer, the pulsing anger in Laurel's stomach subsided a little and she realized that the men in front of her weren't much older than Trent, perhaps in their early twenties. And they looked terrified.

"Wait." Her hands were shaking. She lowered the barrel of her gun. "I'm a doctor. I should take a look at your hand." She was speaking to the one she shot.

"Are you kidding me? You shot me!" He shook his head, eyes wide. He looked terrified. Then he turned and ran, leaving his gun behind.

14

BEAR

For a long moment, Laurel didn't move. She remained stock still, her chest rising and falling as she fought to keep her breath steady. Gesturing for Trent to stay where he was, Bear walked slowly toward her. She was still holding her gun at her side, but her fingers were trembling.

Gently, Bear curled his fingers around hers. She twitched, but let him take the gun from her.

Putting the safety back on, he slid the gun into his own belt, then pointed to the empty truck. The doors were still open.

"Come sit down." He guided her to it and she slid onto the front passenger seat. Sitting sideways, her legs dangling, she leaned onto her knees and exhaled a loud shaky breath.

Bear took his water bottle from his pack and offered it to her, then reached for a candy bar. "The sugar will help."

Leaving her for a moment, he returned to Trent. He had picked up the kid's abandoned gun and was looking at the small spatter of blood on the ground.

"Is she okay?" he asked quietly, looking furtively around Bear at Laurel, who'd taken her glasses off and was staring at the space between her knees.

"She'll be okay." Bear took the gun from Trent and slung it over his shoulder. He'd never seen Laurel lose control before. Not in a combat situation. Not when weapons were involved. No matter what, she'd always been able to put her emotions aside and focus. He sincerely hoped this was a one-off.

He was studying her expression, trying to decide between tough love and empathy, when Jess bounded out of the undergrowth. She was practically grinning, a limp creature clamped between her jaws, her tail wagging.

Trent crouched and held out his hand. Jess dropped the animal into it.

"Cool. Rabbit!" He ruffled her ears. "Good job."

Jess was still wagging her tail, but looked past Trent at Laurel and tilted her head. Immediately, she trotted over and pawed Laurel's leg. Laurel reached down and Jess jumped into her arms. She lowered her head and pressed it to Jess's forehead. She was whispering something, but there was no way Bear would have heard what it was even if his hearing aid hadn't been on the blink.

"Shall we make a fire?" Trent asked, looking at the rabbit.

Bear scratched his bearded chin. He was looking forward to the weather warming up, so he could at least go back to a defined stubble rather than the Sasquatch look. "We're not far from her friend's farm. I think we should keep going. Offer him the rabbit as a welcome gift."

Trent's shoulders dropped a little. As if in answer, his stomach growled fiercely.

"Grab some water and a snack. We'll eat properly when we get there." Bear motioned for Trent to take a seat by the side of the road, then walked slowly over to Laurel. As he walked, he made a decision. Tough love.

"What was that?" He folded his arms in front of his chest. With him standing and her perched in the truck, they were eye level with one another. His jaw twitched.

"I'm sorry. I… lost control." As Laurel's eyes grew watery, Bear bit back the urge to soften his tone.

"That's not good enough, soldier." He fixed his gaze on hers, refusing to look away.

Laurel blinked slowly and returned her glasses to the bridge of her nose. "I know."

"Rivera, you need to talk about how you're feeling. Talk about your grief. If you bottle it up and pretend it's not there…." Bear looked back toward the smudge of blood on the ground. "You'll either implode or explode. And we can't afford for that to happen. Not if we want to find our daughter and get to her in one piece."

Inhaling through her nose, Laurel pressed her lips together. Her cheeks dimpled as she sucked them in a little. Then a flicker of the resolve he recognized came to her eyes. She bit her lower lip and nodded. "Understood."

Finally allowing himself to unfold his arms and put a hand on her knee, Bear said, "This can't happen again, Laurel."

"It won't." She squeezed his fingers briefly before taking her hand back and rubbing her thighs. "I promise."

The approach to Roundacre Farm was down a long, straight road. Fields stretched out on either side, covered in snow but with grass beginning to peek through from below. In the distance, a quaint-looking farmhouse stood proudly. However, as they drew closer, Bear began to feel uneasy.

"It's pretty quiet." Trent narrowed his eyes, staring into the distance. "Can't see many animals."

"They're probably under shelter. It's still cold out." Laurel adjusted her scarf and looked up at the sky. It was gray and mottled with clouds. But for the first time in a long time, it looked like it was threatening rain rather than snow.

Next to the farmhouse was a large barn. Perhaps the animals were in there.

"It's pretty open out here." Bear tugged off his hat and shoved it into his pocket. The warmth in his muscles from walking for two straight hours was making him hot. "Exposed."

"That's risky, right?" Trent asked.

Bear tilted his head from side to side, rubbing his neck. "Could be in the spring, if it's obvious someone's living and working here. So far, he's only had winter to contend with."

"Even in winter, the smoke from the chimney would let people know there's someone here, right?" Trent gestured to the farmhouse, which just as he said was releasing plumes of smoke into the air.

"Cai knows how to take care of himself." Laurel's tone was clipped, her Texan accent seeping through as it always did when she was irritated. She shoved her hands into her pockets, but the gesture made Bear smile; he'd rather see her annoyed with him than the way she was earlier. He still didn't even quite know how to describe how she'd looked, how she'd sounded when she promised him it wouldn't happen again.

"I'm sure he does." Bear diverted his eyes back to the farmhouse. Laurel's gun was still in his waistband. Without saying anything, he took it out and handed it to her. She took it without saying anything.

After twenty-or-so minutes of walking the long path to the farmhouse, Bear scooped Jess into his arms and strapped her back into her carry pack. The last thing he wanted was her getting herself shot again because she spooked the guy.

As they approached the steps, Bear took in the façade of the farmhouse. It was old, more weathered than it had looked from a distance. If it hadn't been for the smoke from the chimney, it would have looked empty. No plant pots, no throw on the porch swing, nothing to indicate that someone was actually living here.

But if Cai Vong really was as careful as Laurel said, he'd have noticed them well before now. Letting strangers approach your property without giving them a clear sign that you weren't going to put up with any trouble was *not* a good way of doing things. Not in this world, anyway.

Leaving Bear and Trent standing at the bottom of the stairs, Laurel took them three at a time and rapped on the door hard with her knuckles. "Cai, it's Laurel. Are you here?"

She waited, straining her ears, then looked round at Bear.

"Try again," he suggested, a heavy sensation forming in the pit of his stomach.

"Cai. Are you there? It's Laurel." She knocked again, but still there was no answer. Briefly, she closed her eyes, steeling herself. Then she lifted her gun and tried the handle. The door swung effortlessly open and she stepped inside.

With one hand on Jess, in her carry pack, and the other on his gun, Bear padded up the steps behind Laurel. Trent followed. Bear motioned for him to stay back a little.

When Bear entered the farmhouse, he found Laurel standing in the middle of a wide wood-floored hallway. She bent down and picked something up. When she turned, Bear narrowed his eyes. She was holding a picture frame.

"The glass is shattered." She looked at the spot on the wall it must have fallen from, clearly outlined by a square of more brightly colored wallpaper and an empty nail.

Bear took the frame from her. The photograph inside was of a middle-aged man and a middle-aged woman, a small boy standing between them, in front of the farmhouse steps.

"Is this him?" Bear pointed at the man.

"No, I think that's his father." Laurel pressed her fingertip to the boy's face. "This must be Cai when he was young."

"We should check the rooms." Bear looked down the hall and told Trent to stay in the doorway until they'd confirmed the place was empty. Then, one by one, they checked the place was clear.

Living room, empty.

Washroom, empty.

Dining room, empty.

Each room looked frozen in time, as if it hadn't changed for years.

In the kitchen, they found the source of the smoke: a fire in the grate. They also found chaos. Plates abandoned at the large oak table, covered in remnants of food. Empty packets strewn across the floor, broken ornaments that had been knocked from shelves.

"What the…?" Laurel strode into the room and whirled around as if she might find the answer staring her in the face.

"Looks like he's been robbed." Bear strode back to the kitchen door and called for Trent to join them. "Or left in a hurry." He swept his finger through a dusting of white flour on the worktop, and then opened the cupboards above it. They were empty. Completely empty.

Striding over to the kitchen window, Laurel peered out at the farm.

"What does he farm?" Bear asked.

"Corn, I think." Laurel pointed to the barn, visible through the window. "But I know he had horses. We should see if they're okay." She looked at him and held her palm up to indicate he should stay put for a moment. "I'll go sweep upstairs first."

"I'll come—"

Laurel shook her head quickly and swallowed hard. "No, stay with Trent. Just in case…."

She didn't specify in case of what, but Bear did as she asked and shrugged his backpack from his shoulders. As he removed it, Jess wriggled, but he stroked her ears and said, "Best stay where you are for now. Until we know it's safe."

Copying Bear, Trent freed himself from his pack, then flopped into one of the dining chairs. He squinted at one of the plates in front of him as if he was considering whether or not the substance dried onto its surface was worth tasting. Clearly deciding against it, he pushed it away and sighed.

"Still got that rabbit?" Bear asked.

Trent nodded and reached for his belt, where he'd tied the rabbit's carcass by its ears. He set it down on the table with a thud. "When we've figured out what's going on, we'll cook," Bear promised, keenly aware that Trent's stomach hadn't stopped growling for the past thirty minutes.

Straining his ears, he tried to make out the sound of Laurel's footsteps above him. He couldn't. The hearing aid was alternating between beeping at him to tell him it needed recharging and becoming patchy and muffled. When the sound dipped, he'd turn it up. But then it would return again, momentarily, at full volume and make him wince. Right now, it was in a muffled cycle.

"Maybe this Kermit guy of yours has a secret stash of hearing aid batteries." Trent nudged the rabbit with his index finger as he watched Bear fiddling with his ear.

"Maybe." Bear was tempted to take the darn thing out, but since they didn't know what the heck was going on here, he knew he should keep it in. At least for now.

The pricking of Jess's ears told him that Laurel had returned to the hallway. A moment later, she stepped into the room. "Nothing," she said. "There's no one here."

"Does it look like he left?" Bear asked.

"Hard to tell." Laurel was lingering in the doorway. "No obvious signs of a bag being packed, but I'm not sure I'd be able to tell."

"Let's go check the barn." Bear left his pack on the floor. Before Trent could stand up, he said, "You stay here, kid, with Jess." He unstrapped her from the chest harness and hooked on the leash they used when they didn't want her running off.

At the door, he glanced back and fixed his eyes on Trent's gun. "Stay alert."

Trent nodded solemnly and put the gun down in front of him on the table.

Outside, Laurel turned to Bear. "There was blood in the bathroom."

"Blood?" Bear looked back at the house.

"Lots. Smeared on the sink. On the floor." She pushed her fingers through her hair and shook her head solemnly.

"Maybe he hurt himself and went for help." Bear rubbed his jaw with his thumb and forefinger.

"He's a doctor," Laurel replied, a little snappily. "Why would he need to leave to get help? Besides, we didn't see any blood in the snow. If he left, he'd already stopped the bleeding."

"Maybe he ran out of supplies and had to go find someone to stitch him up properly? Bandaged the wound enough to stop it bleeding while he—"

Before he could finish, Laurel strode off through the snow in the direction of the barn.

When she reached the large barn doors, she stood in front of them and attempted to push them open. When they didn't budge, she pressed her ear to the door.

"Hear anything?" Bear asked.

"Nothing." Laurel stood back, then banged on the door with her fist. It rattled. "Cai? Are you in there? It's Laurel."

Still nothing. Motioning for him to go the other way, Laurel took off around one side of the barn. They met at the rear. Here, a smaller door with a black handle had been positioned to the left of the back wall. Laurel tried the handle. Of course, it didn't open.

Then... a voice. Bear strained his ears. Laurel's eyes widened.

"I'm armed!" The voice was shouting, but Bear was having to concentrate overly hard to make out the words.

"Cai? It's Laurel Rivera. From South Minneha. Are you all right?" Laurel had pressed her palms to the door. Her face was etched with worry. It gave Bear a strangely uncomfortable feeling in his stomach.

When the door opened, the feeling worsened; the guy who stepped out was far too handsome for his liking. More like a TV doctor from one of those shows Mae used to watch than a real-life one. Sure, he was disheveled, with a dishcloth wound around his upper arm and a bruise on his face, but all the same Bear's fist tightened at his side.

"Laurel?" Cai Vong lowered his gun, slung it over his shoulder, then took two small steps forward and threw his arms around Bear's wife. "I can't believe it's you." Cai stood back and stared at her. A smile fluttered on Laurel's lips. Bear's jaw twitched. "What are you doing here, Laurel?"

"We're trying to find our daughter. Mae. We were passing by, so I wanted to check in." Laurel's hands were on Cai's forearms. "Are you all right?" She looked behind him into the barn. "What on earth is going on? The farmhouse looks...." She lowered her voice, but Bear was pretty certain that what she said next was, "I found blood in the bathroom."

Briefly touching his fingertips to his upper arm, Cai grimaced. "It's a long story, but I'm glad you arrived when you did. Twenty-four hours earlier and you'd have—" Cai stopped and shook his head, then rubbed the back of his neck. "The house is empty?" His gaze flitted from Laurel to the farmhouse.

"Yes." She was studying him, trying to figure out what he wasn't saying.

"And you saw no one on your way here?"

As Laurel hesitated, no doubt thinking about their encounter, Bear answered, "No one. Property's clear."

Cai inhaled slowly, nodding at Bear but not asking his name. Over his shoulder, he called, "I'll be back." Then he stepped out into the snow. He was wearing nothing but a pair of cargo pants and a fleece. No winter jacket, no hat, no scarf.

"You must be frozen." Laurel pulled off her hat and offered it to him. "How long have you been in there?"

Shaking his head at her offer, Cai shivered. "I'll explain when we're inside. I promise." At the farmhouse steps, he finally turned to Bear and extended a hand. "I'm sorry. I was rude. You must be Laurel's husband. Bjorn?"

Bear cast a surprised glance at Laurel, trying to figure out whether the fact she'd told this guy about him was a good thing or a bad thing.

"Yes." Bear shook the hand of Cai's good arm as vigorously as he felt he should.

"It's nice to meet you." Cai sounded sincere, which made Bear feel a little guilty. But not too guilty; something was going on here, and until this guy explained himself, Bear wasn't going to trust him. Even if Laurel said he was one of the good guys.

"I should tell you, we brought company." Laurel shoved her hat into her jacket pocket as they headed down the hall toward the kitchen. "Our..." she hesitated, searching for a word to describe Trent.

"Our foster kid and our dog," Bear interjected. "They're in the kitchen. It was warm in there."

Cai nodded. "The fire hadn't gone out. Good." When he reached the door, he winced with the effort of pushing it open. Something about his movements made Bear think his arm wasn't the only injury he'd suffered.

Laurel noticed too — Bear could see it in her eyes — but she didn't say anything.

As they entered the room, Trent sprang up from the table. Almost instantly, he relaxed. At his feet, Jess barked, but as soon as Bear said, "It's okay, girl, Cai's a friend of Laurel's," she relaxed and wagged her tail instead.

"Here. Sit down." Laurel pulled out a chair, but before she could usher Cai into it, he stumbled. His eyes rolled back in his head, and he fell to the ground.

15

LAUREL

Laurel and Bear reached for Cai at the same time, but they weren't fast enough; he hit the floor with a thud. Sinking quickly to her knees beside him, she pulled off her scarf and lowered her cheek to his mouth.

"He's breathing," she said, feeling small puffs of warm air on her skin. Putting her hands on his shoulders, she tried gently to rouse him. When he didn't respond, she looked at Bear and said, "Raise his feet."

"Huh?" Bear's voice was becoming increasingly loud. His hearing aid was muffling everything, and he wasn't aware of his own volume.

"Raise his feet for me." Laurel pointed to Cai's feet.

Darting over from the table, Trent scooped up one of Cai's legs. Bear watched him, then did the same.

"I think he just passed out." She pressed the back of her hand to his forehead. No fever. She was about to start unwinding his bandage when his eyes fluttered and he groaned loudly.

"Trent, can you get him some water and a blanket? There are some in the living room. I'm not sure how long he was out there in the barn." She gripped his hand and rubbed it between hers. He was ice cold.

"Laurel?" Cai opened his eyes and instantly tried to sit up.

"Take it easy." She put her hand on his shoulder.

Cai raised a hand to his head and winced. "I'm sorry. What happened?"

"You passed out, buddy." Bear helped Laurel lift Cai to his feet and lower him into the chair she'd pulled out. It was close to the fire. Returning with a blanket, Trent wrapped it around Cai's shoulders and handed him a bottle of water.

Shakily, Cai held the blanket close, then opened the bottle and took a long thirsty drink from it. "Thank you, young man." He smiled at Trent, a shiver running through him. "I appreciate your kindness."

"Cai." Laurel touched her fingers to his bandage. "What happened? The blood upstairs...."

"There's blood upstairs?!" Trent looked, wide-eyed, from Laurel to Bear as if he wasn't quite sure why they'd kept such information from him.

Laurel nodded curtly but remained focused on Cai.

"Maybe we should let Cai catch his breath," Bear suggested. "It looks like he's been through an ordeal."

Nodding slowly, Laurel said, "Of course. But I'll need to look at that wound. Are there any others?"

"Perhaps... I think I should eat something." Cai pushed his fingers through his hair. "It's been a few days since I ate anything."

"A few days?" Laurel's stomach clenched. What the heck had happened here?

"We have rabbit." With a spring in his step, Trent walked over to the table and picked up Jess's find. "And a fire to cook on. Won't take long."

"Rabbit?" Cai smiled. "That sounds great."

As Trent scoured the empty kitchen cupboards for ingredients and Bear skinned the rabbit, Laurel asked Cai whether he had any source of fresh water.

"The tap." He smiled. "My father made this place self-sufficient years ago."

"I'll make tea." She'd already located the kettle. "Then you're going to let me look at that arm."

Ten minutes later, Laurel handed Cai a cup of milkless tea with two spoonfuls of sugar.

"Sugar?" he asked.

"We brought some rations with us from the hospital."

Cai wrapped his fingers around the mug and nodded. "How has it been?"

Smiling, Laurel shrugged out of her jacket. Having stoked the fire, it was now extremely warm sitting beside it. "Ah-ah. You first." Laurel gestured to the arm and Cai rolled his eyes at her.

Nudging the blanket aside, he turned so she could unfasten the bandage and continued to sip his tea one-handed.

"It was militia." Cai's tone darkened as he spoke. Next to them, crouched so he could cook the rabbit over the fire, Bear looked up. "I thought they were the Army, but they weren't." He shook his head. "Well, I think some of them were, but others were...." He trailed off. "*Not* soldiers. Wannabe soldiers."

Laurel and Bear exchanged a look. He was thinking what she was thinking; this didn't sound good.

"At first, they were friendly. Asked if they could make a pit stop. There were twelve, maybe fifteen of them and one of me, so what was I going to say?" Cai shook his head. "I made them tea, gave them some food, told them to fill up their water supplies." He winced as Laurel finally freed his arm from the bandage.

"A bullet wound." She examined his arm.

"Bullet went straight through. I cleaned it as best I could."

Laurel reached for her pack and pulled out the medical kit she'd prepared at the hospital. "You stitched it yourself?"

"Hack job, I know. I was in the barn. All I had was my horse kit."

As Laurel set about cleaning and fixing the job Cai had done of fixing himself, she held her breath, waiting for him to explain.

"They stayed two nights. On the third day, I told them they needed to leave. They were arguing between themselves, then one of them lost it and shot me. The others told him he was an idiot. I went upstairs to try and clean it up. I was coming down for my bag when I heard them talking." Cai shuffled in his chair. "They said maybe they should get going. Then they started talking about the horses." He swallowed hard. "One of them said they didn't need any more horses. They already had the ones pulling the wagons. Then another said they should just take them anyway and use them for meat when their supplies ran out."

Laurel bit her lower lip. She was trying to focus on Cai's fresh stitches, but her heart ached for him at the thought of his precious family horses being taken for slaughter.

"I went out the back, headed for the barn. I keep a shotgun hidden in there. They hadn't thought to look for it." As Laurel finished, Cai nodded his thanks and sat up a little straighter, shrugging off the blanket. "They found me, but I told them they'd have to kill me if they wanted my horses." Cai shrugged. "They argued about it a while, but ultimately I guess they decided it wasn't worth the fight."

"And this was three days ago?" Laurel pressed a protein bar into Cai's hands. He ripped it open and took a large bite, nodding.

Next to her, Bear exhaled loudly. "You say some of them were Army?"

Laurel gestured for him to lower his volume a little. His cheeks flushed and he looked away quickly. She kicked herself a little for embarrassing him.

"Yes." Cai took another bite. "On their way to some kind of base to meet with other groups. I don't know how they were coordinating it without radios."

"Did you get a location?"

"I think they said Fort Stillwell."

"Stillwell? Aren't we headed in that direction?" Trent chimed in from over by the table.

"Kermit's place is closer. Hopefully our paths won't cross." Bear returned to the rabbit, his face telling Laurel he was lost in thought already.

"Kermit?" A smile crossed Cai's lips.

"Long story." Laurel smiled back. Then she reached for his hand and squeezed it. "I'm very glad you're okay."

"I'll survive." He grimaced and looked around his kitchen. "Although it looks like they pretty much cleaned me out of food. So I'm not sure what I'll eat for the next few months."

"We can leave you with some things," Laurel offered.

She expected Bear to disagree, but he didn't.

"We took some supplies when we left the hospital."

"Ah yes. The hospital. So, are you going to fill me in?"

For the next hour, Laurel filled Cai in on everything that had happened since the two of them parted ways, stopping just after their return to South Minneha. In turn, he explained how he'd slotted back into life on the farm without too much trouble. His father had stores of food in the cellar, his own water supply, and plenty of candles. So he'd been all set to ride out the winter.

As Bear and Trent cleared the table, throwing Jess a rabbit leg, Laurel and Cai went to the lounge and he helped her light a fire in the grate. When they sat back on the dark burgundy couch, which they'd pulled across the room, they stared at the flames for a moment, neither of them speaking.

When Cai did speak, his voice was low. "I thought of you often. Wondered about you and your mom. How she was doing."

Laurel didn't look at him, just focused on the flames. "She passed a few days ago."

Cai pressed his eyes closed and breathed in slowly. "I'm sorry, Laurel."

She didn't need to look at him to know he meant what he said, truly. He had lost his father just a few short months ago.

"It's strange, isn't it? Existing in a world without your parent? My brain still forgets. I think, *I must tell Dad that* or *Dad will crack up when he hears this one*... and then I remember he's not around anymore."

"It was hard to leave," Laurel replied. "I felt like I was abandoning her, even though she's not there anymore."

Cai nodded. He must have felt the same when he left to return to the farm. "But you left to reunite your family. She'd be proud of you for that."

"Yes," Laurel said. "She would."

16

BEAR

With a strong black coffee in each hand, Bear paused outside the living room. Silhouetted in front of the fire, Laurel was speaking in hushed tones to Cai. He couldn't make out what they were saying, but it looked... intimate.

Stepping back into the hall, feeling as though he shouldn't interrupt them, Bear looked at the coffee.

"They're talking about her mom." Trent was at Bear's elbow.

Without waiting for the okay, Jess trotted past them and bounded up onto the couch next to Laurel. Laurel turned, saw Bear and the coffee, and waved. "Come in, it's nice and warm."

But after handing them the coffee, he remained standing. "I think I'll hit the hay. Is it okay to light a fire in one of the rooms upstairs?"

Cai nodded. "Sure. At least they didn't take my firewood. Take any room you like."

"Kid? You coming?" Trent looked from Bear to Laurel as if he was waiting for him to ask her too. When he didn't, he nodded.

"Sure, PB."

At the door, Bear paused. "See you soon?" he said, fixing his eyes on Laurel's.

"I'll drink this, then be up." She looked brighter. Or was he imagining it?

He let the door swing closed after him, then headed upstairs and chose a room with two bunk beds. A grandkids' room, with brightly colored bedding and a toy plane strung from the ceiling. "Top or bottom?" Trent asked as Bear lit the fire.

"Bottom."

"Cool." Trent hopped up onto the top bunk. Sometimes, he still looked like a little kid. Other times, he was so grown up.

Settling into the lower bunk, looking across at the empty one, Bear tried not to count the minutes until Laurel padded up the stairs and settled in the bed opposite him.

He was drifting off when he thought he heard her voice. But he couldn't be sure.

"You need any help with anything before we head out?" Bear asked.

He and Cai were standing on the porch looking out at the rising sun. Neither had been able to sleep. Laurel and Trent, however, were still sleeping.

"Nah, you three should get moving." Cai smiled and glanced sideways at Bear. "You've done enough. Really."

Bear rubbed his hands together. The snow might be thinning, but the air was still cold and the ground frozen. He'd left his gloves inside, so he cupped his palms and blew warm air into them. "What about security?" he asked, turning back around to look at the farmhouse.

"Security?" Cai winced as he turned to face Bear, shifting his arm back and forth as if it was causing him trouble.

"From the approach, it's obvious this place is inhabited. Smoke from the chimney's always a giveaway. You can't help that. In spring, you'll have crops growing, animals... plenty of signs that there are resources here that folks might find useful."

Cai nodded thoughtfully, tilting his head from side to side. "I have to admit, things like that aren't my forte. I thought having a gun would be enough of a deterrent. I didn't expect...." He trailed off, pressing his lips together.

Gently, Bear put a hand on Cai's good shoulder. "There's plenty we can do to make it look a little less inviting. Let me give you a hand before we leave."

For a moment, Cai hesitated. But then he smiled and said, "Okay. Thanks, Bear. Where do we start?"

"We'll secure the perimeter."

"Not sure we've got time to build a wall," Cai quipped.

Bear chuckled a little, adjusting his hearing aid because Cai's voice was going from too loud to too quiet.

"You all right?" Cai asked, noticing.

"Darn thing's on the blink. I was lucky to find a working one, not sure I'll be so lucky again."

"Can you hear without it?" Cai had raised his voice, as most people did when they realized Bear wore an aid.

"Hardly." Bear gestured to his other ear. "Completely deaf in this ear. This one, without the aid, it's like…." He tried to think of a simile. "Like whoever's talking to me is stuck down a really big hole. With a manhole cover on top. Speaking in a quiet voice."

Cai shook his head and laughed, but before he could ask any more questions, the door behind them swung open and Trent strode onto the porch. "Morning, guys." He was beaming, as always, hands casually in his pockets. "What's the what?"

Bear frowned at him.

"It means 'what's happening?'"

"I gathered that." Bear shook his head, but he was smiling all the same. "I'm just about to help Cai reinforce his perimeter. Want to learn something?"

Immediately, Trent grinned. "Do I!"

"What do we need?" Cai asked, heading for the door.

"Well," Bear said, scratching his chin. "Do you have any mousetraps?"

Having gathered the items from Bear's list—mousetraps, bullets, fishing line, tent pegs, a hammer, a hand drill, and some nails—the three of them headed for Cai's workshop.

"What are the bullets for?" Trent asked, peering over Bear's shoulder as he set the mousetrap.

"Loud noise," Bear replied. Without warning, he triggered the trap and the metal trap hammer sprang back with a loud snap.

Cai and Trent continued to watch as Bear sprang the trap another three times.

"Why are you doing that?" Cai asked, tilting his head.

"So I know where to position the bullets." Bear pointed to the faint grooves that had been left in the wood. Then he took his drill and made two holes, one on either side. Holding up a bullet, he showed it to Cai and Trent. "We put this in the hole. We rig the fishing wire to the trap, like a tripwire. Then if someone trips it, the trap—"

"Springs back and hits the bullets," Trent said, open-mouthed. "Coool."

"And the bang tells me someone's here."

"With the added bonus of scaring them off if they think there's someone with a gun watching them." Bear handed a trap to Trent and one to Cai. "We'll set up a tripwire on the road coming toward the property, then we'll do the perimeter. Eight traps should do it."

"What if an animal triggers it?" Trent asked as he loaded and sprang his trap.

"It's possible, but we'll pull the wire taut. It'll take some force to trip it. Small animals likely won't set it off." He looked at Cai. "But don't freak out if you hear it. Investigate first. Safely."

Cai nodded. His cheeks flushed a little. Was he embarrassed that Bear was having to teach him this stuff? If so, he shouldn't be. He didn't have combat experience or experience living off-grid. How would he know this stuff? What would he have used it for?

"There's no sense setting them till we're gone, but let's go get them in position, and then you can hook up the trip wires later." Bear gestured for Cai to follow him, and the three of them headed outside.

Bundled up in their coats, they banged in their mousetraps (which were now attached to tent pegs) at appropriate intervals. When they were all in position, Bear showed Cai how to rig the wire and make sure it was taut.

"Next up, we'll reinforce your locks." Bear had already started back toward the house. However, when they got there it seemed Laurel had the same idea.

They found her in the kitchen. Jess was sitting on a chair at the table watching while Laurel did something with a saw and a large piece of wood.

"Thought I'd make a wooden bar for the door."

"I can help with that." Cai moved to the table to hold the end of the wood while Laurel continued to saw.

Bear raised an eyebrow; he'd never seen his wife doing DIY before. It was something she'd always left to him.

"What?" she asked, looking up at him as her glasses slid down her nose. "You didn't think I knew how to cut wood?"

"Not at all." Bear smiled at her. "I'm certain you're capable. Just surprised, that's all."

For a moment, as their eyes locked, Bear thought Laurel was about to fire back a witty retort, but she resisted. Returning to the task at hand, she asked Cai to pass her the nails as she fixed three smaller pieces of wood—the latch for the large wooden bar—onto the wall.

Bear offered to do the same for the windows, but Cai declined. "I know it's probably sensible to block them, but I can't sit here in the dark all day," he said. "I'm sure the tripwires and the bolted door will suffice."

"In that case, I'll make a sign."

"A sign?" Cai asked.

"Might as well let people know you're not to be messed with." Bear gestured for Trent to follow him and jogged down the steps into the cellar. There, they painted a large leftover pallet with the words "TRESPASSERS BEWARE".

By the time midday arrived, most of their tasks had been finished. The only thing left to do was to help Cai clear the snow from the top of the outdoor wood store. Single-handed, it would take him forever, and he wanted to move some kindling out while he could.

Hesitating, Bear looked up at the sky.

As if he'd read his mind, Cai said, "You'll want to be going soon."

"I think we should, yes." Bear was mentally calculating how far they'd get before nightfall, and whether they'd make it to Kermit's or have to camp in the open again.

"I've been thinking." Cai looked from Bear to Laurel. "You should take the horses."

For a moment, no one said anything. Laurel narrowed her eyes as if she hadn't heard him correctly. "Take them? But Cai, you risked your life for those horses…."

"I know, and I want them to be safe. But I also want them to be useful. I'll keep two, Dante and Flock. You can take the other three. I know you'll take care of them." He met Laurel's eyes with a force that made Bear feel as if he should look away. "Please, Laurel. Take them. Use them to help you find your daughter."

After a long pause, Laurel nodded. She clasped Cai's hands in hers. "Thank you." She looked at Bear, smiling. "Isn't this great? Horses. We'll move so much quicker."

Bear nodded back and extended his hand to shake Cai's. "Great. Thanks, buddy."

He looked at Trent, expecting the kid to be bouncing with excitement. Instead, an uneasy expression had settled on his face. "Horses?" he said a little croakily.

"Yeah, horses." Bear frowned. "You don't like horses, kid?"

"Like them?" Trent licked his lower lip and giggled nervously. "Ah, sure. If they're like in a field. A far-away field. Where they can't kick me or trample me or bite me."

"Bite you?" Laurel was fighting back a surprised giggle. "Horses don't bite."

"Are you kidding? Have you seen their teeth?" Trent wiped his brow with the back of his hand. The kid was visibly sweating.

"Hey." Cai stepped up and wrapped a gentle arm around Trent's shoulders. "I promise you, my horses *do not* bite. They'll take good care of you if you take care of them. I'll introduce you. Okay?"

Trent nodded in reply, but his entire body had stiffened up. "Sure," he said shakily. "Sure."

"Why don't I take you to see them now?" Cai asked. "While Laurel and Bear clear the wood store? You can help me get them saddled up."

Trent glanced at Bear. He was physically trembling. Dipping to meet his eyes, Bear said firmly, "Kid, you've come up against wolves and men with guns. Horses ain't nothing compared to that."

He didn't look away until Trent exhaled and said, "Okay. Okay. Sure. A horse is better than a wolf, right?"

"Right." Bear stood up straight and reached for his shovel. "You go with Cai. Laurel and I will join you when we've cleared the store."

As Trent and Cai headed for the barn, Laurel and Bear waited a moment, watching them. At Bear's ankles, Jess tilted her head. Bear looked down at her. "Coming with us? Or do you wanna go protect Trent?"

Jess wagged her tail. For now, she was sticking with him.

"Did you know he was scared of horses?" Laurel asked as they struck off in the direction of the outdoor wood store.

"No idea," Bear said.

"He'll be fine once he's met them."

"Yeah." Bear looked over his shoulder at Trent's figure in the distance. "I hope so."

17

LAUREL

Cai's underground wood store was well and truly snowed in. Slightly sheltered by the overhang of the farmhouse roof, it had been shielded from the warmth that had begun to melt the more exposed snow out on the fields. It had also, clearly, been victim of the almost constant northerly winds that had blown snowdrifts in the direction of the house. However, between the two of them, it didn't take much time for Bear and Laurel to clear the snow from the opening to the hatch.

With no flashlight to illuminate the dark space beneath them, Bear reached for a packet of matches and handed them to Laurel. Cai had given them a kerosene lantern, which she managed to light, and held out in front of her as they descended the steps.

"Strange set-up for a wood store," Bear muttered behind her.

At the bottom of the steps, Laurel stopped, holding the lantern up to throw the store into a muted light. "That's because it's not a wood store." She turned to look excitedly at Bear. "It's a *food* store."

Taking the last step, Bear nudged past her and turned slowly around, taking in the shelves that surrounded them. "Cai's dad was better prepared than we thought."

"And thank heavens the snow was covering the hatch. If the militia had found this...."

"There's wood, too." Bear pointed to a neatly arranged woodpile in one corner of the cavernous space.

"Canned fruit, pasta, flour, matches...." Laurel was running her finger along one of the shelves. "This will keep him going a while."

"Sure will." Bear clapped his hands together. He looked suddenly eager to leave. "Let's go tell him."

"You want to check on Trent, don't you?" she asked as they ascended the stone steps.

Bear shrugged, but she could tell he was quickening his pace.

Saying goodbye to Cai was harder than Laurel had expected. As they rode away from the farm, Trent clinging to his horse's reins as if it was about to bolt at any second, a lump formed in her throat. Concentrating on the road ahead, she fought back the urge to cry.

They'd left Cai waving to them from the porch. As they'd loaded up the horses with the food he'd insisted they take from his newfound store, he'd presented them with one last gift: his father's old hearing aids.

"I'm not sure if they're any good, but you're welcome to them." Cai had handed Bear a small metal box containing two hearing aids and some spare batteries.

Bear had looked at them as if they were made of solid gold, an uncharacteristically broad smile breaking out on his face.

"One right, one left," Cai had said. "But maybe you can do something to make the wrong ear work for you."

Bear had nodded. "I'm sure I can." Then he'd pulled Cai into a tight, back-patting hug and said. "Thank you, Doc. Thank you."

Now, Bear was watching her. She could feel it. "You'll see him again." He was beside her on a black mare. When she turned, he met her eyes.

"Will I? When we've found Mae, we're heading for Thunder Bay. I'm not sure we'll see any of our friends again."

Bear didn't reply, just pressed his lips together—the way he did when he was deep in thought—then fell back so he was riding next to Trent.

"Looks like I'm not the only one who doesn't approve of this mode of transport," Trent quipped. Laurel looked over her shoulder. He was gesturing to Jess, who was strapped back into the carrier on Bear's chest, looking decidedly uneasy at being so far off the ground.

"Sorry, girl." Bear shrugged a little. "Can't be helped."

"Are you going to put the new hearing aid in?" Trent asked.

"Soon. I'll get what I can out of this one first." His nose twitched and he added, "At some point, I might have to ration myself. Go back to written communication."

Laurel turned back to look at the road but said, "Maybe Kermit will have more working batteries."

"Maybe," Bear replied. "But even if he does, it won't be a lifetime's supply."

"You think the power's gone forever?" Trent's question was blunt and loud, and not one that any of them had dared to ask out loud before.

"At this point, kid," Bear said gruffly, "yeah, I think it is."

After that, the three of them settled into silence. So far, Laurel had focused on one task after another. One crisis after another. She hadn't spent much time considering what the future might hold. The idea that this was now the way things were—forever—made her feel a little queasy.

Could they really spend the rest of their lives in a world full of darkness?

As the sun dipped lower in the sky, Laurel wrapped one arm around her waist, keeping the other on the horse's reins. She'd been lost in a daydream, imagining she was back in Texas, riding in the sun with her face turned up to the sky.

"Your mom liked riding, didn't she?" Trent's question broke Laurel's train of thought.

She frowned at him a little, wondering how he knew that about her mom.

Shrugging, as if he knew what Laurel was thinking, Trent added, "She told me the two of you used to go riding up to this creek near your house. Have picnics after school."

A smile parted Laurel's lips as she remembered rushing home at the end of the school day and finding her mom waiting by the porch with the horses saddled and ready to go. "She always loved horses." Laurel glanced at Jess. "She loved all animals, but being around horses was different."

"Did Mae learn to ride?" Trent asked, looking from Laurel to Bear.

Chuckling loudly, Bear shook his head. "Laurel wanted her to." He met Laurel's gaze and raised an eyebrow at her. "Don't I remember you and your mom trying to get her into dressage?"

"Dressage?" Trent said the word as if he had no idea what it meant.

"It's where horses dance around in a big ring." Bear straightened his shoulders and tilted his chin up, adopting the pose of a dressage rider.

"It's a little more complex than that," Laurel tsked, rolling her eyes. Although she had to admit — looking back — she wasn't sure why she *ever* thought Mae would want to get involved in a sport like that.

"Mae *hated* it," Bear said, shaking his head at the memory of their ten-year-old daughter stomping her feet and refusing to go to lessons because she'd rather be playing soccer or climbing trees.

As their laughter faded, Trent yawned and said, "You must be real excited to see her again."

Laurel glanced at Bear. The two of them exchanged a knowing look. Yes, they were excited. But with the excitement came a sense of dread. First, because it had been years since the three of them were together. Second, because one of the first things they'd be faced with would be telling Mae that her grandmother had died.

Picturing Mae's face, and the conversation they'd have to have about her illness and what had happened in the months after the EMP, Laurel sucked in a deep, shaky breath. Seeing Cai had helped her find her footing again, after feeling as if grief was going to swallow her up. But thinking of telling Mae the news made her wobbly all over again.

Changing the subject, she rubbed her horse's shoulder, enjoying the warmth beneath her hand, and asked Bear how much farther they had to travel until they reached Kermit's place.

"Not too far. Might make it before sundown." He looked at the sky, then at his map, seeming totally at ease on horseback.

"How come we never did this?" she asked quietly.

Bear tilted his head, the way he did when he was waiting for her to elaborate on something she'd said.

Waving her arms at their surroundings, Laurel smiled a little. The woods around Sollon Falls were quiet and picturesque. Deep green pine trees, a dusting of snow blanketing the ground between them, big pinkish-blue sky above. There was even the sound of a river somewhere in the distance.

"We never went riding together. I never even knew you liked it."

Looking down at his horse, Bear shrugged. "We didn't do much together in the last few years, did we?"

Laurel watched as her husband rubbed his chin and shook his head. She was about to speak when Trent interrupted.

"Making up for it now, though, aren't you? Looks like you'll be spending every day together for a while. Especially if the plan is to head back to Thunder Bay and set up home at Bear's cabin." He paused as the two of them looked at him. "Right?"

Biting back a smile, Laurel nodded. "Right."

"Laurel?" Bear asked. She expected to see him smiling, but when she turned to study his face, she realized he was frowning.

"What is it?"

"Is your horse limping?"

Laurel looked down at Shadow, the black stallion she'd chosen from Cai's three horses. She'd assumed his unsteady gait was due to the uneven terrain, but Bear might be right. "We better stop. I'll take a look." Tugging gently on the reins, she pulled Shadow to a stop and swung herself down from his seat.

As Trent and Bear remained in their saddles, she encouraged Shadow to walk and closely examined his legs. Bear was right; he was limping on his front right.

"Hop down, guys, take a break. I need to look at this properly." Laurel helped Trent down to the ground. Bear followed, quickly releasing Jessamine from her carrier so that she ran off full-pelt into the woods, tail wagging, thrilled to be free.

"Is he okay?" Trent asked, skirting nervously around Shadow's side while Bear tethered the other two horses to a nearby tree.

Laurel crouched down and flexed Shadow's leg. When she lowered it to the ground, he immediately shifted his weight onto his other feet. "Shoot," she muttered, cupping her hand around the troublesome foot. "He's warm."

Inching forward, Trent bent down next to her. "What's up with him?"

"I can't be sure, but it looks like laminitis."

"What's that?" Trent's eyes widened.

"Bad news," Laurel muttered, pinching the bridge of her nose.

Shrugging off his pack, Bear headed over and put his hand on Laurel's shoulder. "Can we do anything?"

"He needs to rest, and probably some painkillers and a vet."

"We brought some from the hospital," Trent said, motioning to Laurel's pack.

She stood up, bracing her hands in the small of her back because it was starting to ache after several hours in the saddle. Grimacing a little, she shook her head. "I have no idea which of them he could take. Some could be toxic."

"So, what do you want to do?" Bear asked, glancing at the sky. "We could set up camp here tonight? Let him rest? Then it's a short journey to Kermit's in the morning."

Laurel nodded. "Yes. Let's do that. In the meantime, I'll see if I can forage anything that would work for a compress to take the heat out. Can you two start the fire?"

"Sure." Trent was about to turn away when he stopped, turned slowly back around and patted Shadow's nose. "You'll be okay, boy," he said gently. "Laurel is good at fixing things."

18

MAE

"How are you this morning?" Lisa was carrying a small silver tray. Mae pushed herself up on her elbows and yawned. Daylight was streaming through the window, illuminating the interior of the medical RV she'd been allocated. It had been a long time since she slept alone. Years, maybe. After two nights, she was growing to like it. Although she had wondered more than once why she was the only injured soldier the Freemen decided to bring back to their camp and treat.

Reaching down to rub her leg, Mae winced. "Slept better."

"Did Shane check you over yesterday?" Lisa asked.

Mae nodded. An ex-EMT called Shane, with startling blue eyes, had been there when she first woke up two days ago. He'd come again yesterday to check her wound and give her painkillers. She'd been hoping he might come again today, but it seemed Lisa was taking a turn.

A little loudly, Lisa set the tray down on the table next to Mae's bed. It contained a glass of water, some painkillers, and some eggs.

"You have chickens?" Mae asked, her mouth watering at the thought of fresh eggs.

Lisa nodded. "And goats."

"Here?"

Again, Lisa nodded.

Mae couldn't understand how the Freemen had gotten set up here so quickly. They only took the depot from those civilian soldiers a few days ago. Surely they couldn't have been that well organized? She wanted to ask, but was also keenly aware that she was currently being treated extremely well. If she started to seem like a threat, they might seal her off, stop her having access to anyone or anything else. And that wouldn't do because, right now, her main objective was to find out as much as possible about the Freemen and the way they were running themselves.

Since she arrived, she hadn't set foot outside the RV, but the sounds and smells filtering in from outside told her she was in the middle of some kind of campsite. She'd been cataloging them—because she had nothing else to do—and had so far listed kids, dogs, chickens, something that sounded like a large gate, a second RV, a guitar, and plenty of cooking smells.

Today, she was determined to get a proper look at the Freemen's commune.

Mae downed the painkillers quickly, then picked up her fork and shoveled a large portion of eggs into her mouth. Closing her eyes, she made an *mmm* sound.

"Good?" Lisa sat down in a chair opposite the bed.

"So good." Mae ate three more mouthfuls. Then there was a knock at the door.

Lisa turned and told whoever it was to come in, and a young girl entered holding two flasks of what smelled suspiciously like coffee. "There's a little sugar in each," she said, handing them to Lisa.

"Thanks, Ellie." Lisa took the coffees and, as Ellie left, offered one to Mae.

Holding it under her nose, Mae inhaled the scent. "Oh, that's good. It's been weeks since I had coffee."

"We're pretty well stocked here," Lisa replied, sipping hers and watching Mae over the top of her flask.

For a moment, they sat in silence. Mae still hadn't worked out what Lisa's role here was. She knew Art King was in charge; everyone knew the name *Art King*. But Lisa could have been anyone at any level. She could have been Art's most trusted confidant or just a woman who was in the wrong place at the wrong time and who stumbled across Mae, and subsequently was entrusted with looking after her.

"I think I should take a walk today." Mae edged to the side of the bed and swung her legs around. Her right leg, the one with the gunshot wound in its thigh, throbbed. "I haven't moved much. I need to get up and about."

Lisa looked her up and down. If she was suspicious of Mae's motives, she didn't let it show, just nodded in agreement. "I was going to suggest the same thing. I've asked our carpenter to make you a walking stick. He'll bring it by later. Then we can take a tour."

"Of the depot?" Mae made a mental note to chart every room and corridor, every person, every sign. If she could catch sight of a floor-plan, even better. Maybe find a way to peel off on her own and find blueprints for the place.

"The depot?" Lisa frowned at her, then laughed a little. "We're not at the depot, Mae."

"Oh, I know, but I thought...." Mae's throat was suddenly dry. She knew she wasn't inside the military depot; that much was obvious. But she assumed they were camping on the grounds. Set up outside for whatever reason. Perhaps to avoid whatever was so important *inside* the depot.

"We're about a twenty-minute walk up into the woods," Lisa said, already heading back for the door. "Not sure you'll make it on your leg." Lisa glanced at Mae's lower half. "Even with a walking stick."

"Oh." Mae pinched the bridge of her nose. "I didn't realize we were so far away."

"We've been camped here for a while. The depot isn't safe."

"The Army took it back?" Mae's heartbeat quickened. Had Cornell succeeded after all?

"Oh, no." Lisa shook her head firmly. "We're still holding it. The militia...." She paused and raised an eyebrow at Mae. "Your friends retreated. But until it's completely secure, Art wants the majority of us out of harm's way."

Mae swallowed hard. She had no idea what had happened after she was shot. The last thing she remembered was Lisa's face, then waking up here. "Why did you bring me here?" she asked suddenly. "Am I a prisoner?"

Lisa stopped near the door, then turned around and headed back to Mae. Sitting down, she crossed one leg over the other and leaned onto her knee. "Mae. You are not a prisoner. We brought you here to help you. Art wanted to send you back to your friends—put you on a stretcher and deposit you outside their dingy warehouse."

Mae sucked in a deep breath; the Freemen knew about the warehouse.

"But you're not like them. I can see it, and Art trusts me. So he agreed to let you stay."

"Not like who?"

"Your boss. Cornell." Lisa raised an eyebrow, as if she anticipated Mae being surprised by the mention of the captain's name. "The rest of your company. The so-called *militia* who wanted to join forces with you."

"How do you figure that?" Mae asked, an indignant twang to her tone.

"You're a soldier because you want to help people." Lisa stood up slowly. "They're soldiers because they want to control people."

She stood up, this time making it to the door before glancing back over her shoulder.

"And what do you want?" Mae asked, meeting Lisa's eyes.

"Me?" Lisa asked, a slow smile crossing her lips. "I'm someone who wants to survive. But who's not willing to forget her humanity to do so."

It was nearly sunset when Lisa returned. Mae looked at her hands, expecting to see her holding a food tray. Instead, she was holding a walking stick.

"If you think you're strong enough, how about that guided tour?" Lisa asked, standing in the doorway.

Mae swung her legs around and put her feet firmly on the ground. It wasn't as good as getting an inside look at the depot, but she wasn't going to pass up the opportunity to assess the Freemen's camp; if she was here, and they were willing to let her leave the RV, she might as well gather intel. At least *that* might please Cornell.

"So you can see what we're about." Lisa handed her the stick, then gestured to the door.

Mae stood up gingerly. Three days of bed rest had made her wobbly on her feet. Lisa handed her a coat and a scarf.

"It's chilly out," she said, adjusting her own scarf at her neck.

Shrugging on the jacket, Mae realized just how much her muscles were still aching. She shuddered. A breeze whipped through the door. "Is this the only RV?" Mae asked. "Or are there others?"

"We have two. One for people who need medical care. One for anyone who just feels like they need a break from tent life." Lisa smiled a little, pushing open the door.

"How did you get them up here?" Mae asked, frowning at the idea of them pushing two broken RVs through the woods.

"They were already here, actually. Abandoned." Lisa shook her head, as if she was thinking of whoever might have left them here and why, then stepped outside.

Following her, Mae was greeted by a darkening sky. Orange around the edges, it was the kind of sunset she hadn't seen in a long time, clear and crisp. She squinted up at it. It was good to have fresh air on her face, but she didn't give in to the temptation to close her eyes and soak it in. Instead, she surveyed her surroundings.

Holding out her arm, Lisa waved at the scene in front of them. "This is our home. For now, anyway."

Mae wrapped her arms around her waist. She couldn't believe what she was seeing. Behind her were the two RVs. In front, a clearing with two large awnings. Tables beneath them. A cooking area. A laundry area. Further back, in the woods behind the RVs, more tents. In front, a fence that seemed to wrap around the perimeter of the clearing and through some of the trees too. Everywhere, people were milling about.

Lisa started walking toward the clearing. "This is where we cook and eat." She pointed to a brick-built stove and lines of trestle tables. "And this is where we socialize in the evenings." Beneath the second awning, a fire pit sat in the center and was surrounded by a combination of picnic chairs and logs.

A few people were sitting, chatting and drinking what looked like tea or coffee, and in the tent next door, dinner was being prepared. The smell of the food made Mae's stomach growl. As she shifted position, she spotted a hog being roasted over the fire and a small group of men and women preparing what looked like a large bowl of potatoes and onions.

She was about to ask how long they'd been here when she felt something brush against her calf. She stepped back, alarmed, and saw a chicken trot past.

"It's sunset. She's off to bed." Lisa chuckled. Turning to the woods, she motioned to the tents. "Most of us sleep in the tents in the woods. We take it in turns to patrol, cook, clean."

Mae leaned heavily on the walking stick, squeezing it with both hands, and shrugged her shoulders up toward her ears. What she was looking at was almost idyllic. As they wandered toward the food tent, lanterns sprang to life around the perimeter of the camp. A gong sounded. People began to emerge from the woods.

How could *these* be the same people who'd been ruthlessly killing civilians?

Mae tried to count the people walking past her, but when she reached thirty, plus three dogs and five babies, she stopped.

"You look very happy here." Her mind was whirring. These people captured the depot and slaughtered soldiers in cold blood? It made no sense.

"Would you like to join us for dinner, or would you like to eat in the RV? It's entirely up to you." Lisa stood still, waiting for Mae's answer, blinking slowly.

Mae looked back over her shoulder. Part of her wanted to race back to the warmth and safety of her own company and slam the door shut. But a bigger part wanted to find out what was lurking beneath the surface of this seemingly perfect setup.

"I'd love to join you." She straightened her shoulders and smiled, but in her head, she readied herself to catalog every single thing she could glean about the Freemen's existence here. Starting with *exactly* how far away she was from the depot, and what their intentions were now they'd captured it.

19

BEAR

The expression on Laurel's face told Bear that Shadow hadn't improved overnight, despite the chamomile compress she'd made, and several hours' rest.

"What's the plan now? Can he make it to Kermit's? It's about an hour's trek from here." Bear pointed at Kermit's location on the map as Laurel wrinkled her nose and examined it.

On the other side of the campfire, Trent was feeding Shadow some dried grass they'd brought with them from Cai's farm. Seemingly, the horse being in pain had softened Trent's distrust of him.

"He'll have to. We can't leave him here. I just hope the journey isn't too much for him." She swallowed hard and held out her hand as Bear offered her a mug of coffee. "But he can't bear any weight. I'll have to ride with Trent."

Bear nodded. By the fire, Jessamine was lying on her back, wriggling into the ground as if she wanted to coat herself in every scent she could find. He took a dog treat from his bag and tossed it to her, causing her to flip over and gobble it up in one swift movement.

"Don't worry." Bear squeezed Laurel's elbow. "He'll be okay."

She pressed her lips together and nodded. It was a face he'd seen many times before; the one she showed him when she was trying to hide how she truly felt about something.

Leaving Shadow, Trent sauntered over, pulling his jacket close against the early morning chill. His breath plumed in the air as he spoke. "Did anyone else hear those noises last night?" He picked up a mug of coffee and winced as he drank from it, still having to force himself to find it enjoyable, then yawned.

Bear frowned. He hadn't heard anything. He'd switched his hearing aid off, trusting that Jess, Laurel, and Trent would alert him if something was wrong.

Laurel nodded, caught Trent's yawn and pressed the back of her hand to her mouth to stifle it. "Wolves," she said to Bear. "We were safe with the fire, but it was unsettling."

"You should have woken me." Bear put his hand on Trent's shoulder; he knew the kid must have been more than a little unsettled after what happened to them in the Boundary Waters. As Trent shrugged, pretending it was no big deal, Bear stooped and took the new hearing aid Cai had gifted him from his pack. It was no use putting it off. If he was lucky, the new aid would last until they returned to Thunder Bay. It made no sense to continue with the old one if it meant he was unable to hear what was going on around them.

"Here." Laurel opened her palm and Bear dropped the old hearing aid into it. The new one was the wrong size, far too small, and pinched his ear viciously. But when he turned it on, immediately, everything became more focused. The crackle of the fire, birds in the trees… background noise that had blurred into one indistinguishable crackle came to life.

Sighing, Bear turned his head slowly and took it in. He liked silence, but he missed this too. The nuances of the wild.

Suddenly, closing his eyes and focusing on absorbing the sound of the woods, his stomach lurched with the desire to be back in his cabin. Back in Thunder Bay, except this time with Laurel, and Mae, and Trent to keep him company.

By the summer, they could be holed up safely, prepping for winter, enjoying long evenings under the stars and blocking out whatever was happening beyond the woods.

"Okay?" Laurel asked, her voice a little too loud. When Bear tapped his ear, she smiled and lowered it. "Sorry. Are you okay?" she repeated.

"Good." He adjusted the hearing aid, turning it down a notch, then gestured to the campfire. "We should get ready to head out. If we make it to Kermit's before midday, we can get the information we need, stay overnight, and leave first thing tomorrow."

"Will he be up for visitors?" Laurel asked, adjusting her ponytail. "From what you've said, he doesn't sound like the kind of guy who'd take kindly to house guests."

"He's a touch paranoid, but he's a good guy." Bear nodded firmly. "He'll be happy to help."

The look on Laurel's face told him she didn't quite believe that, but she didn't say so. Instead, she downed the last dregs of her coffee and set about putting out the fire.

A few minutes later, they were ready. Fire out, bags packed. Laurel was riding Robin with Trent behind her, arms looped around her waist. She was holding onto Shadow while Bear took her pack and Trent's to try and even out some of the weight. His horse, Lucy, was thick and sturdy and didn't seem to notice the extra burden.

By his reckoning, they were just half a mile away from Kermit's when Shadow's limping became so bad they were forced to stop.

With a furrowed brow, Laurel examined his foot. "We'll have to leave him here, let him rest, then come back for him later."

Bear bit the inside of his cheek. That meant doing the same distance twice. A waste of time. But the way Laurel folded her arms in front of her stomach told him she wasn't making a suggestion; she was giving him an order.

As she tethered Shadow to a nearby tree, Bear checked the map. "We'll dismount up there." He pointed to a spot near the river ahead. "Do the last part on foot. Kermit's place will be booby-trapped. We can't just—"

"Booby-trapped?" Trent asked loudly, in a mixture of excitement and horror. "What kind of traps?"

"No idea." Bear folded the map and tapped his horse's side with his foot to encourage her to start walking. "But we'll soon find out."

By the river, he climbed down and tied Lucy—stupid name for a horse—to a tree, leaving her enough slack to allow her to reach the river for a drink and forage for grass or berries nearby, but not so much she could get tangled or into trouble.

Laurel had followed them on foot the short distance from where she'd tethered Shadow. He was blinking at them through the undergrowth, clearly confused as to why his two friends were up ahead and he'd been left behind.

Helping Trent down from Robin, Laurel took the horse's bridle and guided her over next to Lucy. When both horses were secure, she brushed down her pants, took her pack from Bear and shrugged it onto her shoulders, then nodded at him to lead the way.

"Now, if I know Kermit, the coordinates I had for his cabin would be deliberately off." Bear scanned the map, narrowing his eyes. "So, keep a close watch on your surroundings."

"What are we looking for?" Trent asked, shifting from foot to foot as if he might be standing on a trap of some kind.

"Signs of life. Disturbed earth. A flash of metal. Anything that looks too carefully positioned."

"What about the alarm system you made for Cai? Something like that?" Laurel asked, glancing at her ankles, clearly picturing stumbling into a line of wire and setting off a gunshot.

Bear nodded, tugging his hat from his head. Now that the weather was warming slightly, when the sun came out, he preferred the feeling of fresh air on his ears to the sensation of them being cocooned by wool.

"Kermit's probably got something a little more sophisticated set up, but, yeah, something like that."

Laurel nodded. A look of determination had settled on her face. He liked that look; it was the expression she wore when the thrill of solving a puzzle or finding a way out of a difficult situation settled in her stomach.

"Okay then," she said, waving her hand at him. "Let's go, Papa Bear."

As Trent chuckled, raising his eyebrows at Bear, Bear scooped Jess back into the carrier on his chest and began to walk slowly forward.

At least in this situation, his eyes were more important than his ears. In fact, not being distracted by the sound of leaves, or twigs, or bird song, allowed him to focus on what he was seeing. Quickly, he turned down his hearing aid, scouring the ground before each step he took.

On either side of him, Trent and Laurel were doing the same. Trent looked terrified to move, but Laurel was moving deftly, scanning the trees, bushes, and snow as she walked.

"There, up ahead." Bear could only just make out her voice. He turned his hearing aid back up and followed the direction of her stare. "Something flashed."

Bear lifted a finger, indicated that the two of them should stay still, and inched forward. Passing Laurel, he brushed her arm with his fingers, and nodded. When he reached the spot she'd pointed to, he stooped down. Sure enough, there was a trip wire. But this one wasn't attached to an alarm system.

Crouching down, Bear gently scraped some leaves aside and raised his eyebrows at Laurel. "Net," he said.

Laurel walked over and bent down beside him to examine what she'd spotted; a metal pulley attached to a cord that ran up the side of the tree. The net had been hidden beneath leaves and a light dusting of snow.

"Is that for humans or animals?" Trent asked.

Bear shrugged and stood up, leaving the trap as he'd found it. "Either." He motioned for Trent to skirt around the trap. "Come on, this way. Let's keep going."

They continued through the trees, following the map. Soon, they came across a wire like the one Bear had installed at Cai's farm. He spotted it before Laurel and stuck his hand out to stop her from tripping it.

"Maybe we should trip it?" she asked. "I mean, don't we want him to know we're coming?"

"We don't want him coming out pointing a gun at us," Bear said. "Especially if he's… fragile."

"Fragile?" Laurel tilted her head and raised her eyebrows. "What do you mean, *fragile*?"

Before Bear could answer, from up ahead, a yelp shook the trees. *Trent.*

Bear looked at Laurel, unsure which direction the sound came from. "This way." She started running and he ran after her.

"Be careful! There's a pit!" Trent yelled.

This time, Laurel stopped Bear from going any farther as she looked down at her feet. He followed her gaze. There, right in front of them, the ground gave way to a large muddy pit.

Peering over the edge, Bear saw that Trent was lying on his back, his pack having cushioned his fall.

"Kid? You okay?" he called down.

Trent pushed himself up onto his elbows and nodded. "Yeah. Just broke my butt, is all."

"We need to find something to get him out of there," Bear said to Laurel, who was already shrugging her pack from her shoulders and searching the ground for a long branch they could use to heave Trent back up to ground level.

"Um. Guys...." Trent's voice was shakier this time.

Bear crouched and waved. "It's okay. We'll—"

Trent cut him off, shaking his head and starting to crawl back into the corner of the pit. "Guys... you know what else I hate? Apart from horses?"

"I thought you'd gotten over that," Laurel chimed in, chuckling a little as she pulled a large branch from the undergrowth.

"Snakes." Trent's voice went up in pitch. "I *really* hate snakes."

Bear narrowed his eyes. Something was moving in the shadows. Some *things* were moving in the shadows. "What kind of snakes are native to Minnesota?" Bear looked at Laurel, her expression changed, and she dropped the branch.

"I have no idea." She looked down and reached for his hand as not one, not two, or even three, but a whole quiver of snakes moved into the light.

"Stay where you are. You'll be okay. They're more scared of you than you are of them," Bear called down.

"I highly doubt that!" Trent stumbled to his feet and backed up toward the rear wall of the pit. Waving up at them, he added, "Why the blue heck would your friend have a pit of *snakes* outside his house?"

Under his breath, Bear muttered, "He's always been a fan of theater."

Turning to Laurel to ask for the branch she was holding, he noticed her eyes widen. She looked at Bear, then at something behind him. Something in the near distance.

Before he could ask her what it was, a gunshot blasted in their direction, narrowly missing Laurel and hitting the tree behind her.

"Nobody move!"

20

TRENT

As Trent's fingers dug into the cold mud wall behind his back, he tucked his knees up under his chin and tried to slow his breathing. In front of him, more snakes than he could count were slithering slowly from the shadows. What Bear said made sense; he was bigger than them. They should be scared of *him*. Plus, Minnesota didn't have venomous snakes... right?

As one inched closer to his foot, Trent looked up. Whatever they were doing up there, they needed to hurry the heck up and get him out!

He couldn't see Laurel, but Bear was holding out his hand as if he was gesturing for her to pass him something. Good. Any second now, they'd be pulling him back up to solid ground. But as Trent watched Bear, something caught his eye. Movement from the bushes. Trent checked Bear's chest; Jess was still strapped to it, so it wasn't her. Trent fixed his gaze on Bear, hoping he'd notice and turn so he could mouth "be careful."

Before he could, the slow shuffle of bushes turned into a figure. A large, camo-clad figure with a gun. In one swift movement, the figure lifted the gun and fired. Trent's heart hammered in his chest. The bullet hit the trunk behind Laurel, sending shards of bark flying.

"Nobody move!" the figure shouted.

Slowly, Laurel held up her hands, still grasping the branch.

Bear raised his too, his back still turned toward the man with the gun.

"Put the branch down," the man yelled.

Laurel nodded and slowly lowered it. Her eyes flicked from Bear to the guy behind him; if this was PB's friend Kermit, surely he should be speaking up right now. Telling him, *hey, buddy, it's me, why don't we put the gun down.*

Instead, Bear seemed to be simply following Kermit's instructions.

"Both of you, keep your hands in the air." The guy inched closer. His face was almost completely obscured by a bandana, but Trent could see a shock of almost pure white hair beneath his hat.

He approached Bear slowly, then nudged him with the barrel of his shotgun. "Turn around, then back up to that tree. One quick move, and I'll shoot."

Bear didn't answer him, just did as he was told. Slowly, he turned around. This was it. Surely, Kermit would recognize him now.

Trent held his breath as he watched, but Kermit simply took a step back and nodded at the tree. "I said back up. Both of you."

Everything in Trent's belly was telling him to shout up at them, but maybe this guy wasn't Kermit. Maybe he was someone else. Some *other* guy with traps who lived alone in the woods.

Reaching for his pocket, the man took out a pair of handcuffs and tossed them to the ground in front of Bear's feet. "Cuff her hands."

Bear looked at Laurel. He nodded, just a tiny bit, and took her hands gently between his. Trent's fingernails were now encrusted with mud, digging so hard into the wall behind him that a clump of dirt came loose into his hand.

He'd clean forgotten about the snakes, but when he glanced down at his feet, he found that one was slowly slithering across the toes of his boots and had to bite down a yelp.

Shaking, he forced himself to remain still, but began scanning the pit for anything he might be able to use to get out.

"Now yours." The man threw Bear a second pair of cuffs. "Behind your back. Then lie face down on the ground."

Bear fastened his cuffs, but then looked at his chest. "My dog," he said quietly. From her pack, Jess was watching closely.

"I don't give a rat's ass about your dog. Lie down."

Awkwardly, Bear dropped to his knees and lowered himself to the ground, keeping his chest raised and his weight off Jess's back in some kind of sphinxlike yoga pose.

Next to him, Laurel was pressed flat against the cold ground.

The man stalked over. Finally, he looked from them to the pit and noticed Trent. "Well, well, looks like I caught a guppy." From his tone of voice, he sounded as if he might have been smiling. But with the bandana still wrapped around his face, it was impossible to tell.

"I'm going to search you. I recommend you remain very, very still," he said, looking at Bear. Then, turning to Trent, he added, "You should stay still too. My snakes don't like creatures that make sudden movements."

A wave of nausea crept up Trent's arms and into his throat. A long brown one was still on his shoe. He was desperate to kick it off, and wishing he was a bit more like Liam; the kind of kid who'd have known precisely how to identify the snakes and whether they were dangerous or just for show.

As the man approached Laurel, Trent clenched his jaw and breathed out hard. How was Bear being so calm?

Tugging Laurel back to her feet, the guy swept his hands over her arms, legs, and stomach, like one of those security guards at the airport. She remained stock still as he removed her gun from her waistband and the knife she'd been keeping in her boot.

"Back down," he said sharply, pressing on her shoulder so that she sank back to the ground.

Next, it was Bear's turn. He clambered to his feet. The guy looked at his chest, at the carrier containing Jessamine, and tilted his head as if he wasn't sure what to do with her.

"Is she the biting kind?" he asked as Jess snarled, uncharacteristically baring her teeth.

"Only when threatened," Bear replied. "You could say she's a white raccoon."

Trent's brow furrowed. White raccoon? What the heck was he talking about?

"White raccoon?" the man repeated.

Bear nodded slowly. "A white raccoon, skating in Central Park."

The man blinked at him, slowly. From the ground, Laurel looked up.

Bear didn't move, just held the man's gaze, then said, "Kermit… it's me."

Trent's muscles relaxed, ever so slightly, as Kermit tilted his head. He tugged down his bandana, as if it might help him see more clearly, and took a step forward, peering into Bear's face. With a gloved hand, he pinched Bear's cheeks and turned his face from side to side.

"White raccoon, skating in Central Park," Kermit muttered. Then his eyes widened, and his face broke into a huge toothy grin. "Ha!" He shouldered his shotgun and slapped Bear on the shoulder. "Ha! Bjorn Peterson, what in God's name are you doing out here?" He gestured to the pit. "And who have you thrown in my pit?"

Laughing, Bear shook his head, then wriggled his arms. "How about you uncuff us, help me get the kid out of there, and then I'll explain." He chuckled as Kermit pulled him in for a tight embrace. "It's a long story."

"Of course! Of course!" Instantly, Kermit pulled a ring of keys from his belt and started fumbling for the correct ones. After unlocking Bear, he helped Laurel to her feet and unlocked her too.

"This is my wife," Bear said, soothing Jess with a rub between the ears because she was still growling at the back of her throat. "Doctor Laurel Rivera."

"And that…" Laurel stepped closer to the edge of the pit and waved down at Trent, "is our kid. Trent."

For a moment, Trent's ears lost focus. As if he was swimming underwater, the rest of what Laurel said was muffled and seemed a very long way away. *Our kid.*

A lump formed in his throat. Suddenly, he didn't care that a snake was on his foot and that three more were slinking toward him looking hungry. *Our kid.*

"Kid? Kid? You okay?" Bear was calling to him.

Trent looked from the snake back to Bear. "Yeah, yeah, I'm good. Would kinda like to get the heck out of here now, though, if I'm honest."

From next to Bear, as Laurel lowered a branch, Kermit said, "Just kick him off. He's not dangerous. Just looks ugly."

"You're sure?" Trent asked, voice shakier than he'd have liked.

"Sure as Christmas," Kermit shouted down.

Trent took a deep breath, closed his eyes, and kicked. When he opened his eyes, the snake had retreated. He stood up quickly, turned around, and grabbed the branch. Then, with more strength than he knew he had, used it to climb back up toward the daylight.

A short while later, the four of them emerged from the trees into a small clearing. Trent looked around, expecting to see the cabin Bear had mentioned. But Kermit didn't seem to be ready to stop.

"This way." He beckoned to them over his shoulder.

As Laurel strode on, close behind Kermit, Trent reached for Bear's elbow. "How come it took him so long to recognize you?"

Bear shrugged. "It's been a while since we saw one another. Plus...." He rubbed his chin. "I'm a lot more bearded these days." Patting Trent's shoulder, he added, "But I knew he would eventually. Important thing with Kermit is not to spook him."

Trent nodded. "Right." He was about to ask Bear whether he'd noticed what Laurel had said—*our kid*—when Kermit interrupted them. Calling through the trees, he shouted, "Here we are!"

They came to a stop next to Laurel. She was standing with her hands on her hips, looking around at seemingly nothing but trees and shrubs.

"Ah, Kermit?" Bear moved closer to his old friend, but Kermit waved him off and started kicking at the ground.

After a few seconds, something appeared beneath the scrub. "Is that a hatch?" Trent crouched down.

Kermit turned to him and nodded. "Sure is, boy." He crouched too, grabbed the large metal handle and pulled.

Slowly, the hatch opened. A soft yellow light flickered inside the hole.

"Ladies first," Kermit said, gesturing for Laurel to swing herself down into it. Without hesitating, she positioned herself at the rim and lowered her legs down. Finding her footing, presumably on a ladder, she disappeared.

Trent followed her. At the bottom of the ladder, there was a small drop onto hard concrete. They were standing in a tunnel, lit by two dim gas lamps.

Bear landed with a thud next to Laurel. When Kermit was fully on the ladder, he pulled the hatch closed and said to Bear, "There's a net attached to the hatch door. It pulls the covering back in place when it's closed."

"Ingenious," Bear said, clapping his friend on the shoulder.

"This way." Kermit took one of the lamps from the wall and edged between Laurel and Trent as he headed off down the dark concrete tube.

They walked for several minutes, then finally, came to a large metal door. It was round, like the hatch, with a huge combination lock on the front.

Angling his body so that none of the others could see the code he used, Kermit unfastened the lock and ushered them through.

The room they emerged in looked like the inside of a survival store's warehouse; floor-to-ceiling shelves, crammed with boxes, camping equipment, hunting supplies, bottled water, canned food. All neatly sorted and given their own allocated, and labeled, spaces.

Moving slowly through the room, Trent's stomach lurched as he noticed a box labeled *candy bars*.

At the end of the storage area, an archway led to another room, the living area. There was a camp bed in the corner, a fireplace—which Trent assumed had been set up to release smoke above ground—and a huge desk covered in maps and papers.

Immediately, Kermit swept the maps up into a bundle and put them into the top drawer of a nearby filing cabinet. This, too, had a lock.

In the corner of the room, a small kitchen area had been set up, beside which was a large old-fashioned-looking radio.

"Bit of a mess all this, isn't it?" Kermit said as he removed his jacket and boots, hanging them on a hook near his bed.

"I think you've got the place looking pretty neat, actually," Bear replied.

"No, not *this*." Kermit waved at their surroundings. "*This*. The end of civilization as we know it."

"Ah," said Bear. "That." Before Kermit could say anything else, Bear glanced at Jess. "Is it okay if I let her loose? She's friendly, and house trained."

Kermit nodded, as if he really didn't care, and placed a heavy hand on the top of his radio. "We knew it was going to happen." He folded his arms and fixed his stare on Bear. "The network. We'd been preparing for years."

Trent glanced at Laurel. She moved closer to him and gestured for him to sit next to her on the bed. Clearly, it was best that Bear handled this one.

"You know what it was, don't you?" Kermit lowered his voice and leaned in conspiratorially.

Trent waited with bated breath; since this whole thing started, no one had actually ventured an explanation for it. They'd just accepted that something terrible happened and no one knew how long it would last or if this was now their permanent way of life.

"Actually, Kermit, before we get into that I should probably explain what we're doing here."

Kermit blinked slowly, then stood up straight and nodded. "Of course." He turned to light a camping stove. "I'll make coffee. Then you can tell me everything."

21

MAE

"I'll go wake her now, Lisa. See you in a minute." A voice Mae didn't recognize jolted her from her sleep. Someone was outside the window of the RV, speaking far too loudly.

As she sat up, pain shot up Mae's leg. She sucked in a sharp breath, squeezing her eyes closed until the pain subsided. Reaching for the bedside table, she searched for some painkillers but found just a bottle of water.

Outside, dull morning light was visible through the window. Large droplets of condensation snaked down the inside. The fire in the corner of the RV had almost gone out, but Mae was grateful for the warmth it had created overnight.

Rubbing her temples, she rolled her sleeping bag down to her waist and folded her arms. Her hair was scraped back into a ponytail, and the mirror opposite the bed told her that her skin these days was far paler and more blotchy than it used to be. "Too many candy bars, not enough vegetables," she muttered to herself.

Although she had to admit, the meal the Freemen had cooked last night had gone a long way toward easing her craving for something fresh and unpackaged; they'd served a huge dish of pasta with root vegetables and a tomato sauce. Sure, there wasn't any cheese, but Mae could forgive that. Plus, there was the roast pig, which tasted better than anything she'd had since leaving Texas.

Swinging her sleeping-bagged legs over the side of the bed, Mae scanned the room. She was looking for something to use as a notebook and, not for the first time, missing the heck out of her cellphone, when the door opened.

"Morning." A long-haired woman, slightly older than Mae, ducked into the RV. "Did you sleep well?"

Mae frowned. The woman was talking to her as if they'd met before, but Mae had no idea who she was.

"I'm sorry. I'm Sharon. I helped Shane treat you when you were first brought in, but you were a little out of it." The woman thrust out a hand. Mae took hold of it and shook it firmly. "I'm Lisa's partner."

"Nice to meet you." Mae's stomach lurched into an angry growl that made Sharon laugh.

"Don't worry, breakfast isn't far off." Sharon pulled up a stool and sat down opposite Mae. "First, though, let me check that leg."

"Are you a doctor?" Mae asked nervously as Sharon helped her out of her sleeping bag and rolled up her pants leg.

"Vet." Sharon laughed. "Don't worry, Shane has been teaching me how to treat humans. He's a good tutor." As Mae turned her face away, Sharon examined her leg. "Looking good." She patted Mae's knee. "You can roll these back down."

"How long do you think until I don't need the stick anymore?"

Sharon tilted her head from side to side. "That's completely up to you. I'd say maybe a week. Two." Sharon stood up and gestured to the door. "After breakfast, I'll show you the tent Art has allocated you."

"A tent?" Mae reached for her hat and pulled it down over her ears.

"The RV's only really for those who need medical attention." Sharon smiled. "You're doing well. You can move to a tent." When Mae's expression didn't change, Sharon squeezed her arm. "It's good news, Mae."

"And if I want to leave?" Mae asked, leaning back on the bed. "If I don't want to be allocated a tent?"

Sharon's forehead crinkled into a frown. "Well, that's entirely your choice. You're not being held captive." Her tone had sharpened. She laced her fingers together and flexed them in front of her. After a pause, Sharon drew a deep breath and bit her lower lip. "Lisa thinks you're one of us. She thinks she sees something in you."

Mae didn't speak, just met Sharon's eyes, and tried to keep her expression as steady as possible.

"I'm not sure I agree, but maybe you'll prove me wrong." She shook her head a little, then glanced at the door. "Are you coming?"

"I'll be there in a minute." Mae nodded. "Thank you."

When the door had closed, Mae stood up and tried putting weight on her leg. It hurt, but she was determined not to use the stick. So, taking a deep breath, she took two strides. Big ones. On the third, she yelped with pain and stumbled back searching for the stool. Grabbing it and lowering herself down, she cursed at the ceiling and leaned forward, breathing deeply between her knees to fight the slight panic in her chest.

Were the Freemen playing mind games with her? Did Lisa really think she'd seen something in Mae? Or was she just saying that to throw Mae off her guard?

Reaching for the walking stick, Mae stood back up. They might not be keeping her prisoner, but right now they didn't need to; she'd never make it out of camp on her own with her leg the way it was.

Glancing back at the bed she'd slept in for three nights now, she inhaled slowly and straightened her shoulders. She'd vowed to find out what she could about the Freemen. If Sharon was right, and it would be several weeks before she could walk properly, she'd just have to make the most of it. And she'd have to get better at acting because, if she was going to find out what the heck was inside that depot, and how the Freemen managed to defend it so easily, she'd need them to believe she was having a change of heart.

Outside, breakfast was already in full swing. Some kids were playing soccer over by the chicken coops, causing the chickens to cluck and flap loudly. Mae chuckled as she watched an older woman with wispy gray hair rush over and shoo them away.

"Go play in the woods," she shouted loudly. "But don't go past the fence."

One of the kids stuck his tongue out at her. Another grabbed the ball and kicked it down the slope toward the trees.

Folding her arms, Mae stood for a moment and watched them. She tried to remember the last time she'd seen something as normal as children playing. Even before the power went out, it had been a while since she'd had any leave. When she did get some, she usually chose to spend it alone close to wherever she was stationed. Gideon had always found it odd that she didn't want to go home and see her folks; she never even complained about being away for Christmas. "You don't know my family," she'd tell him, to which he'd always respond with, "Well, you're welcome to come spend the holidays with mine. My folks would love to see you."

Thinking of Gideon, Mae's stomach twisted uncomfortably. She wondered if he was out looking for her, if Cornell noticed or cared that she was missing. Then she shook her head and in her internal voice—which always reminded her of her mother's—told herself that Cornell had to think of the unit. He couldn't risk the safety of his soldiers for one missing sergeant; it was up to Mae to ensure her own safety.

Mae was still thinking of Gideon, and all the jokes he'd have made about her wonky leg, when she spotted Shane, the EMT, helping himself to a large bowl of oatmeal and a mug of coffee. When he saw her, leaning heavily on her walking stick, he raised a hand and waved.

"Mae, how are you? I'm sorry I couldn't check on you today. I had a pregnant mother with Braxton-Hicks."

Mae caught his eyes and realized she was smiling. "No problem. Sharon says it's all good."

"Here, sit down." Shane gestured to an empty spot at the table, put his own food down opposite it, then returned to fetch a portion for Mae.

As she lowered herself onto the bench, she felt eyes on her from all directions. When Shane returned, she accepted the oatmeal and the coffee gratefully. "Thank you."

Shane sat down and instantly began spooning oatmeal into his mouth. Wiping his stubbled chin with his sleeve, he said, "Sorry. Still not used to the sheer *lack* of food, you know?"

"I do." Mae nodded, blowing across her coffee to cool it. "Army portions have gotten distinctly smaller lately."

"Ah, yes," Shane said a little uncomfortably. "You're militia."

"I'm *Army*," Mae replied sharply. "There's a difference."

"Is there?" The question seemed genuine but it got Mae's hackles up all the same.

"I'm a trained soldier. I'm part of the US Armed Forces."

"But the Army is *joining* forces with untrained soldiers? Militia? So, doesn't that make you part of the militia too?" Shane tilted his head.

His logic was tripping up Mae's thoughts. She put her coffee down with a thud. "No," she said. "It doesn't."

A few seats down, an older man rolled his eyes and grumbled loudly. "She sure looks like militia to me. No idea why Art brought her here."

"Me neither," someone else chimed in. "She shouldn't be here."

"Hey, come on." Shane raised his palms and glanced at Mae. "This woman needed help. She's too injured to leave. She's no threat to you."

The older man tutted and rolled his eyes. The woman next to him muttered something under her breath.

"Sorry." Shane shook his head. "They don't mean it."

"I think they do," she replied, spooning some oatmeal from her bowl. "But I don't blame them. I probably wouldn't trust me either."

"Especially after what the militia have been doing around these parts." Shane watched her over his coffee mug as he took a long sip.

"The militia?" Mae frowned. Her mind flicked to the store. Cornell. The woman. "It's the Freemen who've been slaughtering people."

At that, Shane almost spat out his coffee. "Slaughtering? Are you serious?"

"You took the depot from the civilians who were guarding it for us. We were supposed to rendezvous with them. I saw it with my own eyes."

As Shane opened his mouth to speak, another voice cut in. "We did not kill civilians."

Around the table, a hush settled. "Art," Shane said, nodding at the large figure standing next to Mae.

The man, Art, slid into the seat next to Shane and leaned forward onto the table, looking Mae up and down. "Miss...?"

"Peterson," she said, her mouth a little dry.

"Miss Peterson, you seem to have some misconceptions about us. Let me dispel them for you."

Mae pressed her lips together and swallowed hard.

"I am the leader of this community and I do not condone violence. Especially violence against civilians. But we will respond with force if we are attacked." He tapped the table hard. "Your facts are inaccurate."

"Then maybe you should correct them for me? Explain to me why I'm so wrong about you?" Mae knew she was being too direct, but as her eyes flashed with defiance, Art nodded slowly.

A smile spread across his face. "Come," he said. "Take a walk with me." He stood up and held out his hand.

Ignoring it, Mae picked up her stick and glanced at Shane. "Art's a good guy," he said. "You can trust him."

Not sure yet whether she could trust either of them, Mae leaned heavily on her stick as she followed Art away from the crowd of eating Freemen toward the perimeter fence.

"Miss Peterson, you need our help. You're injured and, right now, you're relying on us for food, shelter, and medication. It's due to our goodwill that you weren't left to bleed out."

Mae put one hand into her pocket. Her army fatigues were gone, she had no idea where. Since she arrived, she'd been using a selection of clothes given to her by Lisa. Thermals, pants, fleeces, and a large, padded jacket. "My friends would have helped me," she said, continuing to look ahead as they walked—very slowly—along the fence. "Besides, I wouldn't have been injured if *your* people hadn't shot me."

Sighing a little, Art chewed the inside of his cheek. He seemed like the kind of man for whom everything was thought out and considered, not the kind of person to say things he didn't mean or behave irrationally. "For a moment," he said, "let's put aside who has the right to occupy the depot and why someone might want to do so." He glanced at her sideways. "That's a separate issue."

Mae pressed her lips together. If Art wanted to talk, she'd let him talk. Somewhere in there, she might discover something of use.

"In which case, Miss Peterson, you were shot because you were trying to infiltrate the already-occupied depot. You intended to kill my people. Did you not?"

Mae didn't reply.

"Yet, when they fought back and you were injured, it was *my* people who rescued you and cared for you. Not your own."

"You didn't give them a chance—" Mae began to speak but Art raised his hand to cut her off.

At the same moment, a jolt of pain shot through her leg and she stumbled forward. Art caught her arm, steadied her and asked, "Okay?"

She took her arm back and nodded at him. "Yes. Thank you."

After a brief pause, checking she was all right to continue their slow crawl beside the fence, he said, "My people left you after you were shot. You passed out. Do you remember Lisa being there?"

Mae frowned. "Yes."

"Well, Lisa and the others went to secure the gates. After the militia were driven back, they were reinforcing the exits when they found you. Still lying on the ground where they left you."

A cold shiver ran down Mae's spine.

"Your friends, your unit, walked straight over you. Abandoned you. *My* people saved you."

Silence settled between them. Mae swallowed hard. Gideon would never.... But would Cornell? If he thought she was already dead or that treating her would take too many precious resources?

"It is, of course, up to you whether you believe me." Art put his hand on her shoulder and indicated that they should head back toward the main body of the camp. Mae's leg was throbbing. She was desperate to sit down, and now her head felt a little woozy too.

Quietly, they walked back to the tables where Shane was still waiting for her. When they reached it, Art fixed his gaze on hers. "We did not steal the depot from civilians, Miss Peterson. We were protecting it. The civilians, who I believe wanted to join your *militia*, tried to take control of it, and we fought back." Art King stood back and folded his arms in front of his chest. "And that is what happened."

The authority with which Art spoke made the hairs on the back of Mae's neck stand on end. She nodded, lacing her hands together in front of her. "Thank you for explaining," she said contritely.

For a moment, Art simply looked her up and down. Then he nodded and said, "You may stay here as long as you wish. All I ask is that you try to keep an open mind." Then he walked away, leaving Mae with far more questions than answers.

22

LAUREL

Kermit was *not* how Laurel expected him to be. She'd pictured him being older; gray hair, bristles on his face, deep lines around his eyes. In actual fact, he looked quite young. Younger than Bear, at least. He had bleached white hair, which fell in unruly locks around his face, bright blue eyes, and a nice smile.

When he was pointing a gun at her, however, she was also keenly aware that he seemed like someone who wasn't necessarily inhabiting the same world as everyone else.

Now that they were down in his bunker, that sense had only intensified.

After making coffee for them, he unfolded some camping chairs and shooed Laurel and Trent off his camp bed. Sitting down on it, he waited until they were in their chairs, Jess at Bear's feet, then waved his hand at them. "I'm listening," he said, eyebrows raised.

Taking his cue, Bear took a deep breath and launched into their story.

He told Kermit a surprising amount of detail, but perhaps that was because he knew Kermit was the sort of person who needed detail. There was even some that Laurel hadn't been aware of before.

By the time Bear finished, their coffees were almost stone cold.

"So, we left to find Mae. When we've tracked her down, we're hoping she'll accompany us back to Thunder Bay." Bear sat back, looking a little exhausted from the effort of speaking.

Watching him, Laurel tried to stop her lips twitching into a smile; this was quite possibly the most she'd heard her husband say throughout the entire course of their marriage. Even before his hearing loss, he wasn't a big talker. In fact, when it came to wedding speeches, Laurel had been the one to stand up and thank their friends and family.

For a moment, Kermit didn't speak, just nodded his head slowly.

Next to her, Trent kept glancing at his ankles as if he was still feeling snakes on his legs, but he hadn't spoken or interrupted while Bear told his story.

"Why now?" Kermit tapped the side of his mug with his fingernails.

"I'm sorry?" Bear asked.

"Why did you decide to try and find her now? Why not before?" There was a note of suspicion in Kermit's voice, as if he had a feeling something didn't add up about their tale. Of course, it didn't. But that was because Bear had left out the part about Laurel's mother passing. "Everything you've told me leads me to believe that your wife, Doctor Rivera, was *beyond* dedicated to her hospital and her patients. She only left before because someone was threatening to hurt them. So, why would she leave now?" Kermit stood up, slowly. His hand moved to his waist. "Unless someone *told* you to come here."

As Bear raised his palms to try and calm his friend, Laurel bit her lower lip. Then, unable to simply sit there any longer, and worried that the situation could descend into something much more dangerous if they weren't careful, she said, "My mother died."

Just like that, she said it. Was it the first time?

"The reason I went to South Minneha was to enroll her in a cancer trial. Her meds ran out. The new ones didn't work. She died." Laurel rubbed her thighs and breathed out hard. Saying the words hit her chest like a bullet. "That's why we decided to leave; there was nothing left for me at South Minneha."

Kermit scanned her face then narrowed his eyes. "But your patients—"

"Are all gone. The only ones left are medical staff and those who are well enough to take care of themselves. They decided to stay together, as a family. But…." She glanced at Bear and reached for his hand. "Now it's time for us to find our family."

"They're telling you the truth," Trent spoke up. "I guess you probably have no reason to believe what I have to say, but Bear and Laurel are two of the best people I've ever met. They're telling the truth. They risked coming here because they thought you could help them."

As Bear winced, clearly worried that Trent had given away too much too soon, Kermit's eyes snapped to Bear's face. "You need my help? What kind of help?" He sat back down, moving his hand away from his gun.

"Well," Bear answered slowly, looking around the room, "I knew you'd have a setup like this." He smiled. It was a smile Laurel recognized; the smile he used when he was being charming. "Of all my contacts from the old days, if there was anyone who'd have been prepared to ride out this storm, I knew it'd be Kermit."

Kermit's cheeks pinkened. He smiled and brushed his fingers through his pale hair.

"So, when Laurel asked how the heck we were going to find Mae, there was only one person I could think of who might—just *might*—be able to help us." He squeezed her fingers.

Laurel nodded. "Bear said you were the only one he'd trust."

Kermit's expression became suddenly more serious. For a moment, Laurel wondered whether she'd said the right thing. But then he nodded at her. "Darn right, you can trust me."

In one swift movement, he stood up, paced across the room, and grabbed a swivel chair from beneath his desk. Sitting down, he pushed himself over to the filing cabinet and pulled out the maps that, a short while ago, he'd hidden.

"Okay," he said, "what's your daughter's last known location?"

Bear stood and walked over to the table. Laurel and Trent joined him. "That's just it," Bear said solemnly, "we have no idea."

Looking up, Kermit left his palms flat on the map and bit his lower lip. "You have *no* idea where she last was?"

He glanced at the radio nearby. He'd begun tapping his foot. Speaking to himself, he said, "If you knew, I could radio…."

"Radio?" Trent's voice brightened. "Your radio works?"

Looking a little annoyed by the interruption to his train of thought, Kermit nodded dismissively. "I have contacts who operate on the HAM network, but we have an agreement that radio communications will be for emergency situations only. If you knew the exact base, I could reach out, but I can't justify contacting every single one of them."

Laurel's heart lurched in her chest. This was their shot, and he was saying no? She tugged Bear's arm and he nodded at her.

"Kermit, there must be a way."

Kermit stood up. He'd begun to pace and was muttering something to himself. Finally, he stopped, arms folded, and looked at them each in turn. "I have a solution."

Fighting the urge to rush forward and ask him to hurry up, Laurel smiled tentatively at him. "You do? That's good. That's *great*."

"What's the solution, Kermit?" Bear asked. Beside him, Jess was scratching his leg as if she wanted to go pee, but he ignored her.

A slow grin appeared on Kermit's face. "The solution," he said, "is birds, my friends. *Birds*."

Barely stopping for breath, Kermit grabbed his jacket and his shotgun, then set about heaving the table away from the wall. Peeling a large stars and stripes flag off the wall, he revealed a door very similar to the one they'd entered through.

Without speaking, he opened it and disappeared into the darkness beyond.

Bear scooped up Jess, deposited her back into her carrier and followed him.

Taking Trent's hand, Laurel stepped in behind him.

Up ahead, Kermit lit a gas lamp and the faint glow guided them down the tunnel. Finally, they reached the end. Not a door, but a ladder like the one they'd used to climb down in the woods.

This one, however, opened into a basement.

Laurel wrinkled her nose. It smelled like a basement; damp and laced with the scent of DIY materials.

Lighting another lamp, which he took from a long wooden workbench, Kermit handed it to Bear, then guided them up a series of wooden steps until they emerged in a cabin.

Wondering why on earth Kermit chose to inhabit an underground bunker when he had a perfectly lovely cabin up above him, Laurel took in the room. A soft couch, a large fireplace, a kitchen with a wood-burning stove and shuttered windows.

"It's kinda like your place," Trent said to Bear.

"Yeah," Bear agreed. "It is."

"This way. This way." Kermit gestured to a wooden ladder in the corner of the room, which led to a mezzanine area above the main living area. From there, he took them out a small wooden door and onto a wrap-around balcony that encircled the entire top floor of the cabin.

Laurel drew in a sharp breath as the cold air whipped her face. The sun was dipping lower in the sky, taking with it the warmth they'd become accustomed to during the day's travel.

Seemingly not feeling the cold, Kermit beckoned for them to keep following. When they turned the corner, as if they were going to take the balcony around the western side of the cabin, a gentle cooing sound made Laurel pause.

In front of them, blocking the way, was a huge cage. Stretching the width of the balcony, and about seven feet high, it contained at least a dozen pigeons, maybe more.

On seeing Kermit, the birds' noise increased in volume. A few ruffled their feathers, while others flapped their wings. All were watching him.

"Pigeons?" Trent's tone was as incredulous as the voice inside Laurel's head. This was Kermit's big idea? *Pigeons?*

"Yes, kid, pigeons." Kermit stood with his back to the cage and folded his arms in front of his chest. Sensing that Trent wasn't a believer in the power of pigeons, he spoke to Bear and Laurel as he said, "Each of these birds has a homing instinct. Each was trained by a contact of mine at a different location." Sensing their confusion, he added, "Years ago, certain members of the HAM network also set up a homing network. We trained our own birds, then swapped them. So, all over the country, there are birds whose instinct is to fly back here. And, in this cage, I have birds whose instincts are to fly to *their* homes."

"Right." Laurel's brain was starting to put the pieces together. "So, you can send each other messages by swapping birds?"

"Precisely." Kermit rubbed his hands together. "Again, not to be used unless it's an important situation, but as the birds are not a finite resource, I think the network would agree to an exception." Kermit nodded to himself. "We'll send them out with a message asking for news of your daughter. If anyone knows of her, or can tell us where she is, they will reply."

"Kermit, isn't that a bit of a long shot?" Bear asked tentatively. "What are the chances someone has bumped into her?"

Frowning, Kermit bit his lower lip. "We are not simply relying on them having *seen* her, Bear. We are relying on the information they have in their possession. Each of our members has been gathering intel on the military base closest to them."

"So, you have information about the base nearest to here?" Laurel asked. "Are you sure Mae's name wasn't on it? Mae Peterson?"

Rolling his eyes a little, Kermit said, "I'm certain, Doctor Rivera. I know every name on my list."

"So, we send the birds out and hope that one of them has information about Mae?" Bear asked.

"Do you have a better plan?" Kermit raised his eyebrows.

Slowly, Bear breathed in. He was looking at the pigeons, probably thinking the same thing as Laurel: was this really their best shot?

"I thought not. In which case, if we hurry and write our messages quickly, we can dispatch the birds before sunset. Come."

Heading back to the ladder, Kermit hastily ushered them back down into the belly of the cabin and, from there, to his underground bunker.

Pulling out a bundle of tiny pieces of paper, presumably small enough to be wound into a coil around a pigeon's leg, Kermit handed them several pieces each. Gesturing to an old, empty tin can full of ball-point pens, he told them what to write:

> Seeking whereabouts of Sergeant Mae Peterson. Respond ASAP. M. McFly.

"McFly?" Bear asked, raising an eyebrow as he copied Kermit's message. "As in Back to the Future McFly?"

As Kermit nodded proudly, Trent frowned. The 80s movie reference was utterly lost on him.

It took them just a few minutes to fill out their pieces of paper, and then they were back up to the roof. Carefully, Kermit secured their messages to ten small pink legs. "All right, my beauties," he cooed gently, the birds getting even more excited. "Ready?"

While Laurel, Bear, and Trent stepped back, Kermit released his birds one by one into the darkening night sky.

"They won't turn around and come back here?" Bear asked. "I mean, how do you know they don't think of *this* as their home now?"

"Because home isn't such a fickle notion to these birds as it is to us humans," Kermit replied, a tear in his eye as he watched the pigeons' silhouettes grow smaller in the distance.

Securing the cage door, Kermit sighed a little.

"Thank you," Laurel said, putting her hand on his shoulder. "Thank you for using your birds to help us. Will they return? The ones you sent?"

"Nope," Kermit said, both eyes watery now. "They've gone home."

Laurel glanced at Bear, gesturing for him to say something.

"Well, listen, Kermit—we really appreciate you using them to help us. I'm sorry we've depleted your flock."

Sniffing loudly, ushering them back into the cabin, Kermit shook his head. "No matter. We intend to rendezvous next summer to conduct another swap."

Noticing Trent looking confused, Kermit added, "Any chicks that are born here will consider *this* their home. They're transferred to a different coop—on the other side of the cabin—and they'll mature with this location as their base."

"Ohh," Trent nodded enthusiastically. "I see. Clever."

"Yes," Kermit said, climbing back down into the bunker. "It is."

After securing the bunker, Kermit allowed them to go up into the main body of the cabin to eat supper. "Rarely eat up here," he said. "But as I've got company...." He headed for the kitchen and began to open cupboards, then shouted over his shoulder for Bear to light the fire.

As Bear stooped down in front of the grate, Laurel walked over to him and handed him pieces of kindling.

"He's odd, but he's doing his best to help," Bear said quietly. "We can trust him. If anyone can find Mae, it's Kermit."

Laurel smiled and rubbed Bear's elbow. "I know. You did good, Bjorn."

Catching her eyes, Bear raised his eyebrows at her. "Bjorn?" A flicker of a smile crossed his face. "I either did something very good or very bad, because I can count on one hand the number of times you've called me *Bjorn*."

Laughing, Laurel pushed her glasses up onto her head and rubbed the dents left on the bridge of her nose. "I'll let you decide which one," she said quietly. Then she headed to the kitchen to help Kermit.

While she and Kermit cooked up a large pot of rice with beans, canned vegetables, and tuna, Trent and Bear played around in front of the fire with Jess. She was pleased to be out of her carrier and her knitted coat, rolling on her back and exposing her belly for rubs as she wagged her tail.

Every now and then, Kermit looked over at them. Eventually, as if he couldn't contain it any longer, he said, "Sorry, Bear… could you ask your dog to stop that?"

Bear looked up and tilted his head as if he'd misheard.

"Wriggling her fur into the rug," Kermit said, rubbing his hands together like it was physically painful to watch Jess rubbing her coarse white hairs into his floor. "Hairs," he added.

"Right." Bear sat up, rolling Jess off her back, and giving her a final pat on the head. "Sure. Sorry, buddy."

"No problem." Kermit turned back to the rice, but Laurel caught his shoulders visibly relaxing now that the dog-hair risk was back to normal.

"Dinner's ready." Laurel tapped a wooden spoon on the side of the cooking pot and gestured for the boys to fetch dishes and cutlery. "Help yourselves."

Taking larger-than-normal portions, Bear and Trent thanked them both and returned to the fire. Laurel joined them, sitting cross-legged on the floor and wrapping her hands around the warmth of her bowl. For a moment, she thought Kermit was going to remain standing. But then he gave a little shake of the head, muttered something to himself, and walked over to perch on the edge of the couch.

For a while, they ate in silence, enjoying the crackle of the fire and the hot food in their bellies. Then Kermit cleared his throat and said, "So, Bear, the plan is to head back to Thunder Bay when you've found your daughter?"

Bear was chewing but nodded. When he'd finished, and swallowed the mouthful, he said, "That's the plan, yeah."

"The four of you?" Kermit glanced at Laurel. Clearly, knowing Bear and Laurel had separated, he was trying to figure out what exactly their current situation was.

"That's the plan," Laurel interjected.

"Well…" Kermit stood up, ready to take his dish to the sink, "when you're settled, you should join the network. We could use a contact up that way."

Bear stood up too, following Kermit to the kitchen. "I'll think about it," he said. "Definitely."

While Bear and Trent slept soundly on Kermit's couch, Laurel spent most of the night unable to catch even a few minutes' rest. Every time something moved outside the window, an owl hooted, or a twig snapped, she jolted awake. Finally, in the early hours of the morning, she positioned herself in an armchair near the fire, occasionally glancing over at the nearest window, searching for the shape of a bird on the sill, waiting to be let in.

After spending so long trying not to think about Mae and what she was doing, suddenly it was all Laurel could think about.

Bear, Trent, and she had gone through so many trials and tribulations since the power went out. The people in South Minneha had each had their own dramas and difficulties to overcome. So it wasn't unreasonable to think Mae had too. And the knowledge that she hadn't been there for her daughter, hadn't even been *close* to being there for her, over the past few months was starting to weigh heavy on Laurel's chest.

The sun was starting to creep up over the horizon when tiredness finally took over. Her eyelids drooped, her breathing slowed, and she was about to slide beneath the surface of consciousness when something startled her.

The sound she'd been waiting for all night; scraping at the window.

Jumping out of her chair, Laurel yelled for Kermit. Instantly, he appeared at the bottom of the stairs. His hair sticking up in unruly tufts, his eyes blurry, he strode across the room and threw open the window. "Tonto!" he cried, opening his arms wide.

Instead of flying into them, the pigeon landed on the kitchen table and began pecking at the leftovers on its surface.

"Tonto, it's been so long." Kermit approached the bird quietly, then scooped it up, cupping it in his hands and holding his cheek to its silky feathers. "My friend. Do you have news?" He examined the bird's leg. His eyes widened. "Here, here...." He beckoned for Laurel to come over. "His leg. A message."

Laurel reached out gingerly and unfurled the message. By now, Trent and Bear had heard the commotion and were sleepily climbing out of their blankets.

"Clever bird," Laurel said, smiling at Kermit.

Pride flushing his cheeks, Kermit straightened his shoulders and puffed out his chest. "But of course," he said. Then he nodded at the message. "But what does it say?"

Mae Peterson, Base 362, Iowa, January. J. Rabbit.

"That's her." Laurel peered at the scratchy handwriting. "That's Mae." As Bear strode over, she grabbed his arm and showed it to him. "Bear, she was in Iowa three months ago. That's not far from here."

Bear swiped his fingers through his hair, nodding slowly. When he looked up, he wrapped one arm around Laurel and the other around Trent. "Well then, kids, it looks like we're heading to Iowa."

23

LAUREL

ONE WEEK LATER

"I don't think I can feel my butt anymore." From the horse next to her, sitting behind Bear, Trent wriggled uncomfortably in the saddle.

"Me either." Laurel lifted herself up out of the saddle to relieve the pressure on her tailbone and rubbed her lower back. They'd been traveling on horseback for an entire week, making their way from Kermit's hideout toward the last known base Mae had been seen.

For the past two days, they'd been in Iowa, and were all sorely in need of a rest stop.

"You said when we reached the next town, we'd stop." Trent leaned sideways to look at Bear. Since being given a potential location for their daughter, he was reluctant to stop, as if, by taking too long, they might lose what chance they had of reaching her before she moved on somewhere else.

"We do need to stop, Bear." Laurel lowered herself back into the saddle and rubbed Robin's mane. "We're running low on supplies and the horses are tired." Playing her trump card, she added, "Plus, Jess must be going stir-crazy in this thing."

While Trent traveled behind Bear, Laurel was taking a turn carrying Jess. The poor dog had spent the majority of the last week being transported via carrier strapped to someone's chest, because Bear didn't trust her not to run off or spook the horses if she caught the scent of something tasty. She was now in desperate need of letting off some steam.

Looking at the big-eyed puppy-dog expression on Jess's face seemed to soften Bear's resolve. "Okay," he said tightly. "Looks like there's a town up ahead. We'll stop if it looks safe."

Breathing a sigh of relief, Laurel adjusted her gun on her shoulder. As well as the one in her waistband, Kermit had let them leave with a shotgun each. This had left Bear almost speechless, but Kermit had insisted. "When we rendezvous to exchange birds, you can return them to me," he'd said purposefully, clearly not willing to let go of the idea that Bear would eventually join the HAM network as well as the homing pigeon one.

He'd also given them an extra hunting knife each, some water purification tablets, paracord, fire-lighting supplies, and—Trent's favorite—a roadkill cookbook. "The worrying thing is," Bear had said quietly, slotting the cookbook into his pack, "Kermit cooked this stuff *before* the EMP."

Food-wise, though, they were running short. While Kermit had seemed happy to share his plentiful weapons, his food supply had been very carefully calculated to get him through the next two winters—taking into account the possibility that his crops might not develop as expected and leaving a surplus for next winter and the one after while he established himself. So, giving away candy bars or cans of beans was not something he was willing to consider.

He'd also grumbled about them leaving the injured Shadow with him. "Another animal to feed," he'd said grumpily, "and not one that's easy to hide, either."

"At least he won't leave hairs on your rug," Trent had quipped, resulting in Laurel giving him a *be quiet* glare.

Now, as they continued their approach into town, Laurel studied the neat rows of houses on either side of them. With overgrown lawns and dark windows, almost every single one looked abandoned. A couple were proudly displaying the American flag, blowing in the breeze. Most were boarded up, and one was nothing more than a burned-out husk of a building. A little farther, a battered sign read: *Welcome to Clancy.*

"Looks like they've had some tough times," Bear said through gritted teeth.

Laurel nodded, tweaking Robin's reins to help her skirt around a large truck that sat abandoned in the center of the road.

"Looks like the town center is up ahead," Bear said, passing the map to Laurel.

She studied it. He was right; if they carried on along this road, they'd come to the main thoroughfare of stores and cafés. "There's a pharmacy at the lower end of the street. I'll stop there and see if there's anything useful, while you two scope out food supplies."

"Don't expect much," Bear said gruffly. "By now, most of it will have been ransacked by locals."

Laurel breathed out through tight lips. In the past day or so, Bear's mood had darkened, and she wasn't sure what had caused it. At the beginning of their journey, he'd been upbeat, but something was bothering him now and she couldn't make out what it was.

"Well, we might be lucky. We found Mae using a guy called Kermit and a carrier pigeon named Tonto. So, you never know." She smiled at him, hoping to see him return the gesture, but his eyes were fixed ahead.

Trent was sensing the change in mood too and looked over at Laurel. She shrugged at him lightheartedly and rolled her eyes, the way parents often do when their other half is being moody and their kid has noticed.

Lowering her head to Jess's, she whispered, "What's up with him, girl? Have you figured it out?"

Of course, Jess didn't reply. But she did lick Laurel's nose, and the momentary warmth was nice.

"Okay, this is me." Laurel pulled Robin to a halt outside the pharmacy and dismounted, looping her reins around her hand. The street was empty, not a soul in sight.

"I'm gonna walk from here too, PB." Trent effortlessly swung himself down from Lucy's back, quite the practiced rider after a week of non-stop saddle time.

"We should—" Bear was about to tell Trent to get back on the horse, but seemed to notice his own tone and corrected himself. Clearing his throat, he said, "Okay. But we can't leave the horses out in the open."

Laurel scanned the street. Opposite the pharmacy was a playpark. Behind it was a copse of trees. She pointed to them and Bear nodded. "I'll secure them. Trent, with me."

"What about Jess?" Laurel looked at the Jack Russell, who was wriggling to be freed now that they were back on foot.

"Okay. But I'm putting her on a leash." Bear pulled a piece of rope from his pack and, as Laurel set Jess on the ground, he looped it around her neck.

Shaking herself all over, despite the leash, Jess grinned at them and furiously wagged her tail.

"Looks like there's a convenience store down the street. Meet you there?" Trent asked, pointing to a sign that read, *O'Donnell's Groceries.*

Laurel nodded, already on her way to the boarded-up pharmacy door.

Inside, it was dark and quiet. The front window had been boarded too, and the only light entering the building came from a dirty skylight above the checkout desk.

Laurel reached behind the counter and took a paper bag from a hook, then traveled down the first aisle, scooping up anything that was useful but not too heavy.

Unfortunately, Bear was right about the medical supplies; most had been looted. But she did manage to find some bandages, some iodine, and a couple of suture kits. Out back, the drug section had been raided too. All that remained were some of the more obscure painkillers and some out-of-date antibiotics. Still, she pocketed them too. Out-of-date drugs were better than no drugs.

She was loading her fresh supplies into her pack when she heard footsteps on broken glass near the front door. Slowly, she stood up and ducked behind the shelves in front of her.

Taking her gun from her waistband, she strained her ears. There was a scuffle, a voice cried out, and then a flurry of white appeared, wagging its tail.

"Jess...." Laurel bent down, laughing. "That leash didn't last long, huh?"

The dog's leash had been chewed clean through, and she was panting proudly as she showed off the bitten-off section that now trailed behind her.

"Darn dog...." Bear appeared, hands on hips, face like thunder. "Didn't even make it to the store. She took off back to find you."

"Oh, come on, Bear. Don't be mad at her. Do you blame her for wanting to keep us all together?" Laurel chuckled, picking up the loose piece of leash and holding out her hand for the other half. Bear handed it to her and she knotted it swiftly back together. Handing it back to him, she let her palm linger on top of his knuckles. "Are you all right? You seem...."

"Fine. I'm fine." He breathed in heavily, held the air in his chest for a moment, then sighed. "Sorry, Laurel. I'm fine. It's just...."

"Guys!" The sound of Trent clattering through the door interrupted them. "You better come. Quick."

As Bear headed for the door, Laurel scooped the last of her supplies into her pack and sprinted after him.

Outside, Trent was moving quickly, jogging down the street, beckoning them to follow.

When they reached the convenience store, all three of them stopped in their tracks. Outside, two dead bodies lay on the sidewalk. Another was in the doorway, half inside, half outside.

Laurel swallowed hard and approached the bodies closest to her, a man and a woman. She crouched down and held her fingers to the woman's throat, even though she knew from the dried blood on the ground and the pallor of the woman's face that she wouldn't find any signs of life.

Turning her over gently, Laurel winced. "Gunshot wound," she said, looking at the woman's stomach. Her puffy blue jacket was soaked with a dark red stain.

Doing the same to the man, Bear sighed in agreement. "Same here."

"There's more. Up there." Trent pointed down the street. Outside a boarded-up café were two more bodies. These looked younger. Laurel didn't examine them too closely.

Slowly, quietly, they traveled the length of the street. As if she knew something very grave was happening, Jess stopped wagging her tail and walked calmly by Bear's side.

Laurel had counted ten dead bodies when she stopped counting.

"What was that?" Bear stopped and reached for his gun. "Up ahead. There. Something in the church window."

A shudder ran through Laurel's body; surely, whoever did this wouldn't attack the church? As she and Trent lifted their guns too, the three of them approached slowly, Bear in the center, Trent and Laurel on either side.

When they reached the church steps, they stopped. There it was again; movement in the window.

"Is anyone there?" Bear called loudly.

"I'm a doctor," Laurel added. "Does anyone need help?"

There was a long pause. The air seemed still, and warmer than it had been a moment ago. Then a crack appeared in the door. Through it, a voice said, "Who are you? Where are you from?"

Laurel stepped forward, shoving her gun back into her waistband. As she did so, Bear tugged her arm, but she shook her head at him and positioned herself in front of the door. Raising both palms, she said, "I'm a doctor. Dr. Laurel Rivera. We're from Minnesota. A town called South Minneha. We're heading south, looking for our daughter. I have medical supplies. Does anyone inside need assistance?"

The sound of muffled voices filtered out from the crack in the door. Then it opened a little wider. "Give us your weapons and you may enter."

"If you want our help, we bring the weapons." Bear stepped forward and wrapped his fingers around the door.

Laurel bit her tongue, tempted to pull him back but aware he was probably right; surrendering their weapons seemed like a very bad idea.

"We cannot allow weapons inside the church."

"Then we cannot help." Bear tugged Laurel's arm. "We're sorry for your troubles." He turned, gesturing for Trent to do the same.

They were at the bottom of the steps when the voice called, "Wait. Please don't go."

24

LAUREL

Laurel looked sideways at Bear. His eyes were closed as if he'd been waiting, as if he knew the people inside wouldn't want them to walk away.

The door opened a crack more. "Please." A woman stepped out. She was elderly and plump, with her hair tied back into a loose ponytail at the nape of her neck. As her fingers curled around the door, Laurel noticed how pale they looked.

With gray-blue eyes, she blinked at them. Taking in the three of them, she stepped outside, leaving the door ajar.

"Are you really a doctor?" she asked Laurel.

Laurel nodded. "Yes, ma'am. Do you need help?"

The woman looked again at Bear, then at Trent. As if she understood that they were trying to make themselves look friendly, Jess gave a small yap and wagged her tail. If she'd still been wearing her bright red sweater, she'd have looked cuter still. But the woman smiled anyway.

"All right," she said, her shoulders drooping as if she knew she had little left to lose. "You can come in."

Taking Laurel's hand, Bear kept pace with her up the steps, Trent jogging up behind them.

As they stepped into the dark belly of the church, Laurel's eyes struggled to adjust. After a moment, shapes began to come into focus.

The church was modern but dimly lit. A stained-glass window behind the altar let in some muted light from outside, and some candles had been lit around the room.

Examining the pews, Laurel inhaled sharply; they were full to bursting with people. Men, women, children. Old and young. All huddled together in silence watching the strangers who had just entered their church.

"What happened here?" Laurel asked.

The woman closed the door. As she did, two young men hurried over and pulled over two huge wooden chests which, it seemed, were being used as barricades. Without answering Laurel's question, the woman gestured to a door to their left. "The injured are this way."

Bear took Laurel's elbow. "Be careful."

She nodded. "Wait here with Trent. I'll assess and let you know what's going on."

He fixed his eyes on hers for a moment, then nodded.

The woman led Laurel through the small door and into what looked like some kind of meeting room. Chairs were stacked up around the edges and boxes of kids' toys were piled in one corner. It reminded Laurel of the kind of places she took Mae as a child; church halls where volunteers set out scuffed and dribbled-on toys for local kids to play with.

In the middle of the room, she counted eleven patients. Two had bloodied bandages on their heads, and were sitting up nursing cups of something. Three were lying down with their eyes closed. The rest had varying degrees of minor injuries, rubbing sore legs, wounded hands, and injured sides.

Laurel swung her pack from her shoulder and set it down. A strong pulsing sensation in her stomach told her to get started. Help the injured immediately and without delay. But she'd been through enough in the past months to know that, sometimes, self-preservation had to come before her instinct as a physician.

Gesturing for the woman to follow her, she headed back through the door. When she reached Bear, she folded her arms and said, "I can help. But first, I need to know what happened here. I need to know that we're safe."

Before the woman could speak, a figure appeared at her shoulder. Another woman, slightly younger. "Mom? I thought she said she was a doctor?"

The older woman smiled at the younger woman and patted her arm. The look that passed between them made Laurel bite the inside of her cheek as a memory of her own mother floated in front of her eyes.

"I am a doctor, yes." Laurel extended her hand. "Laurel Rivera." Turning to Bear, she introduced him and then Trent.

"I'm Cathy," the younger woman said tightly. "And this is my mom, Doria."

"Well, Cathy, Doria," Bear interjected, folding his arms in front of his stomach, "we want to help you but, as Laurel said, we need to know what happened."

Sighing loudly, Doria smoothed her light gray hair over her temples. She looked behind her at the frightened faces in the pews. "Freemen," she said finally, her voice trembling. "They called themselves *freemen*. They arrived a few days ago. Fifty of them at least. We welcomed them, but they weren't interested in pleasantries."

"They raided our stores, our houses, everywhere." Cathy cleared her throat and blinked tears from her eyes. "We'd set up a community hub at the school. They waited until nightfall, when we were sleeping in our dorms, and attacked us. They said they just wanted supplies, that if we gave them what they wanted, they'd leave us alone."

"But," Doria cut in, "how could we simply hand over all our medicine? Our food? We pleaded with them to just take what they needed, but it was no use. They started shooting. In the end, it was futile. We ran for the church, for shelter."

"By the time we emerged, the town was empty." Cathy looked suddenly pale and sat down hard on a chair next to the door. "There's nothing left. Nothing. They took it all."

Laurel closed her eyes and pinched the bridge of her nose, taking off her glasses as a sigh wracked her shoulders. When she opened her eyes, Bear was staring at her. But the expression on his face was not one of shock. Was this what was wrong with him? Had he somehow *known* about these freemen?

"All right. Thank you for sharing that with us." Laurel squeezed Doria's arm. "I'll go and help your friends now."

As she headed back to the meeting room, she heard Trent asking whether they had anything to eat and offering to share what was in his bag. A smile fluttered on her lips. He really was a *good* kid.

By the time she'd treated all eleven patients, the sky beyond the window was darkening. Emerging from the meeting room, Laurel unfastened her hair from its ponytail and refastened it, scraping her fingers through it so that her nails massaged her aching scalp.

"Okay, doc?" Bear asked, handing her a cardboard cup of what looked like extremely weak tea.

"Okay. One head injury from a fall, one from a near miss with a bullet." She grimaced and took a sip of her drink. It tasted of nothing but was, at least, hot. "Broken ribs, from being whacked with a shotgun." She shook her head. "Who the heck are these people? Who would *do* this to a defenseless town? I mean, half of these people are elderly and the other half are kids."

Bear gestured for her to sit down. The look on his face told her she was right; he knew something about these *freemen*.

"Bear? You know something, don't you?"

Breathing out hard, Bear pushed his fingers through his dark blond hair. "Kermit warned me of chatter about a group of civilians calling themselves 'freemen' who've been raiding towns. They seem to be heading east, heading for some kind of camp. He told me to be careful."

"And you didn't think this was worth sharing with me?" Laurel blinked at him, raising her eyebrows.

"I didn't want to give you anything else to worry about."

"I don't need to be handled with kid gloves," she replied, tugging her arm away as he tried to soothe her. "You should have told me."

"I'm sorry." Bear tried again to put his hand on her arm. This time, she let him. "I'm sorry, I should have."

Softening a little, Laurel edged closer on the pew and allowed herself to lean against Bear's side. "Is there anything we can do to help these people? Apart from patching them up? I mean, they have nothing left. Surely we can't just ride out of here and leave them?"

Tilting his head from side to side, Bear wrinkled his nose.

"You've thought of something?"

Hesitantly, he replied, "There's a National Guard base less than an hour from here on horseback. It takes us off course, but if I leave at first light I could fetch help, warn the soldiers what's happening out here, bring reinforcements for the town or ask them to take in those who want to go."

Laurel bit her lower lip. She vowed when she left South Minneha that she wouldn't be thrown off course, that they would stick to their plan and keep going until they found Mae. But how could they just walk away?

"All right," she said quietly. "I'll stay here with Trent and Jess. You go first thing. But you come straight back, okay?"

"I'll fetch the horses now, bring them here to the church where we can keep an eye on them." Bear's hand lingered on Laurel's shoulder. Not for the first time, after being in such close proximity for so long, it seemed as if he was about to slip back into the nuances of being husband and wife. A kiss on the cheek, a hug goodbye. But he stopped himself, nodded, and disappeared before she could tell him to be careful.

That night, they slept on the floor between the pews with the other fifty-or-so residents who hadn't fled the town.

Doria, it turned out, was the wife of the town's preacher. He was killed when the EMP first hit and a truck careened into his car on the highway outside of town. It took Doria three days to find him. When she did, members of his congregation helped carry his body back to town and they held a memorial. Ever since, she and her daughter Cathy had taken on the role of looking after the town.

When the Freemen came, however, they were utterly helpless. Most were unarmed, and those that were had no experience in a combat situation.

"Your husband is going to fetch help?" Doria asked the next morning as sunlight started to filter through the stained-glass window. Laurel was sitting up, arms wrapped around her knees, still inside her sleeping bag while she watched Bear pull on his boots and drink a fast mug of weak coffee.

Laurel nodded, tucking a strand of her loose dark hair behind her ear. "He'll bring military assistance, don't worry."

Doria looked thoughtful, squeezing her hands together in her lap as she sat on the pew beside Laurel.

"Is everything all right, Doria?"

"I...." She hesitated, then sighed a little and said, "I heard some of them talking. They were outside, keeping guard over us while they loaded carts with supplies."

Laurel nodded, waiting for Doria to continue.

"They said something about making it to a camp and backing up the others." Doria looked over at Bear, as if this news might make him decide to stay.

"So you think this is a bigger effort than just one group?"

"From what I heard, yes." Doria pressed her lips together.

"I'll warn Bear." Laurel stood up and peeled herself out of her sleeping bag. "But don't worry, he'll be careful. He'll tell the Army what's going on. They'll help."

As Laurel walked over to Bear, she glanced at the spot where Trent had set up his bed. It was empty, and Jess was gone too. Catching her looking, Bear said, "She needed to pee. Trent volunteered to take her for a walk."

Raising her eyebrows, and wrapping her arms around herself against the chill of the church, Laurel asked, "Are you sure that's a good idea? Is it safe?"

"He's armed, and he's smart. He'll stay out of plain sight, but to be honest, I can't see the Freemen returning. What is there to come back for?"

Laurel nodded, taking Bear's empty coffee cup and placing it on a nearby shelf as he zipped up his coat and wound a scarf around his neck. Glancing back at Doria, she repeated what the elderly woman had told her.

Bear listened intently. "So, they're part of a wider group? A group that's coordinating itself somehow?"

"If Kermit has access to the HAM network, it's not unthinkable that others do too. Although I'm not sure I can picture anyone else having quite the same success with homing pigeons as he has." Laurel smiled a little, remembering the expression on Kermit's face when his favorite bird returned triumphant.

"True," Bear chuckled. His expression hardening, he added, "I'll brief the soldiers at the base, and I'll make sure they bring help. I'll be a few hours at most."

Laurel nodded as Bear tucked his map into his pocket and headed for the door. When he reached it, he stopped and waved.

"See you soon," he said, fixing his eyes on hers.

"See you soon." She waited until the door clicked shut before releasing her breath.

25

BEAR

Traveling without Laurel, for the first time since they were finally reunited, made Bear feel distinctly uneasy. As his horse trotted toward the spot on the map that indicated a mid-sized military base, he found himself looking over his shoulder for her. Being without Trent, too, was a strange sensation.

When he first set off from South Minneha alone to find Laurel, he'd realized just how much Trent had come to mean to him. He hated himself for thinking it, but more than once he'd wondered why it was so easy with this kid he barely knew when—with Mae—it had always been so much harder.

While Trent was easygoing, full of life, and rarely angry or annoyed, as a child Mae had been the opposite. In fact, when she was Trent's age, she'd spent most of her time back-chatting, sneaking out of the house, hiding her cigarettes and tattoos from her parents, and raising Cain if she wasn't allowed to go to a party she wanted to go to.

When she decided to join the military, it got worse. While Bear used to be able to keep the peace between her and Laurel, or at least try to, he found himself unable to soften either female's hostility. Mae simply couldn't understand why Laurel was so against her joining the Army when it was a career that had been passed down through their family for generations. Of course, Bear knew the truth; Laurel wasn't against Mae joining the Army because she feared for her life. Yes, she was worried for Mae's safety. But the unspoken reason both Laurel and Bear were so reluctant to see their hot-headed daughter sign up was because they weren't sure she could handle it.

If Mae had learned that truth, it would have broken her. Bear and Laurel never even said as much to one another, but they each knew what the other was thinking; that the Army could either make or break Mae and they had no idea which.

For a while, after Kermit gave them Mae's last known location, Bear was filled with hope. He could see the excitement in Laurel's eyes, thinking about being reunited with their daughter after everything they'd been through. Deep down, however, Bear had misgivings. Misgivings he couldn't voice to Laurel because the last thing he wanted was for the two of them to end up fighting like they used to.

"What do you mean?" Laurel would ask, her eyes flashing with indignation.

And then Bear would have to explain, with his few words and awkward way of expressing himself, that he was simply worried. Worried that their reunion with Mae wouldn't be as full of flowers and cotton candy as Laurel hoped it would be. Worried Mae wouldn't be pleased to see them. Worried she still held a grudge and, yes, worried that their daughter would drive a wedge between them again.

As he thought these things, Bear mentally kicked himself. He loved his daughter. He'd do anything to find her and keep her safe. All that other stuff was in the past.

Sighing, he tightened his grip on the horse's reins and tapped its sides to hasten its speed. Soon, in the distance, a sign appeared. Fort Long Acre. Two miles.

Bear followed the sign, not slowing down, eager to get there and deliver his message so he could return to Laurel and Trent. When he approached the base, however, it became immediately obvious that all was not well.

Ahead, the barrier that would usually stop cars, trucks, or anything unauthorized from entering the base, had been blasted off its hinges. The guard in the small booth next to it sat slumped forward, a bullet hole in the side of his head.

As his horse slowed, Bear swallowed hard. He contemplated jumping down and continuing on foot, but something told him he might be glad of the speedy getaway.

Continuing through the open gates, Bear scoured the ground. It was littered with dead bodies, mostly men but some women too. Not soldiers. At least, not in military uniforms.

He was in the center of the large stretch of tarmac outside the main building when someone shouted, "Stop! Hands in the air!"

Bear did as he was told, raising his arms as he tried to spot where the voice was coming from. "I mean no harm. I bring news from the people in Clancy. They were attacked by a group calling themselves the Freemen. They need military aid."

A figure appeared, a tall, lanky soldier with dark brown hair and a neatly shaved beard. He moved closer, gun aimed squarely at Bear's chest.

"Who are you?"

"Just a civilian. I was passing through Clancy with my wife. She's a doctor. There are a lot of injured people back in town."

"Sorry. We can't help." The soldier didn't seem like he was going to put down his gun any time soon. "As you can see, we've had some Freemen trouble ourselves."

"Looks like you handled yourselves?" Bear asked, scanning the dead bodies on the ground.

The soldier nodded. "Saw them off. For now. But we're moving out." He nodded toward the gate. "You should be too."

"They need medical assistance." Bear moved to climb down, to have a sensible conversation, but the guy with the gun shook his head.

"Stay where you are. Turn around, and leave." He jerked his head toward the gate. "We can't spare the resources or the manpower. Your friends will have to fend for themselves like everyone else."

Bear opened his mouth to object, but before he could say anything, the man aimed his gun at the ground and fired it.

The noise made Lucy jerk her head back and whinny loudly. Her eyes wide, she started trying to turn around.

"Fine," Bear spat, allowing Lucy to turn. "Thanks for your help."

As they trotted back through the gate, he heard the soldier yell, "You're welcome!"

On the approach into Clancy, Bear braced himself for how exactly he was going to break the news to the people inside the church. There was no help coming; they'd been abandoned.

He'd just finished tethering Lucy to a nearby tree when he heard the church door open.

"Bear?" Laurel was at the top of the steps. Taking them two at a time, she ran to him. He half expected her to throw her arms around him, but instead she stopped. She looked over his shoulder, then at Lucy. "Trent isn't with you?" she asked, shoving her hands deep into her pockets.

Bear frowned at her. "Trent? No. He's not. Why would you think…." He trailed off, then closed the gap between him and Laurel in just a few strides. "Where is he?"

Laurel shook her head. "I'm sorry, Bear. I don't know where he is. Robin was gone, so I thought he'd headed after you." She swallowed hard. "Jess is missing too."

"Dang it," Bear muttered, pulling off his hat and bunching it in his fist. He was about to ask why no one had gone out looking for the kid when something about Laurel's expression made him stop. She was looking past him into the undergrowth.

"Someone's in there," she said quietly, nudging Bear to one side and taking her gun from her belt. She raised her voice. "Whoever's there, come out now."

Bear lifted his weapon too. "Come out now," he repeated.

In front of them, the bushes began to move. Leaves shuffled. Twigs snapped. Then a bleeding woman tumbled out of them. From the ground, looking up, she smiled. "You're looking for a kid, aren't you?" She winced, then narrowed her eyes. "Reckon I can help you with that."

26

LAUREL

Laurel kept her gun pointed at the injured woman, while Bear glowered down at her as if it was taking every fiber in his body not to pick her up by the throat or knock her unconscious.

Slowly and deliberately, he wrapped his fingers around her arm and hauled her to her feet. "What did you do to the boy?" he growled, face inches from hers.

At first, the woman's eyes widened, but then a small smile tweaked her lips. "Oh, so you're his pa, are you?"

Bear's jaw twitched. Laurel edged closer.

"I didn't *do* anything." She tugged against Bear's grip. "But I did see what happened. And if you let me go, I'll tell you." She fixed her eyes on Bear's and tipped her chin defiantly upward.

"How about, you tell us what happened, and we *don't* shoot you?" Laurel raised her gun and moved closer.

"You shoot me, you won't find out what happened."

"If you're not going to tell us, what difference does it make?" Laurel narrowed her eyes. As she scanned the woman's upper body, she noticed a gash in her jacket, a gash edged with blood. "You're injured," she said. "Not just your ankle. You've been shot." She pointed at the woman's arm.

The woman didn't reply.

"How long have you been out here? A couple of days? That's how long it's been since your people attacked this town."

Still no reply.

"I'm guessing you haven't cleaned your wound. By now, it'll be close to getting infected. If it isn't already." She moved closer still. "Your forehead looks moist. Have you spiked a fever?" She shook her head solemnly and looked at Bear. "That's not a good sign."

"Really not a good sign." Bear shrugged, looked at his fingers, wrapped around the woman's forearm, then let go. "If it's infected she'll be dead soon anyway. She's not armed. Leave her."

The woman looked at her ankle, then at her arm, as if she was trying to decide whether to run.

"I'm a doctor." Laurel lowered her gun. "I *could* help you. Take you back to the church. Treat your wound. But I can only do that if you help *us*."

"How do I know you're a doctor? Could be lying." The woman winced as she spoke, moving weight from one foot to the other.

Reaching into her jacket, Laurel pulled out her hospital ID card. She'd made sure to bring it with her for precisely this reason. She held it out and the woman stared at it, her eyes flicking between the card and Laurel's face.

"Fine. So, you're not lying." Her fingers went to the hole in her jacket and rubbed it lightly. "You'll help me if I help you?"

"Information first," Bear said gruffly. "Then Laurel will treat your wound."

For a long moment, no one spoke. Then finally the woman said, "All right. Fine. I was hiding in the bushes. The kid came out early, before you." She jerked her head at Bear. "He had a dog with him. Walked off down the street. Returned after you left. Had some grass in his hand. He fed it to the horse. He was about to leave when the dog spotted me. Started yapping its nasty little head off. Bark, bark, bark. The horse got spooked, broke its tether, and ran. Kid went after it." She folded her arms in front of her chest. "And I'm not telling you which direction they went until you...."

Bear scraped his fingers through his hair. Taking Laurel's arm, he moved away from the woman and muttered, "He should have been back by now. If he went after the horse, he should have made it back."

"We didn't see any tracks." Laurel frowned, pursing her lips. "We looked, but we didn't see horse tracks."

"It snowed." Bear shook his head. "Enough to make it impossible to distinguish between the ones I left and fresh ones."

"So you better hurry up and take a look at my arm, hadn't you? Before my memory starts getting hazy." The woman jerked her arm in Laurel's direction.

"Fine. This way." Laurel kept her gun in her hand as Bear marched their prisoner back toward the church.

When they entered, Cathy rushed over, her face pale. "Who is this?" she asked, eyes wide. "Is she one of *them*?"

"She is." Bear handed the woman to Laurel, who marched her toward the meeting room. As she entered she heard him explaining, to a very reluctant Cathy, why this woman needed treatment, and that as soon as she'd received it, they'd be leaving.

"What's your name?" Laurel asked, peeling off the woman's jacket while she sat stiffly in a chair in front of her.

"Alice." She answered quickly, but that didn't mean it wasn't a lie. Still, Alice was as good a name as any.

"All right, Alice. Let's get your shirt off and look at this wound."

Alice turned her head and looked away as Laurel tugged her bloodied shirt off her arm and left it hanging on the other shoulder while she examined the damage. "Looks like it went straight through, which is good news. But we need to clean you up and give you some stitches."

As Bear appeared at Laurel's elbow, she nodded toward her medical kit. He fetched it and opened it for her.

"And my ankle?" Alice asked, wincing as Laurel began to clean the bullet wound.

"Looks like a sprain if you can walk on it. I'll check it over in a minute." Laurel raised her eyes and locked them onto Alice's. "And then you can tell us where the boy and the horse went."

Alice sucked in her cheeks, but didn't disagree.

By the time Laurel had finished, Alice looked gray around the edges. She was clearly in pain, but refused the medication Laurel offered her. "I'm fine. I don't take pills."

Laurel didn't press the matter; the way Alice answered reminded her of patients she'd encountered before, patients who had a past with pills that they didn't want to revisit. That small piece of knowledge about Alice's life felt strange in Laurel's chest. She respected the woman for her strength, but was it possible to respect someone and loathe their actions at the same time?

"Can I get some water?" Alice asked, rubbing her now-bandaged ankle.

"First, you tell us where the kid went." Bear stood with his hands on his hips. He was *not* going to let this continue any longer.

At first, Alice opened her mouth as if she was going to object. But then she nodded, lips pursed, and said, "North. He headed north. Same direction you went, except the horse veered into the trees at the end of the street."

"That's where we tethered them yesterday. Maybe Robin was heading back there," Laurel said, studying Bear's face.

"Let's just hope she didn't head all the way back to Kermit's in search of Shadow." He strode toward the door, scooping up his pack and jacket. "I'll go. You stay here."

"No." Laurel shook her head. "We stay together. We all go." She tugged Alice's good arm and brought her to her feet. "You too, Alice."

"I can't walk on this foot," Alice groaned. "And I need water."

"You can ride Lucy with me." Laurel picked up a bottle of water and offered it to her. "Here. This is for the road."

Outside, they waved a brief goodbye to Cathy and Doria. "We'll be back," Laurel promised. "But we might have to camp overnight."

Doria nodded. There were tears in her eyes but she wiped them away.

"Don't forget us," Cathy said, a stony darkness in her eyes as if she felt it was almost inevitable that Bear and Laurel would not return.

"We'll be back," Laurel repeated. "When we've found Trent and Jess."

Desperate to get on the road, Bear pulled some rope from his pack and used it to tie Alice's hands behind her back. Then he heaved her up onto Lucy and held the horse still while Laurel climbed up too. Wrapping her arms around Alice to keep her steady, Laurel took the reins. "All right, Alice. Which way?"

"Like I said," Alice replied tightly. "Down toward the woods. After that, your guess is as good as mine."

27

MAE

"Looking good, Peterson." Shane the EMT pointed at the bunting in Mae's hands. She looked down at him from her ladder and nodded.

"I agree," she said. "Not bad, huh?"

"Not bad at all, but I'm not sure you should be up there with that leg of yours." Shane extended his hand and helped Mae down from the ladder.

"I'm feeling good," she said, flexing her leg at the knee. "Much better. No more stick, either."

"Does that mean you'll be fleeing for the mothership soon?" Lisa's snarky tone made Mae turn around.

"I thought we discussed this," Mae said, rolling her eyes. "How many more times do I need to tell you all that I've seen the error of my ways before you believe me?"

"I believe you," Shane said, nudging Mae playfully with his elbow.

"Me too." Lisa nodded firmly. Behind her, however, Sharon was watching them. While most of the others had become accustomed to Mae's presence in camp, Sharon remained uncertain about her motives.

Mae couldn't blame her for that, but she did wish she could find a way to get her on her side. "The couple getting married, they're your friends?" Mae asked, looking from Lisa to Sharon.

"We're all friends here," Sharon replied curtly.

Frowning, Lisa lowered her voice and said, "I thought I was usually the grumpy one? When are you going to stop being so hostile?"

Sharon didn't reply.

"They're a young couple. Francesca and Stewart. Only twenty-one, but they want to make a commitment." Shane shrugged. "Guess they figure life's too short to wait."

"I think it's nice," Mae said, smiling as Shane packed up the ladder and Lisa headed off with Sharon to check on food preparations. "I mean, I think marriage is a terrible idea, bound to end in heartbreak and sorrow, but still nice." She laughed and pulled her hair back, fastening it at the bottom of her neck with a navy-blue hair tie.

"Your divorce? Or your parents'?" Shane asked, ladder under his arm. When Mae frowned at him, he added, "Which was it that screwed you up? Your divorce or your parents'?"

"I've never been married," Mae said firmly.

"Ah, so it was your parents." Shane nodded at her. "Mine too."

"But we can still celebrate for Francesca and Stewart, right?" she asked, helping Shane put the ladder back in the tool store. "Because I heard there was going to be cake."

A few hours later, as the sun began to set, the entire Freemen camp—or at least it seemed like the entire camp—gathered around a large white flagpole. The flag hanging from the top of it had been, until today, a peace symbol with a hand in its middle and a dove above it. Now, it displayed a hand-painted image of two gold rings and some flowers.

Standing toward the back of the crowd, Mae watched as Francesca—a young woman with jet-black hair and a dazzling smile—was escorted down the walkway to greet her groom. Stewart, for his part, looked incredibly happy. Big beaming smile. Barely a bead of sweat on his forehead. In fact, Francesca's father looked more nervous than he did.

When he finally handed his daughter over, he wiped a tear from his eye and patted Stewart heavily on the shoulder. The gesture brought a lump to Mae's throat. Her own dad's face flashed in front of her eyes. The last time she saw him, he'd been sad, withdrawn, not the man she remembered from her childhood. When she thought of him, she remembered the father who chased her around the garden pretending to be a monster, who made up silly songs and wasn't afraid to sing them at the top of his lungs with her, and who covered for her when she came home smelling of cigarette smoke in her angry teenage phase.

Scanning the crowd, Mae's eyes landed on Shane. Head and shoulders taller than the rest of the people around him, he was staring straight ahead. Bizarrely, for a wedding, no one was dressed in party clothes. But everyone had made an effort to do something a little different with their appearance.

Most of the women were wearing headdresses made of leaves and pine fronds. The men had all fixed themselves ties or bowties from scraps of material. Shane's was a jaunty yellow color that clashed with his skin tone.

Reaching up, Mae patted her own headdress. Sharon, of all people, had brought it to her as a peace offering. "I'm sorry," she'd said, extending her hand. "Friends?"

As Mae had accepted it, a cold, heavy weight had settled in her stomach. Now, as she tried to shift it, she focused her gaze on the couple in front of her.

Holding hands, Francesca and Stewart exchanged vows. Then Art, who officiated the ceremony, pronounced them husband and wife. Beaming with pride, as if he was related to the pair of them, he told Stewart to kiss his bride.

As their lips met, the entire camp burst into a thunderclap of applause. It carried up above the trees, and was met in return by the sound of a guitar and some drums. A singer began to sing. People filed back toward the trestle tables and sat down on the benches.

When the sun dipped behind the trees, lanterns and torches were lit around the camp. The cake came out on a tray. Francesca and Stewart cut it, fed each other a large mouthful, then announced the dance floor was officially open.

Remaining in her seat, Mae watched as people left the tables and began to dance. Children twirled, dogs ran amuck, and the music grew louder.

She was about to stand up and head quietly back to her tent when a hand on her arm stopped her. "Care to dance?" Shane gave a little bow and extended his arm.

"I'm not sure my leg is up to it," Mae said, shaking her head.

"You told me you were good as new." He raised his eyebrows at her, then jutted out his elbow.

After a long pause, Mae finally gave in. Taking his arm, she followed him to the dance floor. At first, she was nervous. Looking around expecting to find people watching, staring suspiciously, she was surprised to find that no one at all was watching them.

"So," Shane said, "childhood divorce, or were you a grown-up victim?"

"We're going to talk about divorce at a wedding?" Mae shook her head at him. When he didn't answer, she added, "Actually, they didn't divorce. My dad just left."

"Ah."

"He was injured in Iraq. Came back a different person. My mom didn't help. She's… overbearing. Wants everything done her way all the time. Always believes she's right. Just because she's a doctor…." Mae trailed off. "You know what? Let's not talk about this now. It's a lovely evening. This young couple have just pledged eternal love to one another. They don't need my cynicism ruining it for them."

"All right." Shane grinned at her, stepped back, and twirled her dramatically. Her leg pinged with pain, but she ignored it. "Then tell me what you miss the most."

"About my parents?"

"About your *life* pre-lights-out."

"Oh." As the music slowed, Mae took Shane's hand and he put his other on her waist. "Starbucks. Not the taste of the coffee. The feel of the place. When I was home on leave, I'd go and just sit there. For hours. Absorbing the atmosphere."

"Not sure I've heard Starbucks referred to as 'atmospheric' before." Shane raised an eyebrow.

"Are you kidding? Of course they are. All those people. Moms with young babies, sleep-deprived, connecting with other moms over coffee that's gone cold 'cos they've been talking for too long. Guys with Bluetooth headsets pretending to work on something real important so the pretty girl next to them notices. Teenagers skipping school. College kids skipping class. The smell of the beans. The smell of the *muffins*."

"Okay, wow. You really are a big Starbucks fan." Shane laughed and shook his head.

"Well, what about you? What do you miss? Baseball? Soccer?"

"I look like a baseball or soccer kind of guy?"

Mae tilted her head from side to side. "Maybe."

"Actually, I miss fishing."

Mae frowned. "Fishing? I'm pretty sure you can still do that. In fact, it's now pretty much a requirement."

"Exactly. Fishing used to be my way to escape everything. I'd go out into the wilderness all alone and absorb the lack of sound. The quiet. The stillness. Now everything is quiet and still, it's kind of lost its mystique."

"I've never been fishing." Mae wrinkled her nose. "Never seemed like something you'd say had *mystique*."

"Okay, well, if the world ever stops being crazy, I'll take you." Shane nodded firmly. "And in return, you can take me to a coffee outlet of your choice."

"Deal." Mae nodded. "Although I'm pretty sure the world is going to stay the wrong way up for a while." She hesitated, her breath catching in her chest. "Unless whatever they're hiding in that depot can fix things?" She laughed a little, purposefully not looking at Shane's face, concentrating on moving in time with the music.

When she finally looked at him, his expression was different. "I don't know what's inside," he said, letting go of her hands.

"Shane, I wasn't—"

He stepped back, his lips pursed, his body stiff. "You know what, Mae? Enjoy the rest of your evening."

"Shane...." Mae's throat constricted as she reached for Shane's elbow. But he simply turned his back to her and walked away.

28

BEAR & LAUREL

It was nearing sunset. The light in the woods was becoming muted, the undergrowth harder to see through, the air colder.

On Lucy's back, Alice was asleep. Every now and then, she slid sideways—unable to hold on because her hands were tied—and Laurel had to steady her.

As Lucy stumbled a little crossing a large tree root, Alice jerked awake. Eyes open, she groaned and bit her lower lip. "Can we untie these? My arm…." She looked over her shoulder at Laurel. "I'm not going anywhere. I can barely walk on this ankle."

Laurel hesitated, then looked at Bear and said, "She hasn't had any painkillers. It won't hurt to give her a break for a minute."

Nodding, Bear watched as Laurel unfastened the rope. Immediately, Alice rubbed her wrists, then held on to the saddle in front of her. "Thanks," she said.

Without speaking, Laurel passed her a bottle of water. "Here. You should stay hydrated." As Alice drank, Laurel turned to Bear. "Any luck?"

Trent's tracks had disappeared a few meters back, and for the last twenty minutes they'd been walking in circles, trying to find them again. "Nothing," he said. "It's like he and the horse disappeared into thin air."

He sighed and pushed his fingers through his hair. They were now deep in the woods, approaching nightfall, and no closer to finding Trent. Sure, the kid could look after himself. But something about this felt more sinister than Trent simply wandering off and getting lost. There was something here he wasn't seeing, but a tugging sensation in his bladder was proving too much of a distraction. "I need to pee. Wait here."

"I need to pee too," Alice said, wiping her mouth with her now-free hand and screwing the cap back on her bottle.

"You can hold it," Laurel told her.

Leaving Laurel and Alice with Lucy, Bear skirted around a nearby tree and took a couple of paces back into the undergrowth. He'd finished and was zipping up his pants when his eyes caught on something in the near distance. He walked toward it. There, caught on the bark of an uprooted tree trunk, was a small red piece of thread. He crouched down and picked it up with his thumb and forefinger. It wasn't thread; it was wool. Bear's heart beat faster in his chest. Jess had been wearing her coat this morning. He'd watched Trent put it on her and tell her it was cold out.

He stood up, scanning the ground for another clue. Something moved. He turned, hand poised on his gun. A flash of red. He held his breath, but it was too high up to be Jess. He inched forward just as a flurry of wings emerged from the trees and a woodpecker flew overhead.

He was watching it when he sensed something behind him. He turned, but before he could lock his eyes on it, something shoved him hard in the middle of the back. He stumbled forward. Another shove and he realized that the ground was missing below him. Reaching out to stop himself, he tumbled into the hole left by the uprooted tree, smacking his head hard on a protruding piece of root and landing at an angle that sent a shard of pain up through his elbow.

Blinking hard, Bear shook his head. His hearing aid was squealing, adding to the throbbing sensation in his temples and making him feel as if his head was in a tumble dryer.

He pulled it free from his ear. For a moment, silence descended, and he felt able to breathe again. He stood up, pulling his gun. But when he turned, there was no one behind him.

Scrambling out of the hole, he reoriented himself and ran fast back to where he'd left Laurel. He shouldn't have left them. This was Alice; it had to be.

He found Laurel in a heap on the ground, winded, with a nasty scrape down the side of her face. Lucy was gone. So was Alice.

"Bear…." She struggled to stand and he caught her arm. She started speaking but when he frowned at her, she gently touched his ear. The aid was hanging loose. Bear looped it back over his ear and fiddled with it until the screeching noise stopped.

When he nodded at her, Laurel said, "She knocked me off the horse. I dragged her with me, but she kicked me in the stomach. Winded me. Took off before I could stop her." She studied his face. "Are you okay?"

"I didn't hear you shout." Bear internally cursed himself. He should have turned the hearing aid up louder. He hadn't heard a thing. Without Trent and Jess to be his ears, he'd failed to protect Laurel. And now they'd lost their only mode of transport, too.

Laurel lightly touched his arm, looking up to examine his head. "You're hurt."

"She pushed me." Bear shook his head, annoyed at how pathetic that sounded. "Into a hole."

When he looked at Laurel, a smile was curling her lips. "She pushed you into a hole? Big strong soldier like you… outsmarted by a hole?"

Bear couldn't help laughing, despite his injured pride. "Outsmarted by my ears," he said, fiddling with the hearing aid, which was back to pinching his ear.

"Don't be silly." Laurel was looking up at him. She was taller than a lot of women, but shorter than him. He'd always liked that she could fit under his chin. Her hand lingered on the side of his face. She was staring at him, but he couldn't read her expression. Then the moment was gone. She stood back, cleared her throat, and said, "At least we have our packs. Let's set up camp and I'll see to that head of yours."

"What about you?" He gestured to her scratched face.

"Oh, this?" She rolled her eyes. "This is nothing. You should have seen the other guy."

As they headed toward the overturned tree, and set their packs down beside it, Bear scanned the ground. "It's gone now, I dropped it, but…." He looked up and met Laurel's eyes. "I saw a piece of wool. From the coat your mom made Jess. She and Trent must have been here."

He watched as Laurel breathed out heavily. "So, then," she said, "we just need to figure out where they went next."

"Let's set up over here," Bear said, gesturing back into the trees. "There's a nice hole we can use for shelter."

Rolling her eyes at him, Laurel picked up her pack. "At least I took this with me in the fall," she said, shrugging it back onto her shoulders. "Now, which way was it to this hole?"

Following Bear, Laurel patted the scratch on the side of her face. It didn't hurt too much; it was her pride that was the most wounded. She'd been so concerned with watching out for Bear that she hadn't watched for Alice. She took her eye off the ball for *one* moment and Alice took the opportunity to toss her to the ground. She wasn't stronger or smarter than Laurel, just opportunistic and determined.

"You're annoyed with yourself," Bear said, glancing at Laurel sideways. "Don't be."

Sitting down on an upturned tree trunk, Laurel assessed the hole Bear fell into. As silly as it was, he was lucky he didn't break anything.

"Here." Laurel gestured for him to sit next to her and opened her pack. "What did you bang?" she asked, running her fingers over his head. When she reached the left side, just behind his temple, he winced. Something slick on her fingers told her she'd found the spot. "You're bleeding," she said, pushing his hair apart gently to examine the wound underneath.

"You're not going to shave my hair, are you, Doc?" Bear asked, raising his eyebrows at her. "It's my pride and joy."

"Don't fret, you have other assets," Laurel quipped. Almost instantly, her cheeks flushed. "I meant your smile," she said, avoiding his gaze while her skin burned. "I always liked your smile."

Watching Bear fight a smile, Laurel reached for her bottle of antiseptic and her pocket-sized suture kit.

"You need a couple of stitches, but I can save your hair." She put her hands on his shoulders. "*If* you keep still."

Nodding at her, Bear straightened his shoulders and sat staring straight ahead while Laurel patched up his head.

"Take these too." She offered him two painkillers.

"I'm okay," he said, curling her fingers back over her palm. "Save them for emergencies."

"You're sure?"

Bear nodded. "Certain." Then, looking at the scratch on Laurel's face, he said, "Your turn."

"I'm fine." Laurel moved to stand up, but Bear took hold of her arm. "No, you're not." He gestured to her face. "Weren't you the one who told me the smallest scratch out in the wilderness can turn septic?"

"Bear, it's a graze. It won't—"

"Ah—" He raised his index finger at her. "I've done my fair share of first aid. I can handle this."

Smiling to herself, Laurel gave in and sat still while Bear cleaned the dried blood from her face. "Thank you," she said when he'd finished.

"My pleasure." Bear stood up, offering her his hand.

As they began to gather firewood, Laurel looked at him sideways. "How come you're being so gentlemanly all of a sudden?"

"Haven't I always been a gentleman?" he asked, crouching down to arrange some stones in a circle and stack kindling in its middle.

"Sure," she replied. Then, swiftly changing the subject, "Beans or beans for supper?"

"Is that all we have left?"

Laurel nodded, holding up two cans. "'Fraid so. We haven't been too successful foraging for packaged food." She stuck her hand back into the bag. "But we do have... a family-size bag of chips, and some questionable-looking soda. Do you have anything?"

Bear put down his kindling and opened his own pack. "Two candy bars, some canned peaches, a granola bar—the kind that tastes like cardboard—and...." He frowned, peering into the bag.

"And what?" Laurel watched as Bear pulled out a small metal flask.

"There's a note stuck to it." He peeled off a small piece of paper, taped to the front of the flask. But as his eyes scanned it, Laurel was almost certain his throat grew pink. "From Kermit," he said, bunching the paper in his fist and shoving it into his jacket pocket. "Felt bad keeping his food supply to himself. Thought some homemade hooch might make up for it."

Bear unscrewed the lid, took a sniff, winced, then passed the flask to Laurel. When Laurel sniffed it, however, the smell went straight to her lungs, and she burst into a fit of coughing.

"Well," Bear said, taking the flask back, "if nothing else, it'll keep us warm."

"Hooch and beans it is, then." Laurel sat cross-legged in front of the slowly growing fire. Bear sat down next to her.

For a while, eating cold beans from the can, they sat in silence. When they finished, and Bear started fiddling with the flask—turning it over in his hands—Laurel allowed herself to inch a little closer and rest her head on his shoulder. "And then there were two," she said quietly.

Bear squeezed her shoulder.

"We were so close to finding Mae, but now Trent and Jess...." She trailed off and sighed, pinching the bridge of her nose.

"We'll get them back." Bear stared into the fire. "All of them."

As Laurel's thoughts flicked to her mom, she shook her head and drew in a deep breath. "So, about that hooch."

"Ladies first." Bear offered it to her, watching expectantly.

Laurel moved her lips toward the flask, paused, then took a long, deep swig. Instantly, her throat began to burn. Her lungs too. "Oh, dear lord, it's terrible." She shoved it back at Bear, wiping her mouth. "I've never tasted anything so horrible."

Sliding back from beneath Bear's arm so she could watch him drink, Laurel laughed as he thumped his chest and whistled. "Oof, man, Kermit brews some nasty stuff."

"He does." Laurel watched the flames flicker. The warmth spread to her stomach, then her limbs. "Give me another sip."

By the time they reached the bottom of the flask, Laurel's cheeks were beet red, and she was warm enough to remove both her scarf and her hat. Bear, too, had pulled off his hat and had even rolled up his sleeves.

"So," she said loudly, alcohol-fueled bravado swilling in her stomach, "when we do eventually find Mae, and Trent, and Jess—"

"Ahh ha." Bear poked a stick into the fire.

"What's the plan?"

"The plan?" he asked, raising an eyebrow at her.

"Yes, the plan." Laurel sucked in a deep breath and drew back her shoulders. Her glasses were on her head. She pulled them back down to help her think more clearly.

"Well, I guess it depends when we get up there. Hopefully, it'll be before the end of the summer. Give us chance to—"

"I didn't mean the *plan*." Laurel shook her head. "I meant...." She cleared her throat. "I meant *us*. What are we going to do about us?"

For a moment, Bear's eyes traveled over her face. He frowned as if he was trying to figure out what the heck she was talking about. Then his eyes widened. "Oh. *Us*. Laurel and Bear."

Laurel nodded slowly.

Turning back to the fire, Bear hunched over his knees, still prodding the embers with his stick. "I guess I hadn't really thought about that part."

"We *are* still married," Laurel said bluntly.

"Yes." Bear's reply was quiet and thoughtful.

"But we've been apart for a long time."

"Yes."

"And we have a lot of… history. Complicated history." Laurel nudged him with her shoulder to encourage him to look up at her. "It was pretty rocky toward the end, and I know survival has kind of taken priority the last few months, but those things are still there. We can't pretend they're not."

Bear rubbed his knees. He chewed his lower lip, then reached for her hands and squeezed them between his. "I pushed you away," he said, meeting her gaze.

"It wasn't just you. I didn't give you space—" Laurel began but Bear shook his head to stop her.

"How about we promise that when we get to Thunder Bay, we'll make time to talk." He shrugged and squeezed her hands a little tighter. "I know I'm not the best talker, but if you'll listen, I'll try."

Staring into Bear's face, a rush of emotion swelled in Laurel's chest. The alcohol in her veins wasn't just making her warmer, it was making her less inhibited; allowing her to think things she'd usually push down and try to ignore. "Okay," she said, battling the scratchy sensation of tears behind her eyes. "That sounds good."

Nodding, Bear pulled her against his chest and kissed her forehead.

"I've missed you," she said quietly.

"I've missed you too."

29

TRENT

Trent's eyes were heavy. Pulling them open felt like opening a box with rusty hinges. As his surroundings fluttered into clarity, he lifted his fingers to the side of his face and winced. Dried blood, crusted to his skin. He shuddered as a memory flashed in front of his face; the horse, rearing up on its back legs, kicking out. Legs, hooves, wild scared eyes. Jess still barking despite Trent yelling at her to shut up. Then darkness.

Turning his head sideways, he realized Jess was lying beside him. Her deep brown eyes were locked onto his face. When he smiled at her, she wagged her tail but didn't move her head from her paws.

"It's okay, girl. I'm not mad." Trent tried to sit up. His chest was tight, as if he couldn't fill his lungs with enough air. He pressed his hand to his side and a muffled cry escaped his lips. Jess trotted over and licked his face. Pushing himself across the cold ground, he leaned against the trunk of an overturned tree. Jess's leash was still looped around her neck, but was lying on the ground next to her.

In recent days, Bear had become a little paranoid about her running away. Trent hadn't been able to work out why until Laurel told him what Kermit had said to Bear before they left the bunker; that there was a group of people attacking towns and stealing their resources. That there was "chatter"—as he'd called it—about this group being organized and spreading throughout the state. Coming together for some sort of "grand plan," which Kermit and his pals hadn't been able to decipher.

Just in case, Trent wrapped the end of the leash around his wrist and beckoned for Jess to come and sit next to him.

Resting her head on his leg, Jess pawed him and made a small whining sound.

"I'm okay, girl." Trent stroked her head. The movement made his own head spin and his side hurt. Holding his breath against the pain, he unzipped his jacket and shrugged it off, then pulled his shirt free from his pants. Leaning back, he lifted his shirt and his sweater to reveal ugly bruises on his side, already blue and purple, like storm clouds on his skin.

"Darn," he said through gritted teeth.

Jess tilted her head at him.

"Reckon I broke a few ribs."

She sat up, her ears twitched forward. Trent followed her gaze into the undergrowth, but as he tried to stand to see what she was seeing, his head began to spin. His knees wobbled, and he fell to the ground.

The next time Trent woke, he was lying down, but moving. Above him, flashes of cloud peeked through the branches. Cloud and pale sky. Had it snowed again? Or was it about to snow?

He tried to sit up, but a hand on his shoulder stopped him. A face appeared above his, upside down, a scarf wrapped around its lower half. A man with curly black hair and dark skin. With thick fingers, he tugged the scarf down and smiled. It looked odd from the wrong angle and made Trent's head throb as he frowned at it.

"Don't worry, buddy, we've got you." The hand squeezed his shoulder. Trent looked at it, then realized there were others on either side of him.

"Jess..." he croaked, his voice weaker than he'd expected it to be.

"Don't worry, your dog's here. She's safe."

Trent turned his head, trying to locate Jess, but the movement made him feel nauseated. The movement wasn't helping either. Moving his hands, he realized he was on a makeshift stretcher of branches laced together with rope, hard against his back.

"Where are you taking me?" Trent asked as the smiling man moved so he was walking in line with Trent's shoulders instead of behind them.

"Some place safe. Looks like you've had a rough time. Can you tell me what happened?"

Trent swallowed hard. If these were the people Kermit had warned Bear about, then he needed—as Deb would have said—to play his cards close to his chest.

"My horse ran away. I went after her, but Jess spooked her. I tried to catch the reins, calm her down, but...." He screwed his eyes shut as he remembered hooves raining down on him.

"And where are you from?" A woman's voice. He turned and saw an auburn-haired woman in a black baseball cap staring at him.

Trent's mind had gone blank. He tried to remember Bear's map but couldn't. "You probably haven't heard of it. Small town south of here. Emerald Pines."

"And you were heading where exactly?" the woman asked.

Trent glanced at the smiling man. His eyes narrowed slightly at the woman, as if he thought she was asking too many questions and needed to tone it down. But Trent answered truthfully. "Thunder Bay." He cleared his throat and laced his fingers together on his stomach. "My folks died after the EMP. Our car went off the road. I have family in Thunder Bay. It's all I could think of."

Speaking about his parents, using them as a decoy, guilt tugged at Trent's chest. Moisture sprang unexpectedly to his eyes, and he wiped it with the back of his sleeve.

"You've been alone all this time?" The woman wasn't letting up.

Trent sniffed loudly, biting back tears.

"That's enough, Carol." The man's tone was sharp but when Trent looked at him, he was still smiling. "Let the kid rest. He's been through enough." Casting his gaze down at Trent's face, the man added, "I'm Art. Art King. What should we call you, young man?"

"Trent." Trent extended his hand and shook Art's at an awkward angle.

"Well, Trent. It's nice to meet you." Art patted Trent's shoulder firmly. "Not long now, and we'll have you somewhere more comfortable."

Without meaning to, as Art stopped talking and the movement of the stretcher continued to sway gently from side to side, Trent drifted back to sleep.

A jolting motion woke him. The sky was darker now, and they were veering up steeply through a thick section of forest. In the distance, he could hear people. Voices. Kids. Perhaps a town or a village.

When they emerged from the trees into a clearing, the two people carrying the stretcher set it down on the ground, nodded at Art and headed off toward a large, canopied area with trestle tables underneath it. Immediately, they washed their hands in a trough, then set about putting plates out on the tables.

"You're in time for supper," Art said warmly, helping Trent to his feet. "But first, Carol will take you to the medics."

"Are you coming?" Trent asked, feeling more uneasy around Carol than Art, even though Art was very clearly the person in charge.

"I'll see you at supper. I have some business to attend to." Art waved, nodded at Carol, then strode off in the opposite direction.

"This way." Carol offered Trent her arm and stiffly guided him toward an RV on the other side of the canopy.

Inside, she ushered him onto the bed and told him she'd send a medic to see to him. She didn't look back as she left, but dropped Jess's leash so that the small dog could run over and jump up beside Trent.

A moment later, the door opened again and a tall blond man walked in, rubbing his hands against the cold.

"Didn't expect it to snow again today," he said, smiling. "You're Trent, right? Art asked me to take a look at you."

"You're a doctor?" Trent asked, wishing Laurel was the one helping him and not this stranger.

"'Fraid not." The man grabbed a stool, sat on it, and wheeled it over to Trent. "EMT. Shane McCloud. Nice to meet you."

Trent shook Shane's hand hesitantly; if these people really were the Freemen who'd attacked the town, and who Kermit had warned them about, they sure were doing a good job of seeming friendly.

"I heard you got trampled by a horse, which I personally have a fair bit of experience with." Shane laughed a little. "Never been a fan of horses, myself." Then he gestured to Trent's head. "Let's start with the head, then move on to the body." He took a medical bag from a nearby cabinet and opened it up, taking out a flashlight. "Okay," he said brightly. "Look straight ahead."

By the time Shane had finished, Trent was bandaged both around the middle and around the head.

"I don't think you've got a concussion, just a nasty knock. But to be on the safe side, I'll have someone sleep in here with you tonight." He stood up and brushed down his sweater. "If you feel like eating, supper is almost ready."

Trent stood up gingerly. He felt, quite literally, like he'd been run over by something. But at the thought of food, his stomach lurched into a growl. "Thank you," he said. "Food sounds good."

Outside, the sky was now dark. The area beneath the canopy was lit with a combination of lanterns and candles. The tables were crowded with people. Over by the trees, some kids were playing with some dogs. Noticing them, Jess's tail started to wag. Trent gave her leash a gentle pull. "Not right now, girl, sorry. I need you with me."

She looked up at him, her wide brown eyes making him feel instantly guilty. But he simply shook his head.

"Cute sweater," someone said as they passed Jess.

"There's a spot over here for your guest," someone else shouted to Shane.

Gesturing for Trent to go ahead, Shane followed him over to the empty space and sat down next to him. A few moments later, several large trays of food emerged from the makeshift kitchen. One was placed in the center of each table. Instantly people began to dig in.

Trent was loading his plate with what looked like a stew made of rice, beans, and some kind of game meat with gravy when he felt Jess's tail start to thump against his leg. He looked down to see her sitting bolt upright, her ears pricked.

Following her gaze, Trent let his spoon rest on his plate.

He searched the crowd for a rabbit or another dog. And then he realized what Jess had seen… a tall blonde woman with a splash of freckles on her nose and a profile that looked strikingly familiar.

He recognized that woman. Sure, it was a younger version that he'd seen in the photograph in Bear's cabin. But it was unmistakably her.

He'd just found Mae Peterson.

30

MAE

Mae had the distinct feeling someone was watching her. The skin on the back of her neck prickled. Refilling her mug of coffee, ignoring the small jolt of pain in her leg, she scanned the tables. After last night's celebrations, everyone looked a little worse for wear. Hungover faces were everywhere; clearly, Art's homebrew had nasty after-effects when consumed in large quantities.

At the head of the table nearest the fire, Francesca and Stewart sat huddled together. Usually, lunch wasn't a big deal in camp. Mae had learned during her time with the Freemen that breakfast was a quick affair, getting them set up for the day, and lunch was always on offer but simply grabbed on the go by those busy carrying out chores. Supper was when most of the camp gathered together to talk, play cards, and reminisce about things like Starbucks and fishing.

Thinking of Shane, Mae searched the crowd for his face. She'd contemplated going after him last night but, truthfully, hadn't known what to say.

He was, after all, completely right about her. He'd sensed she was fishing for information because she *was* fishing for information.

Despite the fact she had grown to like the Freemen and respect the way they were living, perhaps even yearn for a little of it herself, her mission remained the same; gather information and get back to her unit as soon as she was fit enough.

She'd worked hard to fool the people around her into believing she'd been converted from hardline militia to part of the Freemen community. Lying didn't come naturally to her, but it was something that had to be done. At least, that was what she'd been telling herself until Shane looked at her the way he did last night.

Since then, guilt had been tugging at her insides. She slept badly, her leg hurting more than it had in days. And she'd woken both determined to speak to him and unsure what to say when she did.

When she finally spotted him, she watched him for a moment. He was busy eating, chatting to a teenage boy she didn't recognize from around the camp. At the boy's side, a small white dog began to bark. Mae tilted her head. Her coffee mug was hot against her palm, a little too hot, so she shifted it to the other.

The dog didn't stop barking, even when the boy started ruffling its ears, and the high-pitched noise was strangely familiar. Mae narrowed her eyes. It was a terrier. A terrier in a red-knitted sweater, who was most definitely barking at *her*.

Mae stepped closer. The dog reminded her so much of her dad's Jack Russell that a shiver crept down her spine. Then she noticed that the boy was staring at her too. He said something to Shane, and Shane turned around.

Avoiding Shane's gaze, Mae looked again at the dog. It couldn't be Jess; it simply couldn't be. Her dad was up in Thunder Bay, hundreds of miles away. And even if he wasn't, what were the chances of his *dog* ending up here?

In a slight daze, she walked through the crowd of hungry Freemen. Without saying anything, Shane slid further up the bench so she could sit down. Mae glanced at the boy. He didn't speak, just watched her.

"Mae? You know this dog?" Shane asked.

Mae didn't reply, just bent down and stared into the dog's face. It stopped barking, bundling itself into Mae's hands and rubbing its face on her, tail wagging. Looking up, Mae caught the boy's eyes. "She reminds me of my dad's dog," Mae said quietly.

"She's mine." The boy finally spoke. "I found her in the woods a few months ago."

"You made her that coat?" Mae asked, tilting her head.

"Found it." The boy shrugged, returning to his stew.

Mae glanced at Shane. He'd been watching her, but now looked away. "Shane," she said quietly, putting her hand on his arm.

Before she could say anything else, Shane stood up. Looking at the boy, not at her, he nodded. "When you've finished up, come find me over in the RV." He pointed to Mae's previous accommodation. "You can sleep in there tonight, then we'll get you set up with a tent."

The boy nodded. "Thanks."

Mae tried to catch Shane's eye as he walked away from the table, but he just kept walking without turning back.

For a moment, Mae didn't say anything, just steepled her fingers together and studied the boy's face. She was about to lean closer and ask him to tell her the truth about the dog, because she didn't believe for a second that he'd found it out in the woods, when Art's familiar booming voice cut through the crowd.

When he spotted her, he raised his hand. "Mae? A word?"

She got up from the table and walked stiffly over to him, still limping despite most of her pain being gone now.

"Art?" She folded her arms in front of her chest. Art *seemed* to trust her now, but she couldn't be completely certain of it.

As Lisa appeared at Art's elbow, Art patted her shoulder. "I'd like you two to spend some time with our new friend." He jerked his head in the boy's direction. He was feeding the dog some meat from his stew.

"The boy?" Lisa's eyes had widened. She glanced at Mae then back at the boy. "Where did he come from?"

"He was injured in the woods. He said he was alone, but I'm not sure I buy it." Art turned to Mae. "Alice is still missing. She went on a supply run. The others returned, she didn't. They said they don't know what happened to her." Art's eyes darkened. "If that boy is with a bigger group, they could have something to do with it." He nodded firmly at Lisa, then at Mae. "Talk to him. Find out if he's lying."

As the tables began to clear, the boy got up and stood in line waiting to wash his dish. Next to him, fastened to his wrist with a loose piece of rope, the dog searched for Mae and once again gave a playful yap.

Mae leaned back onto the table and watched. Lisa had told her to fetch the boy and rendezvous near the chicken coop. Clearly, she thought showing the boy how to feed chickens might soften him up enough to get some information from him.

As soon as he was finished cleaning up his dish and cutlery, Mae beckoned him over. "Art asked me to show you around," she said. "You and your dog."

The boy nodded. "Art's the leader?"

"Yeah, Art's the leader." Mae jerked her head in the direction of the chicken coops. "This way."

As they walked, the boy said very little. He had a bruise on his head and moved stiffly, like his body was aching.

"I'm Mae." She extended her hand.

The boy shook it. "Trent."

"What happened to you?" Mae asked.

Trent hesitated. "Trampled by my horse. Darn thing ran off. I tried to catch it."

"Horses can be dangerous," Mae replied, studying his face.

"That's what I told–" The boy stopped, pressing his lips together. "That's what I've always been told," he corrected.

Mae was about to start digging for more information when, up ahead, she saw Lisa waving at them. Trent saw her too. He stopped walking. The dog yapped. Then Trent yelled, "Lisa!" and hurtled forward.

Staring at the scene in front of her, Mae was at a loss for words. As Lisa wrapped her arms around Trent, Mae walked slowly over and waited for them to notice her.

Cupping Trent's face, Lisa stared into his eyes. "What are you doing here, kid? How the heck are you?" Then she crouched down and ruffled her hands all over Jess's body. "And what did you do to this poor dog? A sweater?"

When Mae looked at Trent, he was wiping tears from his eyes. "Is Sharon here too? And Josh?" He peered past Lisa as if he expected to see them.

"You first," Lisa said quickly, her eyes betraying a flash of emotion Mae couldn't interpret. "What's going on?"

"Kid says he got trampled by a runaway horse," Mae said. "Also says he was alone. But Art thinks he's lying. Thinks he could have been with folks who know where Alice is."

Lisa nodded slowly, pressing her lips together. Then, putting her arm around Trent, she nodded at Mae. "This way. We need to talk."

Behind the chicken coops, Lisa ducked her head to meet Trent's eyes. "Was Bear with you? Is he hurt?"

Mae's blood ran cold. As Trent stuttered a hurried explanation, Mae sank to the ground and stared into the dog's eyes. "Jess?"

Lisa and Trent stopped talking. Both looked down at her. "You know that dog?" Lisa asked.

A tear rolled down Mae's cheek. She wiped it away with the back of her hand.

"She's Bear's daughter," Trent replied for her.

When Mae glanced up, Lisa was frowning. "How do you know my dad?" Mae stood up as Jess leaned against her leg. "Where is he? And how do you know who I am?"

Sighing, Trent pushed his hands over his thick black hair. "I know who you are because your mom and dad have been searching for you. I saw your picture in your dad's cabin. I've been with him since he left Thunder Bay. Him and Jess." Trent's fingers flexed on Jess's leash, as if he wasn't comfortable with the idea of sharing her with Mae.

"And you two?" Mae asked, turning to Lisa.

"I met Bear and Trent on the road. They were heading for your mom's hospital in South Minneha. We traveled together for a while."

Mae shook her head. "This is crazy," she said, pinching the bridge of her nose. "What are the chances…?"

"Art mustn't know about Bear and Laurel," Lisa interrupted quietly, almost as if she was talking to herself. "He's close to Alice. She was his son's girlfriend. If he thinks they were involved in hurting her in any way…"

"They weren't." Trent's eyes widened. "They wouldn't. They were at a church in a small town…." He paused, searching for the name. "Clancy. The place was called Clancy. The people there said they'd been attacked by Freemen. They were hiding out in the church. Lots were injured, and they had no food or water left. Bear and Laurel were helping them."

"Clancy?" Lisa frowned. "That's where the supply party was headed, but—"

"So much for Art's no violence policy," Mae muttered.

"Art would be livid if he knew." Lisa bit her lower lip, thinking. "But until we figure out what happened, both of you need to keep quiet about Bear and Laurel."

Mae folded her arms in front of her chest. Something was bugging her. Something about this boy, and the way he spoke about her parents as if they were somehow *his* family. "So, what do we tell Art? He wanted to know more about the boy. What do we tell him?"

"Tell him we think he's hiding something, and we'll keep asking questions," Lisa said. "Tell him we'll let him know if we find anything out, but that it'll take a while to gain the kid's trust."

As she spoke, Trent edged closer to her.

"If Bear and Laurel are around here, they'll find you. You know what PB's like. We just need to sit tight until he arrives. When Art meets him, he'll see straight away that he's a stand-up guy." Lisa nodded firmly. "We just need to sit tight."

When she stopped talking, Trent nudged her arm. "Lisa?" he asked.

"Yeah?"

"It's good to see you."

Checking no one was watching them, Lisa gave Trent a hurried hug, then stepped back, brushing down her jacket. Clearly, she wasn't the kind of woman for overt shows of emotion.

"So, are Sharon and Josh here?" Trent asked as they continued walking past the chickens toward the log store. "Where are they?" He looked back in the direction of the awning as if he might see them beneath it.

"Sharon's down at the depot today." Lisa glanced at Mae.

Mae had never heard of a Josh. She knew Sharon, but Josh had never been mentioned by either of them.

Lisa put her hands into her pockets and released a small sigh. Staring into the near distance, she said quietly, "Josh isn't here, kid. He's dead."

"Oh." Trent's eyes dropped to the ground. "What happened?"

"We reached his folks' farm." A smile twitched Lisa's lips. "We were happy there for a while. Great set-up. Plenty of food, lovely quaint farmhouse with big roaring fires. It was a little bit like paradise."

Mae listened intently as Lisa spoke, following close behind her.

"Until we were attacked by militia." She looked back over her shoulder at Mae. "They came in the night. Sharon and I escaped. Josh and his family didn't."

Despite the sparse details, Trent drew in a sharp breath and closed his eyes. "Poor Josh."

"A few days later, Art and his people came through. They told us they were going to fight back against the militia. So we joined them." She smiled a little and tried to lighten her tone. "And here we are."

Trent sniffed loudly. "I'm sorry about Josh. He was really nice."

"Yeah, kid." Lisa nudged him discreetly with her shoulder. "He was. But at least *our* paths crossed again. Sharon will be very happy to see you." She paused and looked down at the ground. "And Jess. She'll also be happy to see that ridiculous coat of hers."

"I know it's stupid, but Laurel's—" Trent stopped mid-sentence. His shoulders tensed. He didn't turn around, but Mae got the distinct feeling he'd just realized he was about to say something he shouldn't. "Laurel's a fan. She loves it." Trent shrugged dramatically. "And she's a lady you don't argue with."

"I'll second that." Mae stepped in line with Trent, studying him from the corner of her eye. Trent, however, kept looking straight ahead.

Art was right about this kid; he was hiding something. He was definitely hiding something.

31

BEAR

Bear woke before daybreak. Laurel was beside him, curled in her sleeping bag, face barely visible. Her glasses were nowhere to be seen, and her hair was loose. On top of it, to ward off the cold, she was wearing her mom's knitted hat.

Stoking the fire, Bear tried to fight the feeling of hopelessness that was brewing in his belly. He didn't want to admit it, but he felt like he was being faced with a choice; continue on their way to find Mae or break their journey to find Trent.

He studied Laurel's sleeping face. She'd never ask him *not* to find Trent; she cared for him almost as much as Bear did after what they'd been through together. But would she forgive him if a delay meant they missed Mae completely? Never found her?

Wringing his hands together, so tightly his knuckles whitened, Bear sighed. Last night had meant something to him. Kissing Laurel, after all these years of thinking he'd never be that close to her again, had *meant* something. But what if it hadn't meant the same to her? What if it was just a moment's madness? A swell of emotion or nostalgia that was now gone forever.

He scraped his fingers through his hair and shook his head. He had more important things to worry about than a kiss. He wasn't a stupid teenager; he was a grown man.

But it was *Laurel*. His Laurel. After so long….

The sound of Laurel yawning loudly tripped up his train of thought. He looked down to see her arms snaking their way out of the sleeping bag. Stretching them above her head, Laurel yawned again, then smiled at him. "Morning," she said brightly. "I slept like a log."

"Me too," he lied.

"Breakfast?" Laurel sat up, legs stretched out but still inside her sleeping bag.

"Protein bar or protein bar?" Bear asked, holding up two identical bars from their meager remaining stash.

"Ooh, protein bar." Laurel took one from him and ripped into it with her teeth. She seemed chipper this morning, light-hearted despite the fact that Trent and Jess were who-knows-where.

"We'll find them," she said as if she was reading his mind. "I dreamed up a plan last night."

"Oh yeah?" Bear found himself chuckling. "What's your plan, Doctor Rivera?"

"My plan is to think logically." She held out her hand and wriggled her fingers. "Map please."

Bear handed it to her and she leaned forward, spreading it out in front of them.

"Trent's missing. Gone. Vanished into thin air along with Jess and any signs of the horse."

Bear nodded.

"The only way that could happen is if someone covered their tracks."

Bear nodded again.

"We know that the Freemen, as they're calling themselves, are in this area and that there's some kind of 'bigger' plan behind their movements."

"We only know that from what Kermit said."

"But it makes sense." Laurel rubbed her arms as a cool breeze drifted over them. "Kermit's contacts identified several groups that were communicating, so it makes sense they have a common goal."

"Okay, so what are you saying?" Bear was studying Laurel's face. It was bright, fizzing with energy the way it always was when she was enjoying coming up with a plan.

"I'm saying, there must be a meeting point. Somewhere they're heading toward. Something in this area that they *want*."

Bear nodded slowly, stroking his chin. His beard was getting thicker by the day, but since leaving South Minneha he hadn't had time to even think about trimming it.

Laurel was scouring the map and chewing loudly at the same time. Suddenly, her eyes widened. "There! That's got to be it." She jabbed her finger at the map. "That's a supply depot, isn't it?" she asked, looking at Bear for confirmation.

Bear tilted his head and narrowed his eyes. "Not *a* supply depot, Laurel. *The* supply depot. The biggest one in the area."

"So maybe that's their goal… take over the depot and—"

"And…?" Bear raised his eyebrows at her.

"I don't know… take over the world, set up their own little city guarded from the outside?"

Bear smiled ruefully. Either of those was a possibility. Neither was ideal. "So, you think we should head to the supply depot and hope we find Trent there?"

"I think it's our best shot, don't you?" Laurel sat back, twisting her food wrapper in her hand and crossing her arms.

Bear bit the inside of his cheek. After a pause, meeting Laurel's eyes, he said, "What about Mae?"

Without hesitating, Laurel answered him. "Mae would want us to find out what's going on. She's a soldier. She'd *hate* the idea of a reactionary group like that terrorizing people. Stealing their food and their only means of surviving." Laurel sat up on her knees and reached out to take Bear's hand. "Plus, right now, Trent's the one who we know is in trouble." She nodded forcefully, not letting go of his hand. "We'll find Trent and then we'll find Mae. All of us, together. All right?"

"All right." Bear squeezed her fingers lightly between his. "You're the boss."

"Always have been," she replied.

By the time the sun was fully risen in the sky, they were on the road again, this time on foot. Bear's elbow was still aching from his fall, but his head felt better, and he was relieved that Laurel's ankle didn't seem to be giving her any problems; after their return to South Minneha, she'd limped for several weeks before it began to ease.

They were heading for the biggest military munitions depot in the state. It was just a few miles from the section of forest where they'd lost Alice and, to their surprise and delight, in her haste to get away, she hadn't had the foresight to cover her tracks. So, it seemed, she was leading them precisely where they needed to go.

"Bit of a coincidence that she's heading this way, don't you think?" Bear said, raising his eyebrows.

Laurel nodded knowingly at him; she'd already been convinced she was right. But an extra bit of proof didn't hurt.

"Trees will soon start thinning, then we should hit the highway. We follow that for two miles, then branch off and there will be signs to the base."

"Do we want to go that way? Is there another way we can approach?" Laurel stopped and patted Bear's pocket for the map.

Taking it out, they studied it together. "We could loop around this way. It's longer but—"

"Less chance of being seen out in the open." Laurel met his eyes.

Nodding, Bear folded the map and pointed to his left. "In that case, we need to go this way. Stay in the trees."

As they walked, Bear found himself glancing at the ground almost constantly. Looking for any sign of Trent or Jess, even though he knew in his heart they'd been wiped.

They were nearing the depot, having walked for longer than they would if they'd followed the highway, when Laurel gestured for Bear to stop.

"You heard something?" he asked, straining his ears unsuccessfully.

"Up ahead. Voices." Laurel whispered.

Together, sticking to the shadows, ready to use their weapons if they had to, they inched forward. Through the trees, shapes became visible.

"Soldiers," Bear said, frowning.

"Looks like it." Laurel didn't move, just kept watching. "Could these be the soldiers Mae is attached to?"

"Could be." Bear narrowed his eyes. "They're definitely not Freemen. Too organized."

"What are they doing?" Laurel asked, taking in the line of men and women who were gathered together in a huddle, speaking in low voices.

"I don't know." Bear adjusted his pack on his shoulder. "But I think we should find out."

Following them, staying about two meters behind and only moving when the people ahead moved, Bear and Laurel walked slowly forward.

The soldiers weaved their way through the trees, then stopped. Ahead, through the branches, Bear could make out a wire fence.

"They're doing recon," he said quietly.

"Of the ammunitions depot? Does that mean the Freemen already hold the depot?" Laurel was peering through the branches, trying to make out what was happening.

"I don't know." Bear looked behind him. "But I'm not comfortable here. We should move back."

"We need to hear what they're saying." Laurel gestured for Bear to stay put. "I'll get closer. Wait there."

"Absolutely not, Laurel. No way." Bear reached for her arm, but she slipped free and crept forward.

Heart pounding, Bear watched her inch toward the soldiers up ahead. A few feet away, she stopped. Bear's mouth was dry, his skin prickling as he watched her. *Geez, Laurel, hurry up.*

For what felt like forever, Laurel remained stock still, listening. She looked like she was about to turn around and walk back to him when something moved behind her. Branches parted. A young soldier pushed through them, turned toward a tree, unfastened his pants and began to pee.

Laurel froze. She was barely breathing. Slowly, she backed away. He was just a few feet away from her but hadn't noticed her. If she could just make it back into the undergrowth….

She was almost there when she tripped. Bear saw it coming. Saw the root protruding from the ground. Saw that she was so focused on the soldier's back, making sure he didn't turn around and spot her, that she didn't see it.

She stumbled, reached out to stop herself falling, and grabbed a branch. Almost instantly, it snapped. Loudly.

The soldier whipped around, gun in his hand, eyes locked on Laurel. He paused for a moment, then shot.

His aim was terrible and he missed by a mile, but the noise caused a commotion to break out back near the wire fence. Suddenly, others appeared. Laurel ran, hurtling through the trees toward Bear. More shouts. More gunshots.

Bear grabbed her hand and pulled her with him, running as fast as he could.

They continued to run until the noise behind them died out and their legs burned with the effort of carrying them.

Hurtling through the woods, noise up ahead made them slow their pace. Checking behind them, Laurel released a long breath. "Looks like we lost them."

"Might have just run into something else," Bear said quietly, motioning for Laurel to stay next to him as they walked slowly forward.

"Can you hear that?" Laurel glanced at him.

Bear strained his ears. There was something there; something muffled but too distant to dissect.

"It sounds like people. Shouting." Laurel broke into a run before Bear could stop her. As they drew nearer to the sound, something else broke through. Gunshots. Unmistakable gunshots.

"I heard that," Bear said, tugging Laurel's elbow. "Slow down, we don't know what we're walking into."

Laurel's shoulders quivered, as if she was contemplating ignoring him and charging forward anyway, but then she nodded. "Okay. Follow me."

Stepping in line behind Laurel, Bear followed her path forward, trusting that she could hear things he couldn't which might help dictate their path.

Just a few paces farther, they came to a tall wire fence that stretched out left and right, forming a perimeter in the trees. More gunshots broke out, and this time, Bear could hear children screaming. The sound sent a shudder through him, violently gripping his spine.

"Are they attacking a civilian camp?" he asked, exchanging a worried look with Laurel.

"We need a better vantage point," she replied.

In front of the fence, the ground sloped dramatically up, obscuring their view. Laurel gestured to the tree behind them. "I'm going to scale it to get a better look."

Bear nodded. Ditching their packs on the ground beneath the tree, they began to scale it. Using the branches for leverage, they scaled their way up until they were at least twenty feet off the ground.

"Dang it," Bear swept his hands through his hair. "Militia."

Laurel wrapped her arm around a branch above her and slid forward on the one beneath, narrowing her eyes. "They're attacking a camp full of women and children," she said, fury simmering in her voice. "We have to help them." But just as she looked ready to swing back down the tree, Bear narrowed his eyes.

"Wait." At first glance, the camp looked homey. A dining tent, a kitchen area, some kind of RV with a medical cross on the front of it, and rows of camping tents set up behind it. But when he noticed the large painted flag near the camp's entrance, a peace symbol with a hand in its center and a dove flying above it, he realized what they were looking at. "They're not civilians, they're Freemen."

Laurel frowned at him, but he pointed to the flag. They were both looking at it when an explosion ripped through the air. The flag, and the ground around it, went up in flames. The tree they were sitting in shook from its roots to its tip. In a split second, the militia who'd been outside the camp's entrance were inside it. Freemen ran for cover. Bullets whizzed through the air.

Bear's heart began to hammer in his ears. The sounds merged into one big noise, pressing down on him. His breath tightened in his lungs. He pulled at his scarf, his throat constricting as beads of sweat broke out on his forehead. Suddenly, he felt the whip of chopper blades above him. The noise, thunk thunk thunk, in his ears.

"Bear…." Laurel put her hands on his arms. "Breathe. It's okay."

Bear screwed his eyes shut. *There's no chopper. There's no chopper.*

"Bjorn, listen to my voice. Breathe." Laurel cupped his face with her hands and forced him to look at her. Then she tugged his hearing aid free from his ear. The sounds dimmed. Everything was quiet. "Breathe," Laurel mouthed, inhaling slowly through her nose.

Bear copied the movement of her breath. In and out. In and out.

After what felt like forever but could have been minutes, his body began to return to normal. He swallowed hard, steadying himself on the tree. He was about to tell Laurel he was sorry when her eyes widened.

She was looking at something behind him. She tugged his arm urgently and pointed. Following her finger, Bear returned his hearing aid to his ear and narrowed his eyes. There, through the smoke, he realized what Laurel had seen.

"Trent."

32

LAUREL

"Looks like we arrived at exactly the wrong moment," Laurel yelled as they slammed their bodies to the ground and peered up over the sloping ground.

"Or exactly the right moment," Bear said, his eyes desperately searching for Trent in the crowd. "At least we know he's here."

"But how the heck are we going to get him out?" Laurel slid down and turned onto her back, breathing hard after the effort of climbing down the tree, grabbing their packs, and hurtling through the woods.

In front of them, the Freemen's campsite was under heavy siege. The Freemen were armed and shooting, but they weren't organized. Children were being hurried away from the action. People were grabbing guns and shooting wildly in the direction of the soldiers. The militia, on the other hand, had them surrounded and were inching forward bit by bit.

"They're not shooting to kill," Bear said, pointing to the soldiers who were approaching the perimeter fence. "They're herding them back."

Laurel's mind was racing; without knowing the layout of the camp, finding Trent would be almost impossible.

"We can't wait." Bear locked his eyes on hers. "We have to get in there." He brushed at his jacket, then took in Laurel's. "We look more like Freemen than militia. In all the chaos, maybe we'll go unnoticed and be lucky."

Laurel wasn't a fan of *lucky*. She preferred concrete plans. Logic. Knowing what they were getting into before they decided to risk their lives. But she couldn't see any other way. If they left and went back the way they came, not only were they abandoning Trent to whatever the militia decided to do to the Freemen, but they'd come face-to-face with the patrol they'd just narrowly avoided.

A few days ago, when they witnessed the devastation the Freemen caused in Clancy, Laurel would have placed herself firmly on the side of the soldiers. But these soldiers were attacking people who weren't armed. Instead of attacking the depot, they'd gone for the camp. A camp where children were playing and people were simply going about the business of surviving.

"It's a distraction," she breathed. "The militia, they're drawing the Freemen away from the depot to protect the camp."

"So the patrol can take the ammunitions depot," Bear muttered.

"And they're playing right into their hands," Laurel said as a group of Freemen in rag-tag clothing hurtled past them.

Holding her breath in case they were spotted, Laurel sank lower to the ground. Once they passed, she took a deep breath and nodded at Bear. "Okay," she said. "Let's go."

Sticking to the perimeter, they waited in the shadows of the trees, watching for a break in the gunfire. It came when the militia finally got close enough to start cutting a hole in the wire fence. Freemen and militia gathered in the same spot, half trying to break in, the other half trying to keep them out.

"This way, over the top." Bear pointed to the section of fence in front of them. It was topped with barbed wire so, despite the cold, they each pulled off their padded jackets.

Scaling the fence took all the upper body strength Laurel could muster. When she reached the top, she slung her jacket over the barbs and climbed over. It prickled her stomach but didn't puncture her skin.

Bracing herself for the impact of the cold, hard ground, she counted to three and jumped. Bear landed next to her. He rubbed his elbow, still sore from his fall and now smarting from the effort of scaling the fence.

"Trent went that way." Laurel pointed to a large white camper behind what looked like an outdoor mess hall. Freemen were picking up the wooden tables and turning them on their sides to form shields. A good idea, but a little late.

Together, they darted toward the camper. Beneath the canopy, injured Freemen were clutching bullet wounds. The militia might not have been shooting to kill, but they were certainly shooting to wound.

Catching her slowing down, Bear grabbed Laurel's elbow. "We can't help them," he said sternly. "We have to find Trent and Jess."

Laurel closed her eyes and nodded. Her stomach was heavy, but she knew Bear was right. In this moment, she could not afford to be a doctor.

As they reached the camper and were about to skirt around its side, an explosion boomed behind them and the ground shook.

"They're throwing grenades!" Bear yelled.

"Who?" Laurel looked back, trying to make out whether the explosion had happened inside or outside of the camp, her chest tight as images of injured fighters filled her mind.

"Doesn't matter." Bear turned and charged around the corner of the camper. But then he stopped, stock still.

Laurel ran into his back and jolted him forward. Looking around him, she realized why he'd stopped; a tall dark-haired man with a scarf around his neck was standing in front of them.

He looked them up and down, gun aimed firmly at Bear's chest. "You're not militia," he spat.

"No." Bear raised his hands, letting his gun hang loose to show he didn't intend to use it. "We're not. We're here looking for our kid."

"Kid?" The man looked from Laurel to Bear, then shook his head. "I don't have time for this... Lisa!" He didn't take his eyes from Bear as he yelled over his shoulder.

A moment later, a woman appeared, with short brown hair and broad shoulders. "Take these two, tie them up, we'll deal with them later," the man barked.

"Lisa?" Bear spoke loudly. When Laurel looked at him, he was smiling.

The woman's eyes widened as she examined Bear's face. "Papa Bear?" She started to laugh, but then turned quickly to the man. "Art, I know this guy. We can trust him. He helped me out of some tricky situations a while back. He's a good fighter."

The man, Art, looked from Lisa to Bear. Suddenly, the name rang a bell. Lisa was one of the people Bear traveled with on his way to South Minneha from Thunder Bay. Lisa, Sharon, and....

Before Art could respond, another loud bang shook the camp and someone appeared from the shadows behind Lisa.

"Sharon?" Lisa lurched forward. A red-haired woman was dragging another, clearly injured, woman along with her.

Bear darted forward and caught the injured woman's arm as the redhead lowered her to the ground.

"What happened?" Lisa crouched down. "Sharon?" She put her hand on the woman's face and met her eyes.

"She took a bullet. Her side, I think. Don't know if it went through or just grazed." The redhead nodded at Art. She had a shotgun slung over her shoulder and another gun in her hand. "You got this?"

Art nodded. Bending beside Lisa, he scooped Sharon into his arms. "We can't take her to the medical van. We'll take her into the trees."

"Laurel can help." Bear put his hand on Lisa's shoulder. "She's a doctor. We'll come with you."

Art looked at Lisa. She nodded at him. "He's telling the truth. His wife's a doctor."

"Fine," Art said quickly, standing up with Sharon in his arms as if she weighed no more than a feather.

As the noise behind them grew, Art snapped his head toward the trees and they followed him. When they reached cover, he lowered Sharon back to the ground. Laurel immediately lifted up her coat and sweater. Sharon groaned loudly. "It's okay, looks like it's just grazed the skin." She pulled her pack from her shoulders and opened it. As she took out her medical kit, someone else came running into the trees and tugged on Art's arm.

"Art, they've got us surrounded," the boy said, wide-eyed.

Stepping away, Art talked with the boy in hushed voices while Lisa knelt down next to Sharon and wiped her moist hair from her forehead. "You're okay," she whispered. "You'll be okay."

"Lisa." Bear put a firm hand on Lisa's shoulder. When she looked up at him, he said, "We're looking for Trent. Have you seen him? We thought we saw him running with some other kids."

Lisa blinked at him for a moment and then, as if remembering where she was, nodded. "Yes, yes, he's here. Art found him in the woods. He was injured." Lisa bit her lower lip, then added quietly, "Bear, your daughter's here too. Mae."

"Mae?" Laurel's head snapped up. Her hands still on Sharon's skin, she looked from Bear to Lisa. "Mae is *here*? How?"

"It's a long story." Lisa lowered her voice a little more. "But it's best Art doesn't know the connection between you. For now, anyway."

She stopped talking as Art returned to them. He took in the work Laurel was doing on Sharon's wound, then turned to Bear. "Why are you here? What do you want?" he asked, tilting his head.

Bear answered immediately. "Our kid. Trent. He went missing, and we came here to find him."

Art's eyes narrowed. "Your kid? Trent said his folks died."

Bear screwed his eyes shut. "They did. We've been looking after him. He ran away."

For a moment, neither man spoke. Then Art nodded. "Fine, Lisa will take you to him on the condition you stay and help." Art gestured to the trees. "The camp's about to be taken. I'm moving my men out. We have many injured."

Finishing applying a bandage to Sharon's side, Laurel nodded. "Of course, we'll help." She met Bear's eyes. "Won't we?"

She watched as he breathed in slowly, knowing they had little choice. Trent and Mae were in this camp with the Freemen. If they wanted them back, they had to do what Art said. "Yes." Bear nodded. "We'll help."

33

MAE

Pain spread from Mae's leg to her hip, a lightning rod that took her breath away. Running from camp had been painful, but she couldn't stop. Not until she got the kids to safety.

"The caves," Shane had yelled. "You know where?"

Mae had shaken her head. She'd been trying to talk to him, trying to explain what she'd said at the wedding, when the shooting had started.

"Into the woods behind the RVs. Head north. Keep going until you reach a huge, twisted tree. It went down in a storm. Looks like a sleeping dragon. A little way beyond that are some caves. That's the rendezvous." He hesitated, grabbed Mae's arms. "Can you do this?"

Mae glanced at her leg. "Yes."

"*Will* you do this?" He fixed his gaze on hers. "They're kids, Mae."

"Of course I will. You think I'd—" As an explosion rang out behind them, Shane let go of her arms and nodded.

"Go. Now. Take these." He thrust a small medical bag into one hand and a gun into the other.

"What about you?"

"I'm needed elsewhere." And with that, he was gone.

So, with Trent, Jess, and a whole gaggle of children, Mae had headed for the trees.

Now, as the kids huddled together in the mouth of the cave, Mae leaned forward onto her thighs and took several deep breaths.

"You okay?" Trent dipped his head to catch her eyes. "Mae? You okay?"

"Yeah." She raised her head. "Fine."

"Should we start a fire?" Trent looked at the youngsters, wide-eyed, frightened, then at Mae.

"We can't." She shook her head. "It would give away our location."

As Trent started to chatter at her, Mae's head began to swim. Cornell was attacking the camp. A camp he had to know was full of women and children. Even pregnant women. Mae screwed her eyes shut as she thought of the pregnant woman who'd been having false labor pains for the past few days. And the older Freemen. The ones who were too frail to run fast or fight hard.

"Mae?" Trent took hold of her elbow. "Sit down."

She felt herself wobble and did as he said. Sitting down hard, she put her head between her legs and breathed deeply until the tightness in her chest subsided.

"Mae? Are you okay?" A small girl called Catherine had ventured over and put her hand on Mae's knee. "Is your leg hurting?"

"I'm okay, sweetheart." She smiled, then narrowed her eyes. "You're bleeding."

Catherine raised a small finger to her forehead. Her face paled.

"It's all right. We'll get you fixed up." Mae gestured for Trent to follow her to the cave mouth. "Is anyone else hurt?" she asked, scanning the scared faces in front of her. A couple stepped forward. "Okay, line up right here, and I'll check you over." Mae sat down on a large boulder and swung Shane's bag onto her lap. Opening it up, she took out some disinfectant wipes and some Band-Aids. As if he'd known, he'd given her the ones with cartoon characters on them. "Well, Catherine," Mae said, smiling. "Would you like a unicorn or a fairy?"

"Unicorn please." Catherine smiled.

With the children finally patched up, Mae instructed them to huddle together to keep warm, and take turns telling each other stories. Catherine pulled Jess onto her lap and snuggled into her fur. Jess licked the girl's face.

"I'll be right back," Mae told them.

Gesturing for Trent to follow her, as the sound of distant gunshots bled through the trees, Mae pulled her hair loose from its tie and shook her head.

"Trent, I can get us out of here." She fixed her eyes on his. "I was with the militia." She shook her head and corrected herself. "The unit. *My* unit. If we can get to them, they'll recognize me. They'll get us to safety."

"But you switched sides?" Trent asked, eyes narrow. "You said you'd switched sides?"

"I...." Mae trailed off. "It doesn't matter which side I'm on. What matters is that I can get us away from this fighting. There's no way the Freemen can beat the militia. Not out here. At the depot, maybe, with big fences and places to hide. But out here? Not a chance."

"So, you want to abandon them?" The look on Trent's face reminded Mae of the look on Shane's face when she'd mentioned the depot. A slow realization that perhaps she wasn't the person he thought she was.

"They're safe here." Mae glanced over at the cave. "The others will be here soon. The kids are fine. They're safe. But we should go now." She reached for his arm. "We should go now, Trent."

"No." Trent tugged his arm away from her. "I'm not going anywhere with you. Are you kidding? No." He shook his head, backing up into the trees.

"Trent...."

"I don't care what you say about the Freemen. The people I've met here have been kind. Nice. Good people. I'm not going to betray them. No way."

"Trent, lower your voice," Mae said through gritted teeth.

"I'll tell them." Trent drew himself up to look taller, puffing out his chest. "As soon as they come, I'll tell them. It's not right. They think you're their friend."

"Trent, I said be quiet." Mae strode forward and reached for him again. This time, as Trent pulled his arm back, he stumbled and fell, thumping his head hard on a nearby rock.

As blood pooled at his temple, Trent stared up at Mae with wide eyes.

"Come on, let me help you. Don't be silly." Mae reached out her hand to help him up, but Trent shook his head. Scrambling to his feet, he yelled for Jess.

"I'm going to tell them," he yelled, turning away from her. "I'm telling them." Then, before she could stop him, he took off through the trees, and Jess ran after him.

Mae's heart was beating so hard in her chest she felt it might explode. She wanted to tear after Trent, bring him back, tell him not to be such a hot-headed fool of a kid. But a hot-headed fool of a kid was exactly the kind of kid she should understand; she was the same when she was a teenager. Always thought she knew best. She was stupid to try and convince him to leave, not without explaining everything properly.

Pinching the bridge of her nose, Mae looked back at the kids in the cave. Trent was right. She couldn't leave them alone. What was she thinking? She promised Shane she'd take care of them. Through the pain in her leg, and the knot of fear in her stomach, she smiled reassuringly. "Trent's just gone to see where the grown-ups are, if they're coming soon." She nodded at them. "Don't worry. He'll be back soon."

As she sat back down, she rubbed her leg and breathed out heavily. She was about to roll up her pants leg and check if her bandage was still in place when one of the kids shouted, "In the trees. I see something!"

Mae pulled her weapon from her belt and tossed her hair back over her shoulder. Narrowing her eyes, she searched the trees. Then she saw it too. Movement. Someone coming toward her.

Three someones.

The first she recognized was Lisa. Her chest tightened. Had Trent found her? Had he passed on his message? But Lisa was smiling. Grinning.

Mae's forehead creased into a frown. They were in the middle of a siege and Lisa was smiling? Then Lisa stepped to the side and the other two figures came into focus. Mae stopped in her tracks. Her boots suddenly felt as if they were made of lead. She opened her mouth to speak but no sound came out.

"Mae!" Her mother's voice floated toward her through the trees.

"Mom?" Mae lowered her gun. "Dad?"

Her parents hurtled toward her and wrapped her in their arms, both hugging her so tight she felt she might pass out.

"Mae, we found you," her mom muttered. "We found you. We found you."

"Mae flower," her dad breathed, kissing the top of her head. "I can't believe it's you."

"What are you doing here?" Mae pulled back, wiping tears from her eyes, looking from one parent to the other. "Seriously? How?"

"We were looking for you. We were on our way to Fort Stillwell, but —" her mom shook her head. "You know what? That can wait."

While her parents stroked her arms, her hair, her face, as if they were checking she was real, Lisa set down a large backpack and handed Mae a bottle of water.

Mae took a long swig from it, wishing it was something a little stronger, then sat back down, her leg throbbing. She looked up at her mom, expecting her to be staring with watery eyes, asking if she was okay and offering to take a look at her injury. But she was looking at the caves instead.

"Bear? Where's Trent?" Mom pointed to the kids in the cave. "I don't see him."

Mae looked down at her hands.

"I can't see him either." Her dad stepped closer. "Or Jess." He stopped and turned back to Mae. "Were they with you? Art said they were with you."

When Mae didn't answer, her father crouched in front of her. "Mae? Trent's very important to us. He's traveled with me from Thunder Bay. He's a good kid. Part of the family. Where is he?"

Searching her dad's face, Mae fought back the seasick feeling in her gut. "He took off. Said we were sitting targets waiting here. He wouldn't listen to reason." She met her father's eyes, praying he didn't see the lie quivering inside her own.

34

BEAR

"Which way did he go?" Bear threw his pack from his shoulders; he needed to be fast. Really fast.

Mae stared at him for a moment, her eyes wide, as if she couldn't quite believe he wanted to leave when they'd only just found one another.

"Which way, Mae?" he asked again, his heart swelling with pride as he took in how grown up and sure of herself she seemed, but aching as he thought of Trent out there alone.

"You can't leave, Bear," Lisa said quietly, taking his arm. "They're watching the woods. If they see you, it'll lead them straight to the kids. Trent won't go near the action. He's a smart kid, he'll keep out of sight."

Bear's stomach lurched. Prickly nausea gripped him as he took in the scared faces of the kids huddled behind him.

"Wait until morning." Lisa looked up at the darkening sky. "At first light, I'll come with you. We'll find him."

As Bear growled and turned away, Laurel took his arm. "I know you're scared for him, but I think Lisa's right. If we get captured or shot, we'll be no use to Trent. Will we?"

She slotted her hand into his and squeezed his fingers. Bear noticed Mae tilting her head at them, taking in her parents' surprising closeness. He allowed himself to breathe out slowly. He knew they were talking sense, but Jess and Trent both being gone was something he didn't know how to contemplate.

"Lisa?" A small voice made Bear turn around. A child with dark brown hair was tugging on Lisa's jacket. "My brother Ben… he's got asthma. His breathing is bad."

Lisa swallowed hard and looked at Laurel. "Hi honey," Laurel said, crouching so she was at the girl's eye level. "I'm a doctor. My name's Laurel. Take me to your brother and let's see what we can do to help him."

As Laurel took the girl's hand and headed into the darkness of the cave, Bear screwed his eyes shut and tried to remember how to breathe.

"Dad?" Mae's fingers lightly touched his upper arm. "We will find him. I'll help. I promise."

Her wide eyes brought a lump to Bear's throat. She looked that way when she was a child; when she'd broken her mother's favorite vase and was promising to help fix it. Pulling her into a tight embrace, Bear kissed the top of her head. "Thanks, honey. Thank you."

A few other adults from the Freemen camp had arrived with supplies. Hand-warmers—the kind that you snapped in half to release their warmth—food, sleeping bags, and bottled water.

As darkness fell, the kids asked if they could start a fire. "We can't risk being seen," Lisa told them, "but we have these...."

Lisa dispensed the hand-warmers to the kids and gave them sleeping bags, one for each pair. "Huddle together," she said, instructing them to climb in with the person next to them.

Watching, Bear's heart sank. Barely any adults had turned up. Clearly, all the Freemen knew the rendezvous point. Perhaps they were staying away so they didn't lead the militia to the kids.

"How many of you are there?" Bear asked as Mae sat down next to him and handed him a bottle of water.

"Maybe one hundred altogether," she said, taking a sip from her own bottle. "Half here at the camp, half back at the ammunitions depot."

"The militia used this as a distraction," Bear said. "You know that, right?"

Mae nodded solemnly. As the sound of gunfire had faded, they'd all known what was happening; the fight was moving to the depot.

"Why do they want it so badly?" Bear asked, shaking his head. "It looks like the Freemen have a nice setup here. Why do they need the depot? Why not just hand it over, rather than risk all this?"

As Mae opened her mouth to reply, Laurel walked over, smiling at their daughter. She sat down and, without saying anything, pulled Mae into her arms. Holding her tight, as if she never planned to let her go, Laurel closed her eyes and breathed in the scent of Mae's hair.

"Sweetheart...." Laurel sat back; the joy momentarily gone from her face. "We have something to tell you." She clasped Mae's hands between hers and glanced at Bear as her voice wavered.

Mae frowned, looking from her mom to her dad. Then her eyes softened. "It's Grandma, isn't it?"

Laurel opened her mouth to speak but no words came out, so Bear put his arm around her. "Yes, sweetheart. Grandma passed at the hospital just before we left to look for you."

Instantly, tears filled Mae's eyes. She didn't wipe them away but let them fall as Laurel began to fill in the last few years since they were last in contact. When she finished, Mae shook her head, tears still running down her cheeks.

"I'm so sorry, Mom. I shouldn't have stayed away so long."

"It's okay." Laurel kissed Mae's forehead. "None of that matters now. We're together. We found each other. That's all that matters."

"And when we've got Trent and Jess back," Bear added, "we'll leave all this behind. Head to my place in Thunder Bay." He fixed his eyes on his daughter's and lowered his voice. "We'll be safe. Away from the Freemen and away from the militia."

As he watched her, something flickered in Mae's eyes. Before he could decipher what it was, Laurel yawned loudly and said, "We'll leave to find Trent at first light. Let's get some rest."

Bear was awake, Laurel sleeping on one side of him and Mae on the other, staring at the stars that were peeking through the branches above. The kids were in the cave, Sharon, Lisa, and a few other adults asleep at its mouth.

Thankfully, it wasn't as cold as it had been. But still, the sounds of people shuffling in their sleep told him he wasn't the only one feeling restless.

His back aching from the hard ground, Bear gently tugged his arm loose from behind Laurel's back and stood up. Wrapping his sleeping bag around his shoulders, he paced slowly back and forth, enjoying the sensation of his back loosening and warmth spreading up his legs.

Sensing someone else start moving, he stopped and turned around. Mae had noticed him and was getting up too.

Without speaking, they walked a few paces into the trees. From here, they could still see the others. Mae sat down on a fallen tree trunk. Bear sat next to her. The silence between them reminded him of the many silences they'd had when she was a teenager; all the times she'd confessed something to him that she knew her mother wouldn't be happy about. Smoking with her friends. Going to parties instead of studying. The time she got her navel pierced and it developed a disgusting infection, which she insisted on going to a different doctor for because she didn't want Laurel to lecture her about it.

"Dad?" she asked quietly.

Bear didn't reply, just waited.

"I'm not one of the Freemen." She angled herself toward him, knotting her fingers together in her lap. "I'm with the militia."

For a moment, Bear wasn't sure how to compute what Mae had just said. How was that possible? Lisa, Sharon, and Art had treated Mae as if she was one of them. "Undercover?" he asked.

"Not exactly." Mae sighed and swept her fingers through her long blonde hair, tugging the ends the way she did when she was a kid. "Lisa first found me in the woods and she could have taken me prisoner then, but she didn't. She let me go. Then when my unit tried to infiltrate the depot... It was a setup." She shook her head. "They *shot* me, but then they brought me back here. Helped me. He said…. Art said my unit left me behind, but I don't know. Maybe they couldn't find me in the dark. It all happened so fast." She shrugged a little and added, "I'm not sure if they'd have let me go if I asked to leave, or *why* they helped me, but after seeing this place I decided to stay.

Gather intel." Her eyes widened and she said, "They've done some awful things. Raided towns. Killed civilians. Art says there are different factions, other groups calling themselves Freemen who do things he doesn't approve of, but...." She trailed off and pushed her fingers through her hair, as if she was still trying to work out whether she believed this or not.

Bear nodded. "So, this whole time, you've been working for the militia? A spy?" He tried not to let a note of disapproval lace his tone.

Looking down at her hands, Mae swallowed hard. "The militia was different before. I thought we were trying to keep people safe. But then others started to join. Not soldiers. At least, not *real* soldiers. And it got...." She sighed and shook her head.

"Confusing?" Bear asked.

Mae nodded, but then straightened her shoulders and sucked in her cheeks. "I just have to remember why this started. What my role is. It's not my job to ask questions. If my commanding officers know things that I don't—if they think we need the depot—then I need to do whatever I can to help them achieve that goal."

Tilting his head from side to side, Bear narrowed his eyes. Mae was right; a soldier's job wasn't to ask questions, it was to take orders. But he wasn't so sure that the militia had anyone's best interests at heart. Not when they were attacking defenseless women and children. He also wasn't sure how he felt about his daughter betraying two of his friends; Sharon and Lisa had been nothing but good to him. The idea that Mae had been using them made him very uncomfortable.

"They haven't guessed?" Bear asked, thinking of Lisa's usually shrewd judgment.

"No." Mae rubbed her thighs and blinked into the darkness. "I've maintained my cover, and if I can maintain it until we're out of here, then we can find Trent and I can get us all to safety."

"With the militia?"

"With the soldiers, yes." The way Mae said *soldiers* made Bear feel as if she was trying to remind him that *he* should be on that side too because, once upon a time, he was a soldier and should understand her loyalty.

As they settled back into silence, Bear studied his daughter's face. He'd had no idea she was undercover. The fact she'd managed to lie so easily to people he respected—Lisa and Sharon—made him uneasy. As did the fact that she seemed unable or unwilling to objectively judge their situation.

He was confused himself; Sharon and Lisa were good people. He couldn't imagine them getting tied up with a faction that would condone shooting innocent townsfolk and stealing their supplies. But Kermit had said there were many different factions of Freemen coming together. Art King was in control, but if he didn't know what the others were doing, could he be blamed for it?

Bear looked through the trees at Laurel. This was something he needed to talk through with her. He needed her calm judgment, her logical way of looking at things and seeing the path through the weeds. But he couldn't talk to her in earshot of Mae.

So, instead of waking Laurel, he told Mae he was going to try to sleep and spent the next few hours with his eyes closed, trying to make sense of whose side he should be on. If any.

35

CORNELL

"Captain, it's no use. We should fall back. We're outnumbered." Gideon's pale, pasty face came at him from the darkness of the trees.

Cornell lowered his night-vision binoculars and hurled his fist into a nearby tree trunk. It sent a lightning rod of pain up through his elbow. "How are we outnumbered? How are we being beaten by a bunch of disorganized civilians?" He kicked the bottom of the tree too, then turned around and leaned against it, trying to slow down the tsunami of anger in his chest.

The young sergeant stood behind him and waited silently. Cornell could hear his breathing, hard and fast. A little raspy. The kid was pathetic. When he turned back to face him, he drew up his shoulders. He was a tall guy and enjoyed feeling bigger than others. More intimidating. "Attacking that camp was a stroke of genius," he spat. "Or, at least, it should have been."

The sergeant nodded nervously. "Yes, Captain. It was a good plan."

"I know it was a good plan! It was *my* plan!" Cornell clenched and unclenched his fists. "Except the bunch of pathetic idiots I've got working for me couldn't carry it out, could they? It was so simple.... Attack the Freemen camp. Threaten their women and children, their dogs, and their chickens, and everything else about their precious little homestead in the forest. Backup would come from the depot, leaving it wide open for us."

"Captain, they were," the sergeant cleared his throat, "they were stronger than we thought. More resourceful."

Cornell laughed, a loud thunderclap of a laugh. He raised his eyes to the branches above his head and waved his binoculars in the air. "Yes," he said, the gurgle of laughter turning into a swirling pool of frustration. "They were. Once the Freemen realized that their families were at risk, they should have given up the depot to save them, but instead they doubled down. They're holding onto the depot and protecting those in the camp. But how? How are they managing that when they're nothing more than a bunch of untrained fighters?"

The sergeant swallowed hard. He had a nasty cut on his forehead, blood trickling down toward his chin, but was stoically ignoring it. "Sir, I'm not entirely sure. Perhaps they were just more ready for us than we anticipated."

Rubbing his bruised knuckles, Cornell stared back through his binoculars at the scene unfolding in front of him.

At first, it had all gone swimmingly; they'd caused a distraction at the camp, watched as Freemen poured out of the depot gates, heading for the woods to defend their kin. They'd made it through the first line of their defense. Poor shooters, not enough men.

Then, for a reason he couldn't fathom, the Freemen had started winning. Their shots had succeeded, they'd secured key parts of the depot, reinforcements had arrived and started attacking Cornell's troops from the rear.

The militia were surrounded, moved toward the center of the base, then pushed back toward the perimeter. Now it was the middle of the night, pitch black, and had boiled down to a shootout. His men in the trees, their men behind a big fence. And while the Freemen were holed up in an Army depot full to bursting with weapons and ammo, Cornell's men were almost shooting with fumes.

"Captain, we've lost a lot of men." The sergeant nervously pressed his lips together. "And we're almost out of ammo."

Cornell knew what the kid wanted. He knew what they were all expecting him to do, but to suffer a second defeat so quickly after the first? He'd be lucky if he kept his position and wasn't thrown out on his ear like Mackenzie.

"Fine!" he snapped, shooting Gideon a disgusted glare. "Fine." Pushing the sergeant out of his way, he strode forward until he was within shouting distance of his troops. Then he shouted, "Fall back! Back to the warehouse! Fall back!"

As they retreated like dogs with their tails between their legs, Cornell shot one last glance at the big bulky silhouette of the building they'd been sent to secure. A shiver crept down his spine. "Secure it at all costs, Cornell. We *cannot* let the Freemen have what's inside that place."

Cornell squeezed the bridge of his nose.

"Captain? Are you all right?" Gideon asked quietly.

Snapping his eyes open, Cornell drew himself up so his shoulders were pushed back and his chest puffed out. "When we get back to the warehouse, Sergeant, I want you to find six uninjured soldiers to come back out here with me at first light."

"Sir?" Gideon asked.

Moving closer, Cornell clenched his fists. "We're going to take this place, Sergeant. You mark my words. There is *always* a way, and we're going to find it."

36

LAUREL

Bear was already awake when Laurel stirred. His face looked drawn, crumpled, the way it did when he'd been up all night. Sitting up on top of his sleeping bag, he was quietly rearranging things in his pack. He took out the map and examined it before he noticed that Laurel was watching him.

On his other side, Mae was still sleeping. Even though she was now so grown up, like this, asleep, she reminded Laurel so much of the way she looked when she was a child that it made Laurel's chest hurt.

"Are you all right?" Laurel edged closer to Bear, staying inside her sleeping bag because the chill in the air had made her skin prickle. "You look exhausted."

"Long night." Bear nodded toward the cave. "Don't think anyone slept well from all the shuffling and mumbling."

"The kids are scared." Laurel put on her glasses and pushed them up her nose. "Can you blame them? They don't know when, or if, they'll see their parents again."

Bear took his gaze back from the cave and let it settle on Laurel's face. Then he looked at Mae. Gingerly, he stood up and held out his hand for Laurel to do the same.

She took it and stepped out of her sleeping bag.

"Can we talk?" Bear was speaking quietly, as if he didn't want to wake Mae. The tone of his voice made Laurel feel uneasy.

"Sure." She followed him over to an empty space a few feet away. "What's going on?"

In a hushed voice, keeping his eyes on Mae, Bear said, "Mae told me last night that she's been undercover. She was brought back to the Freemen's camp when she was injured, but she's part of the militia. She's been gathering intel to take back to them."

Laurel's face creased into a frown. She replayed Bear's words in her head. "Mae is *with* the militia?"

"You've seen what the Freemen are capable of. It's not hard to imagine her believing she's on the right side."

"But the militia have done awful things too." Laurel hugged her waist and looked over at her sleeping daughter. "They attacked a camp full of defenseless kids."

Bear's jaw twitched. "Mae thinks there's a bigger plan. A cause for the greater good."

"What kind of plan?"

"She doesn't know. She said it's not her place to ask that question." The note of irritation in Bear's voice told Laurel he believed their daughter was being a little more than short-sighted. Sighing, he added, "She wants to go back to them. When we've found Trent."

"What about Thunder Bay?"

Bear pressed his lips together. His jaw twitched. "We didn't talk about it, but from what she said, she's pretty determined to return to her unit."

Laurel put her hands into her jacket pockets, then took them out again. She wanted to pace up and down but didn't want to do anything that would draw attention to them. "Okay," she said, trying to remain calm, "Okay. Let's just focus on getting Trent back. We'll find him, and Jess, then we'll deal with Mae." She slotted her hand into Bear's and squeezed it. "To be honest, Bjorn, if we have to knock her over the head and carry her all the way to Thunder Bay to get her away from this, then that's what we'll do. I'm not letting her go again now that we've found her."

As she said his name, his real name, Bear swallowed hard. His finger traced her knuckles and a slow smile touched his lips. "Not sure knocking her on the head is the way to win her back, Doc."

Laurel shook her head. "You know what I meant."

"Yeah," he said, pulling her to his chest. "I do."

For a moment, they stayed like that. His chest was warm and his chin rested on the top of her head. She'd always liked that about him; the fact that, despite being tall for a woman, she could fit under his chin.

"Is there something you two need to tell me?" Mae had appeared in front of them. She was standing with her hands on her hips, looking at them as if they were teenagers who'd been caught making out after school.

Pulling away and tucking her hair behind her ear, Laurel caught herself blushing. "We're just...."

"Nothing to tell," Bear interrupted, playfully nudging Mae's shoulder. "Just your mom and dad trying to be friends."

Mae raised her eyebrows. "Friends?" Then she shrugged. "Well, I guess it's better than being at each other's throats." As they walked back toward the cave, where the kids were now waking and stumbling sleepily out into the open, Mae added, "So, when are we leaving?"

"Now." Bear strode to his sleeping bag, rolled it up, and attached it to his pack.

Laurel was doing the same, tossing Mae one of her remaining protein bars and a bottle of water, when Sharon's voice broke through the trees. "Hold it! Someone's coming!"

She'd been on watch with Lisa on the perimeter of the caves, despite her injury, and was backing up into the clearing.

Immediately, the other adults began to usher the kids back into the caves. But then Lisa shouted, "It's okay. It's Art. Relax, everyone, it's Art and Alice."

At the name *Alice*, Laurel glanced at Bear. He rolled his eyes and folded his arms in front of his chest. Immediately, upon entering the clearing, Alice noticed them. She whispered something to Art, wide-eyed, but he shook his head at her. Loudly, he said, "The doc and her husband are our friends."

Alice didn't respond, just pursed her lips and watched as Art strode over to Laurel and extended his hand. "Thank you for helping us."

"She's treated some of the kids." Lisa walked over and began to brief Art. "One had an asthma attack, another had a broken ankle. They're scared, but they're okay. We haven't seen Shane, and Sharon's injured. So, Laurel did it all by herself."

Art nodded appreciatively at Laurel. Then looked from Lisa to Sharon. "And everyone else?"

"We're all fine, Art." Lisa glanced behind him as if she was expecting to see others. "What about everyone else?"

Art kept her gaze for a moment, then slowly shook his head. "Everyone else...." He suddenly wavered on the spot and Laurel lurched forward. Grabbing his arm, she told him to sit down. Lisa fetched a bottle of water. Art swept his forearm over his brow and breathed out slowly.

"Art? Are you injured?" Laurel looked for signs of a head wound or other injury, but saw none.

"No. Just tired." He took the water, drank a large swig, then set the bottle down on the ground. "The others," he said firmly, "are back at the camp. Clearing up. Getting ready to move out."

As Lisa's eyes widened, and Mae stepped closer, Art rubbed his palms on his thighs and breathed out heavily.

"We're moving everyone to the depot. We managed to keep control, but only just. We suffered heavy losses." He pressed his lips together. For a moment, Laurel thought she saw his eyes moisten with tears, but he sucked in a deep breath and shook them away.

Lisa slotted her hand into Sharon's.

Laurel picked up the water bottle and gestured for Art to drink some more.

"The militia seems to be leaving us alone for now. They know they're defeated. But I can't imagine they'll give it long before they strike again." Art squeezed the plastic bottle hard, making it crackle beneath his fingers. "I want everyone cleared out and back at the depot by midday. I have men reinforcing the depot now, but we'll need all hands on deck in the days to come."

"Art...." As a flurry of movement began, and people behind them started packing up their sleeping bags and packs, Mae's voice rose above them.

"You all right, Mae?" Art asked, taking a long drink of water and wiping his mouth with his sleeve.

"I'm fine, thank you." Mae's arms were at her sides. She folded them in front of her stomach, then unfolded them again as if she wasn't sure what to do with them. Laurel exchanged a glance with Bear. What was their daughter up to? "It's just—I don't understand what's inside the depot that's so important. Why not hand it over?"

Slowly, Art rose to his feet. "Mae," he said, "you were with the militia. You saw yourself what they're capable of."

Mae closed her eyes and nodded. She was a good actress; she looked genuinely ashamed to have been a part of what the militia did before she came here.

"There are things inside that depot…. Things that could be disastrous if they got into the wrong hands."

"What kind of—"

Before Mae could finish her question, Bear cut in. "Art, Laurel and I need to find Trent. Mae offered to come with us. She knows these woods."

While Mae shot her father a withering glare, Bear ignored her and simply waited for Art's reply.

Looking from Mae to Laurel to the people surrounding the caves, he nodded slowly. "Yes, I understand." He rubbed his chin and made a clicking sound with his tongue. "But I can't allow all three of you to go. We need help." He turned to Laurel. "You promised you'd help. Our EMT is missing in action, and Sharon's injured and can't treat those who are severely wounded."

"And *I* understand too." Laurel folded her arms in front of her stomach. "But you promised you'd help us find Trent. We can't leave him.

He could be injured too." Expecting Art to rise up and pull his gun, threaten her into staying, Laurel braced herself to stand her ground.

Instead, he stood slowly and put his hand on her shoulder. "Dr. Rivera, I'm asking you as a favor, please stay. There are too many injured. We need you. Please, stay."

Laurel's chest tightened. She turned to look at Bear. He inhaled deeply and nodded. "Stay, Laurel. Help them. We'll find Trent and we'll meet you back at the depot. If he's hurt, Mae and I can carry him between us. We'll get him back to you."

Next to them, Mae was silent. Thoughts flitted across her face, but Laurel couldn't interpret them.

"We'll be back before nightfall." He looked at Mae for confirmation.

"Dad's right. You stay. We'll be back soon."

But as Laurel watched them leave, a heavy sensation settled in her stomach. Tears bit at her throat. This wasn't meant to happen. They were meant to be together. Finally. Not separated. Not again.

37

BEAR

"There are too many tracks in these woods," Bear said, crouching down and examining some broken twigs that indicated people had moved through the area. "We'll never find him like this."

"Shall we go back?" Mae asked. "Fetch Mom, then go to the warehouse?"

"You mean the depot?" Bear asked. "No. I'm not leaving Trent out here alone. He's family, Mae."

As Mae pressed her lips together, she shook her head. "No, not the depot. The warehouse. That's where my unit was last stationed."

"Your unit?" Bear couldn't quite believe she was still so fixated on returning to her colleagues instead of being with her family. "Mae, I'm not going anywhere until I've found Trent." He stood up and fixed his eyes on his daughter's. "And I was hoping that when we did, you'd see sense and come with us. Back to Thunder Bay."

"Thunder Bay? You were serious about that?" Mae put her hands on her hips. "We haven't seen each other in years. The last time I saw you, you and mom *hated* each other. You weren't speaking. You split up. *You* left. And now, just because the world's a little different than it was, you think we'll run off into the sunset and play happy families together? With some kid I don't even know? Who, frankly, you seem to care more about than your own daughter."

A familiar flash of temper colored Mae's cheeks. When she was like this, she reminded him of Laurel; fiery and unable to hold her feelings in. Incapable of not just saying what she was feeling. Except that Laurel had never been as irrational as Mae.

"Mae... we've both been through a lot since this whole thing started." He paused, noticing his voice tighten. A queasy, seasick sensation had lodged itself in his gut. He reached for his pack and took out a bottle of water. "For a long time, our family has had things to fix. I don't deny that. And we will. We'll talk it through, and we'll fix it. Together. But first, we need to be safe."

"And Thunder Bay is safe?" Mae asked, folding her arms in front of her chest.

"Yes. It is." Bear took a drink. "Safer than here." He tried to soften his tone. "Let's leave the Freemen and the militia to their fight. It doesn't concern us."

"You heard what they said!" Mae's voice shook the branches as she began to yell. "Art said that whatever's inside the depot could be dangerous. Clearly, my captain and the rest of the militia are trying to prevent disaster. They're trying to take back control of something that could cause catastrophic—"

"You don't *know* that, Mae." Bear threw up his arms. "Dang it, Mae. Do you have to be so pig-headed? Can't you just listen, for once, to what's good for you?"

"I'm pig-headed?" Mae scoffed, hands on her hips. "You're the one who's utterly fixated on getting back to some cabin in the woods."

She paused and fixed her eyes on his. "You're a soldier, Dad. You should get it. You should understand why I can't leave." She stopped, released a heavy sigh, then added, "Would you really be happy holed up there, looking out for ourselves, leaving everyone else to rot?" Mae asked, her eyes flashing.

Bear knew he should keep his cool. When Mae was younger, he'd refereed hundreds of these arguments between Mae and Laurel. He was always the peacekeeper, the one telling them both to take a break before they said something they regretted. But right now, in the woods, he found he couldn't abide by his own advice. "You think the militia aren't doing exactly that? Looking out for themselves?" Bear was rapidly losing his ability to stay level-headed. "You think they want whatever's in the depot in order to protect people? Did it occur to you that it might be the other way around? That the Freemen are protecting us from what the militia want to do with it?"

"I...." Mae stuttered. "That's ridiculous. You've seen what the Freemen have done. They're not as innocent as you might think." She drew back her shoulders. Her tone stiffened. "I trust that my captain has a reason, a plan."

"A plan he hasn't seen fit to share with the soldiers who are doing his dirty work?"

"You *are* a soldier," Mae fired back at him. "I thought, of all people, you'd get it. Mom never has, but you're supposed to be different." Lowering her voice a little, she added, "You've always been on my side, Dad. You've always trusted me. Why is this any different?"

"Because I'm your father and my job is to keep you safe. You are not safe here, Mae."

"I can take care of myself."

As their eyes met, and a moment of quivering tension passed between them, Mae's forehead twitched. She turned her head.

"Did you hear that?"

Bear looked in the same direction. He hadn't heard anything.

"Someone's there." She peered into the darkness.

Bear handed her his gun and pulled his shotgun from his shoulder, but then a voice from the darkness of the trees said, "Put down your weapons."

While Bear didn't move, instantly Mae obeyed the command. "It's my captain," she said, nodding at Bear to put his gun down as she dropped hers to the ground and kicked it away from her. "I know his voice. Dad, do as he says, it's my captain." Then, raising her voice, she called, "Captain Cornell, it's Mae Peterson. I'm with my father."

As Mae spoke, six soldiers emerged from the trees. At their center was the one Mae had addressed as Cornell.

Seeing him, Mae stood up straight, feet together, arms at her sides. Cornell looked her up and down. "I didn't expect to see you again, Peterson. I thought you were dead."

The tone of the captain's voice made Bear flinch. This guy was *not* a good guy. He wasn't pleased to see Mae; just amused that she was alive after all.

"No, Captain. I was taken back to the Freemen camp. I assimilated myself. Gathered intel."

"And you were on your way back to us, were you?" Cornell said, still not telling the others to lower their weapons.

"We're looking for a lost kid," Mae said a little weakly. "But then, yes, Captain, I intended to return to the warehouse." She looked at Bear. "My father served in Iraq. He'd be a welcome addition to the unit. My mother, too, was a field medic."

"Your mother?" Cornell smirked. "Well, well, well, how lovely. A Peterson family reunion."

"Are you going to tell your men to lower their weapons? Or are you going to continue pointing them at one of your own soldiers?" Bear snapped, moving closer to Mae, already regretting giving up his gun.

Cornell turned a steely gaze toward Bear. "They'll lower their weapons when I'm satisfied that neither of you poses a threat."

Giving Bear a frustrated shake of the head, Mae loosened her arms at her sides and spoke up. "Captain—"

Cornell raised his palm at her. "Ah. That's enough." Cornell paused for a moment. He narrowed his eyes. Then he clicked his fingers and snapped, "Take the father into custody. Restrain him."

"Captain?" Mae shouted incredulously. "He's my father. He's no threat."

Whirling around, Cornell closed the distance between himself and Mae. Pressing his chest against hers, he glowered down at her. "Peterson, you've been gone for two weeks. You say you were gathering intel, but why should I trust you?"

Mae opened her mouth to answer, but Cornell pressed a big, thick finger to her lips and it was all Bear could do to keep from grabbing that hand and breaking it.

"You want to prove your loyalty? You'll shut up, do as you're told, and let me assess whether Daddy Peterson can be trusted." Cornell removed his finger but positioned his face close to Mae's. "If you can't do that, then I'll just put you both in cuffs."

Watching, Bear's entire body twitched violently. A soldier grabbed his shoulder and twisted his arm, sending a shooting pain up his injured elbow. He wanted to knock them out, take them all down and run. But they had guns, and he was unarmed. So he pushed down the anger in his stomach and let them tie him up with duct tape.

Mae's eyes widened as Cornell stepped away from her and took a piece of black cloth from his pocket.

But as he tied the gag tight around Bear's face, Mae said nothing. She just watched, her fists in tight balls at her sides.

Fastening the gag tight, Cornell studied Bear's face. He noticed the hearing aid in Bear's ear and a slow smile spread on his lips. Reaching forward, with two long fingers, he yanked the aid free and left it hanging from Bear's ear. He mouthed something in Bear's face. It looked like *can you hear me*, but Bear had never been good at lip-reading.

Turning to the others, Cornell laughed. They laughed too. Next to him, Mae pressed her lips together and closed her eyes.

For several long minutes, they marched through the trees, Mae ahead, Bear behind with a soldier on either side of him. He could hear nothing, just a muffled, staticky merging of the stomping of feet and the cackles of the soldiers. Every now and then, Mae glanced over her shoulder, caught his gaze, and looked at him with a sorrowful expression.

Rather than being angry with her, Bear's stomach twisted with sympathy; it gave him no pleasure to be able to say he was right about her unit. He just hoped that, finally, she'd seen it too. That right now she was playing it smart; going along with Cornell so she could spring an escape later.

He tried to ignore the dull throb in his chest that told him he might be wrong; that his own daughter had just turned into his captor.

38

LAUREL

With the children ready, and the adults gathered around them, the group made their way out of the woods and back toward camp.

They were on the outskirts when Art told them to stop. "Lisa, Paul, Alice, take the kids down through the trees." He fixed his eyes on Lisa's.

She nodded. "Got it." She swiftly kissed Sharon and beckoned for the youngest Freemen to follow her. Positioning herself at the front of the line, with Paul at the back and Alice in the middle, they led the kids toward a section of fallen-down fencing close to where Bear and Laurel had hidden in their tree.

"Is it bad?" Laurel asked, stepping up next to Art as they approached the camp.

"Like I said," Art growled. "We took heavy losses."

At Art's side, Sharon shook her head. "And Shane is missing?"

"Last seen trying to hold back fire on the depot." Art's expression was a mixture of pride and sadness. "When we get there, we'll need volunteers to—" He swallowed hard. "Identify the dead."

Sharon closed her eyes and wrapped her arms around herself. Away from the shelter of the trees, the sun shone brighter, but the wind was fiercer too. Approaching the camp, Laurel assessed the damage.

The RV was on its side, door now open and facing the sky. The trestle tables, which had obviously been used for communal dinners, were upended and peppered with bullet holes. Grenade damage was everywhere, and the awning of the cooking section was torn in half and flapping in the wind.

"Doc? Think you can climb into the RV and recover the medical equipment that isn't damaged?"

"Of course." Laurel headed straight for it. Sharon followed her, but Laurel shook her head. "No, Sharon, you're injured."

"Then I'll wait out here and pack up the stuff you toss out," she said forcefully.

Laurel hesitated a moment, then nodded. "All right." She shrugged off her backpack, then searched for a way up. Putting her foot onto one of the wheel arcs, she grabbed the side of the vehicle, bounced a few times to give herself leverage, then sprang up high enough to catch hold of the door.

Clambering up onto what was now the RV's roof, she slid along on her belly, then dropped down inside.

Her feet landed on the rear wall of the RV, now the floor. Around her, drawers had fallen open, their contents spilled out. Bottles of pills, bandages, disinfectants, all in chaos. But not unusable.

Searching her surroundings, Laurel grabbed a pillow, pulled the case off it, then pulled a stool over beneath the door, clambered up, and tossed the case out to Sharon. "Use this. I'll toss anything that's not breakable out to you. Anything fragile, I'll pack myself."

"Okay," Sharon called back.

Slowly, methodically, Laurel worked her way through the disarray, mentally cataloging anything that could be particularly useful when they got back to the depot.

As she tossed out a stack of bandages, she called to Sharon, "What are the medical facilities like inside the depot?"

"There's a first-aid room, basic supplies," Sharon replied loudly. "But this stuff will help."

"Okay, good." Laurel gently picked up two glass bottles of iodine and slotted them into her own pillowcase sack. Then, holding it over her shoulder, she climbed back up onto the stool.

"I think that's everything salvageable," she said, hugging the fragile bottles close to her chest as she jumped down to the ground.

"Good." Sharon gestured to the camp's entrance. A wagon, pulled by two large black horses, had arrived. Freemen from the caves, and others Laurel didn't recognize, were loading supplies into it. "The kitchen was destroyed," Sharon said, shaking her head. "But a lot of our food supplies are still good."

"What about…." Laurel's eyes came to rest on a body. A young woman, lying in the dirt with her eyes open as if she was watching the clouds float by. "The bodies?"

Inhaling slowly, Sharon pressed her lips together. She didn't answer Laurel's question, just said, "Let's take this to Art."

At the wagon, Art took the sacks of medical supplies and stowed them up front beneath the driver's bench. "Thank you," he said. "These are precious. Thank you for salvaging them."

"Art," Sharon said tentatively, "we were wondering what you'd like to do about the deceased." She said the word "deceased" in a matter-of-fact tone, but her eyes betrayed the sadness behind them.

Turning to look at the now-decimated camp, Art shook his head. "We'll take the supplies to the depot first. They need to be secured. Tomorrow, we'll return for the dead."

"Tomorrow?" Sharon asked, a little incredulously. "We're going to leave them out here all night? What about wolves?"

"We could light torches," Laurel said. "Keep the wolves away."

"Why not just move them tonight?" Sharon looked from Art to Laurel.

As Art screwed his eyes shut and turned his head away, Laurel put her hand on Sharon's arm. "Because the people who are still alive have to come first, which means securing our supplies and the depot itself."

Without looking at her, Art put a large, firm hand on Laurel's shoulder. He squeezed her, silently, then nodded. "You two light the torches. By the time you're done, we'll be ready to move out."

As the last torch was lit, Laurel caught Sharon wiping a tear from her face. "Sorry," she said. "This is bringing back a lot of memories." When Laurel didn't reply, she continued, "We were traveling with a man named Josh when we met your husband."

"I remember. Bear told me about him."

"We were heading for his parents' farm. We made it, but—" Sharon swallowed hard. "Militia found the place. Ransacked it. Josh was killed trying to protect us."

Laurel screwed her eyes shut. A thought floated through her mind; was Mae part of it? Had Mae been part of any of it?

"That was why we joined the Freemen," Sharon said, sniffing loudly and wincing as the movement made her side hurt. "We wanted to fight back."

Silently, Laurel patted Sharon's arm. They were watching the last of the supplies—two huge canisters of water—be loaded onto the wagon when a noise in the trees made Laurel step forward.

"Is that...?" she asked, glancing at Sharon.

"A dog?" Sharon's eyes widened.

Laurel had barely made it to the camp's entrance when a flash of white hurtled toward her, a red-knitted coat hanging off her, a trail of wool in her wake. Spotting Laurel, she raced forward, running straight beneath the horses at the front of the wagon.

The horses huffed and shuffled nervously.

Jess began to bark. Her eyes were big and dark, her bark incessant, high-pitched.

"She must have been out there all night with the explosions and the gunfire." Laurel glanced at Sharon. "She looks terrified."

Still barking, Jess raced over to Laurel, but then sped off again, running in frantic circles.

As she tore through the horses' legs a second time, one of them whinnied loudly.

"Someone stop that dog," Art shouted. Nearby, a big guy with a thick neck attempted to catch hold of Jess as she raced past him. But she simply wriggled out of his grip and kept on barking.

The third time she ran beneath the horses, the bigger of the two lost its cool. It jolted suddenly backward, sending a canister of water tumbling from the unsecured cart.

"Give me something," Sharon said, running over to the wagon. "Food. Something. Anything." Someone passed her a granola bar. Sharon frowned at it. "Something a dog would eat."

Someone else handed her a can of hot dog sausages. "Better." Sharon waved her hands. "Open it, open it."

Now Jess was standing in front of the scared horse, barking at it. Every time someone tried to grab her, she ducked, ran, then returned to bark at the horse.

"You're making it worse," Sharon shouted. "Leave her alone." She turned to Laurel. "Find something to use as a leash. I'll try and lure her away from the horses."

Laurel nodded, pulling the scarf from her neck, ready to loop it around Jess as soon as she got close enough and still enough to capture.

While Art had the others hastily secure the back of the wagon, and slowly start leading the horse off, Sharon backed away. Holding the sausage in the air, she waved it. "Jess. What have I got here, girl?"

Jess ignored her.

Still backing away, Sharon tried again. "Mmm. Jess. What's this?"

For a moment, nothing happened. Then the wind changed. Jess stopped barking. Her nose twitched. She stayed still, sniffing the air. Then, slowly, she began to follow Sharon.

Still holding the hot dog, Sharon crouched down. She glanced at Laurel, gesturing for her to be ready. Jess continued her slow approach. A few inches from Sharon's knees, she stopped. Sharon held out the hot dog. Laurel tip-toed slowly behind Jess. She met Sharon's gaze. Sharon allowed Jess's jaws to clamp around the end of the meat but, just as Laurel reached to loop the scarf around Jess's neck, she bolted again.

Hot dog in mouth, Jess hurtled underneath the wagon and ran a crazy figure eight around the horses' legs.

This time, the horses couldn't remain calm. They bucked and pulled away from the Freemen holding their reins. They turned frantically in a circle, the wagon moving with them. Jess started nipping at their heels. And then the horses bolted, taking the wagon with them.

Laurel dove out of the way, and Sharon did too. Art stepped in front of them, waving his arms. "Woah. Woah." But to avoid him, the horses swung the opposite way and sent the wagon careening into the flagpole.

As the horses bolted into the woods, Jess racing after them, the flagpole wavered.

Laurel's breath caught in her chest.

The flagpole was falling. Art saw it too. On the ground, Sharon realized too late; the pole smacked into her, pinning her flat on her stomach.

"Sharon!" Art dove to the ground beside her and heaved the pole from her back, turning Sharon over so she was lying face up.

"Art, don't—" But Laurel was too late; he'd already moved her. Scrambling over, Laurel placed a gentle hand on Sharon's head. "Don't move. Don't even turn your head. Just stay still."

She sat back on her heels. She and Art were the only ones there. Everyone else had run after the wagon. The pole was large, made of white painted metal, clearly moved up here from the depot itself. "How heavy is it?" Laurel asked.

Art's mouth fell open. He seemed unable to speak.

"Art—how heavy is it?" Laurel gripped his hand. "The flagpole. You brought it up here, how heavy?"

"I don't know, maybe eighty or a hundred pounds."

"Okay." Laurel tried to slow her thoughts.

"We could really use an EMT right now, huh?" Sharon asked, her face pale.

"Shane will have to miss out on this one." Laurel squeezed Sharon's hand. "Now, Sharon, listen—"

"I shouldn't have moved her, should I?" Art's face had paled. He sat back on his heels, swiping his hand through his hair. "Did I hurt her? Is her back—?"

"Art," Laurel said sternly, "now isn't the time. We need to focus on helping Sharon, okay?"

Art pressed his lips together and swallowed hard.

"Do you have another wagon?"

He nodded. "Yes. One more."

"At the depot?"

He nodded again, unable to speak.

"Good. And a stretcher?"

"I think so." Art paused, then nodded. "Yes, we have one. I know we do."

"Go fetch them and bring some strong helpers. We need to get Sharon to the depot so I can examine her." As Art stood up and hurried off through the trees, Laurel squeezed Sharon's hand. "It's going to be all right," she said gently. "I'll get you some pain meds, and we'll fix you right up."

A slow smile spread over Sharon's face. "I don't think I'll need the meds, Doc."

"There's no need to put a brave face on it." Laurel glanced at the pole. "Weight like that, from that height, with that force–"

As she looked back, a tear rolled down Sharon's cheek. "No, Laurel. I'm not being brave. I just don't think I'll need the drugs because I can't feel my legs."

END OF DIVIDED WORLD
EMP AFTERMATH BOOK FOUR

Broken World, July 13, 2022

Chaotic World, August 10, 2022

Dangerous World, September 14, 2022

Divided World, May 10, 2023

Collapsed World, June 14, 2023

Lawless World, July 12, 2023

PS: Do you love post-apocalyptic fiction? Then keep reading for exclusive extracts from **Collapsed World, Burned World,** and **Crumbling World.**

THANK YOU

Thank you for purchasing 'Divided World'
(EMP Aftermath Book Four)

Get prepared and sign-up to Grace's mailing list
to be notified of my next release at
www.GraceHamiltonBooks.com.

Loved this book? Share it with a friend, www.GraceHamiltonBooks.com/books

ABOUT GRACE HAMILTON

Grace Hamilton is the prepper pen-name for a bad-ass, survivalist momma-bear of four kids, and wife to a wonderful husband. After being stuck in a mountain cabin for six days following a flash flood, she decided she never wanted to feel so powerless or have to send her kids to bed hungry again. Now she lives the prepper lifestyle and knows that if SHTF or TEOTWAWKI happens, she'll be ready to help protect and provide for her family.

Combine this survivalist mentality with a vivid imagination (as well as a slightly unhealthy day dreaming habit) and you get a prepper fiction author. Grace spends her days thinking about the worst possible survival situations that a person could be thrown into, then throwing her characters into these nightmares while trying to figure out "What SHOULD you do in this situation?"

You will find Grace on:

BLURB

When the world ends, all they have left is family. But can they survive what's coming?

Laurel and her husband, Bear, have finally reunited with their daughter Mae. But their daughter's loyalties are divided, leading both Bear and Trent to get swept up in the turmoil as Mae is forced to pick sides.

With her family separated once again, Laurel needs to figure out how to save them and remind their daughter that family comes first in the battleground of post-apocalypse America. And it isn't long before a new crisis threatens everything they've worked so hard to build. Now Laurel must work out how to rescue not only the Freemen but the Militia as well.

People are dying as the two groups clash, loyalties are tested, and Laurel and Bear must make the hardest choice of their lives. In the fight for survival, they struggle to answer a single burning question: how much can the ties of family withstand?

Get your copy of Collapsed World
Available June 14, 2023
(Available for pre-order now)
www.GraceHamiltonBooks.com

EXCERPT

Chapter One

Bear

For several long minutes, Bear was marched through the trees. He could hear nothing except a muffled, staticky duet of stomping feet and cackling soldiers. He kept expecting his daughter to turn around and look at him. Instead, she marched ahead, shoulders back, head held high.

Rather than being angry with her, Bear's stomach twisted with sympathy; it gave him no pleasure to say he was right about her superiors, and no pleasure to see Mae being manipulated the way she was. From just the few brief minutes he'd spent in the presence of Captain

Cornell, Bear had figured out precisely what kind of man Mae's Captain was. Bear had worked with guys like him before. He'd had *captains* like him before, and all of them had shared a common trait; their personal ambition, not their sense of duty or morality, was what drove them. This one, though, possessed an added streak of cruelty. Bear could smell it a mile off. He saw it in the way Cornell looked at Mae and had heard it in the way he spoke to her—before he'd ripped Bear's hearing aid from his ear, of course.

Surveying their route, committing any noticeable landmarks to memory, Bear realized they were not heading in the direction of the ammunition depot. He'd expected them to pass it, but instead, they stayed clear and stuck to the trees. Clearly, Cornell was avoiding it, which at least meant that Art King and his Freemen were holding the Militia back. For now.

Despite coming nowhere near any action between the Militia and the Freemen, they passed too many dead bodies. Soldiers who looked too young to be soldiers. Militia who'd been killed by the Freemen.

Looking at the face of a young female soldier with dark hair, a pale face, and open, unblinking eyes, Bear swallowed hard. The branches above her were reflected in her empty pupils. As Cornell's men averted their eyes and tensed their jaws, Bear understood how easy it would have been for Cornell to persuade his troops that the Freemen were the enemy if this kind of confrontation had happened before.

The more Militia lives the Freemen took, the more ammunition Cornell had to fuel his assertion that they were the bad guys.

Bear breathed in slowly, noticing his nostrils flare with frustration.

Neither side was right in this. Neither side could take the high ground. Someone needed to capitulate—give up the depot and whatever was so important inside it—but that didn't look likely any time soon.

Eventually, they emerged from the forest onto a wide country road, which they followed toward the nearest town. Bear studied Cornell carefully. He didn't seem nervous or particularly alert, which implied the Militia had been camped out in Gentry for a while. This in turn implied that the Militia had the townsfolk under their thumb, or at the very least, frightened into submission.

The streets on the outskirts were deserted. From the movement of the sun, Bear calculated that they walked for another twenty minutes before turning off the main thoroughfare. With the sun hovering just past midday, they reached a large, imposing warehouse, which stood alone on a dusty plot of land. Corrugated steel walls, no windows, and large double doors at the front told Bear it was probably used for storage, but that Cornell had decided it would make an ideal bolt-hole while the Militia waited to take control of the depot.

With rough hands on his arms, Bear was marched toward the warehouse. Mae still hadn't looked at him. All he'd seen since they started walking was the back of her head. While Cornell rapped his knuckles on the door, Mae stood back with the others.

A face appeared, a young man about Mae's age. When he saw Mae, his mouth dropped open a little. Bear couldn't see his daughter's face, but the look in this kid's eyes told him he knew Mae and was shocked to see her.

The young soldier said something that looked like, "You're alive?" his breath catching in his chest as Cornell gestured for Bear to be brought forward.

As he was shoved toward the door, Bear finally caught a glimpse of Mae's face. Without looking at her father, she dipped her head and said something Bear couldn't interpret to the soldier at the door. Then her lips twitched. Not a smile, just recognition of the fact they were perhaps more than colleagues.

Shakily, the young man stepped aside to let Cornell pass. He strode through the entrance, beckoning for Bear to be brought along behind him.

Inside, it took a moment for Bear's eyes to adjust. He scanned the room, expecting to see signs of a camp: supplies, beds, weapons. But the interior of the warehouse was dark and completely empty. It was just a huge, cavernous space with small windows of natural light illuminating it through cracks near the ceiling—perhaps so that, to potential intruders, it would look at first glance like nothing more than an abandoned warehouse rather than a Militia hideout.

Ahead, Cornell stopped, said something to the soldiers who were holding Bear's arms, then spun on his heel and disappeared through a smaller door to their right.

For a moment, no one moved. The young man who'd been shocked to see Mae said something to one of the others. For the first time, Mae's eyes darted toward Bear. Then she gestured to his mouth, to the gag. Was she asking them to remove it? Bear was trying to interpret what she was saying from the movement of her lips, but he'd never been good at lip reading.

In unison, the soldiers shook their heads. The three of them argued for a moment. Then, finally, the young man stepped in and seemed to talk Mae down.

As Bear was led farther into the belly of the building, Mae walked beside him. He couldn't be sure whether she stayed silent because she knew he couldn't hear her or because she didn't know what to say. Either way, her lips remained tightly pressed together.

Finally, they reached another door. The young man unlocked it with a large key, hanging from a ring of other large keys.

It led to a large yard, enclosed by a tall metal fence and barbed wire. The light stung Bear's eyes. He blinked. In front of them was a stack of rusty-looking shipping containers.

The boy pointed to one of them. The other two soldiers nodded. Then, leaving Mae and the boy hanging back by the doors, they dragged Bear forward.

As they heaved open the container, Bear's stomach lurched a second time. His throat constricted. He felt like he might vomit. They were going to lock him in? For how long?

A pair of hands landed on Bear's shoulders, spinning him around. The tallest of the soldiers who'd escorted him squared up to Bear and stared into his face. The guy had a shock of jet-black hair, and a scar on his upper lip. His cheeks reddened as he spoke loudly, the sound just about breaking through the static in Bear's ear.

Beneath his gag, Bear tried to yell, "I can't hear you, you idiot," but before he'd finished, the soldier planted two firm hands on Bear's chest and shoved him backward.

Stumbling, Bear tried to catch Mae's eyes. She was too far away. The door began to close. Before sealing it shut, another soldier—not the dark-haired one—paused and yanked the gag from Bear's mouth. Perhaps he was worried Bear would suffocate inside if he couldn't at least take full breaths.

Immediately, Bear turned his head and shook it, indicating his hearing aid needed to be put back on his ear. The soldier who'd taken out the gag moved as if he was going to help, but the dark-haired one held him back. Mae looked away. Then the door was closed, and Bear was alone.

Sealed in the dark, Bear's heart beat faster and faster. He tried to slow his breathing, but his skin was hot and prickly, and he still felt as if he might vomit. He could hear nothing. As if he was underwater, his ears were filled with nothing but a kind of muffled static.

He was trying to slow his thoughts when the slight movement of air near his shoulder made him jump. He froze, stock-still, staring into the darkness.

Slowly, he turned. "Who's there?" he said loudly, hoping his voice was scary enough to stop whoever was in here with him from doing something stupid. "Listen, buddy, I can't hear you. Those assholes took my hearing aid so—"

Something moved behind him and awkwardly brushed against his arm. His entire body stiffened. Then, suddenly, fingers caught Bear's wrist and squeezed gently. In his bound hands, the fingers traced a shape in Bear's palm: T.

"Trent?" Bear's breath caught in his chest. "Is that you, kid? Squeeze once for no, twice for yes."

Two squeezes of his hand caused Bear to breathe out heavily. "Okay. Okay, kid. You tied up too?"

Squeeze, squeeze.

"Right, okay… give me a second to think this through." Slowing his thoughts in line with his breathing, Bear sat down. His arms were twisted at an awkward angle. He stretched his shoulders back, ignoring the pain in his elbow, and tucked his hands underneath himself. Then, drawing his knees up to his chest, he moved his tied hands beneath his butt, tucked his feet inside them, and jerked them up so they were now in front of his chest instead of behind his back. Reaching up, he looped his hearing aid back on his ear.

Immediately, he heard Trent's voice. "Bear? Where'd you go?"

"I hear you, Trent. I'm here," Bear replied, leaning forward and tugging at his bootlaces. "Sit down."

"Sit down?" Trent's voice was shaky.

"Do as I say." Bear reached up, hands still tied, and tugged Trent's pant leg. "Sit down, then sit on your hands and loop them forward over your feet, so they're in front of you." He waited, hearing Trent grunt as he followed the instructions. "Have you done that?"

"Yeah, yeah, I've done it."

"Right, now take out one of your laces." Bear pulled his own lace free from his left boot. "Tie it *tight* around your foot. The tightest knot you can. Leave a length spare."

"Okay...."

"Now tie the other part of the lace around the duct tape between your wrists. You're going to use your feet to snap the duct tape with the lace."

"Will that work?" Trent asked, incredulously. "I'm not as strong as you are."

"You don't need to be strong. It'll work. Ready? We'll do it together."

"Gimme a sec." Bear thought he heard grunting before Trent added, "Ready."

"One, two, three...." Bear leaned back at the same time as he pushed his foot forward, using all the strength in both his legs and his arms to put pressure on the lace and the tape. After just a few seconds, the tape snapped and he jerked backward with a grunt of his own.

"It worked!" Trent cried. "Holy moly, it worked!"

"Hate to say I told you so." Bear stood up, reaching out with both hands until he found Trent's slim frame in the darkness. "It's good to see you kid," Bear said, pulling Trent in for a hug.

"You mean it's good to *not* see me," Trent replied.

Chuckling, Bear shook his head. "Actually, despite your ugly mug, I'd prefer to be seeing you right now," he said, his eyes still trying desperately to fix on anything except darkness. Reaching out, squeezing Trent's shoulders, he added, "Are you hurt?"

"Nah, I'm good, PB. Apart from being alone in the dark thinking I was going to be murdered for the past who knows how many hours."

"Right." Bear shook his head. "About that… you better tell me what the heck happened."

**Get your copy of *Collapsed World*
Available June 14, 2023
(Available for pre-order now)
www.GraceHamiltonBooks.com**

Burned World

BLURB

The apocalypse is over. But the struggle for survival has only just begun...

A hard-won peace has been earned by the McDonald family's Georgia settlement, Hickory Falls. The rural community offers shelter, food, and safety. At least for now...

But in the aftermath of the solar flare, and the fall of the old world, danger takes many forms. It begins with a drought that threatens crops. Then a flood of refugees arrives, driven from their homes by a raging wildfire. They've lost everything, and the inferno is spreading.

Taking in the dispossessed means more mouths to feed—but it also means willing hands to do vital work. And one refugee in particular has valuable skills. Greyson was a firefighter, and he's got a plan to make Hickory Falls safe from the encroaching fire.

But there's something a little off about the man. Beth, the McDonald matriarch, doesn't trust him—though she can't say why. But, like it or not, he's part of the community now.

Will his preparations save Hickory Falls? Or plunge the community into fiery doom...

**Get your copy of *Burned World*
Available October 11, 2023
(Available for Pre Order Now!)
www.GraceHamiltonBooks.com**

BLURB

Family comes first—and he'll do whatever it takes to protect his from the looming storm.

Even before becoming a husband and father, safety had been Shane McDonald's priority for most of his forty-five years. As a nuclear engineer, it's his responsibility to keep the Sequoyah Nuclear Plant functioning at optimum levels to avoid what protesters fear most—a meltdown.

But when a coronal mass ejection from the sun wipes out power across the globe, stopping a nuclear chain reaction is no longer his primary concern.

Now Shane must trek across hundreds of miles to ensure the safety of his loved ones in a world rapidly disintegrating into lawlessness. Yet with few functioning automobiles and a blind teenage daughter to protect, it'll require careful planning to reach his prepper mother-in-law's and reunite with his family.

His wife has her hands full as well. When her brother's chemo drip suddenly stops working and her son gets stuck in the hospital elevator, all Jodi McDonald wants is the security of her husband's steady presence. But with a weakened brother and inexperienced son to look after, Jodi must remain strong amid the chaos and help guide them to her mother's.

However, even the best laid plans go awry as the miles stretch out between them. Supply thefts run rampant. Those who have necessities prey on those who don't. Minds broken by hardship kill on sight.

But the fatal mistake comes when thugs threaten the McDonald's little girl.

Shane must find the strength to do the unthinkable—or watch his family suffer the consequences.

Grab your copy of *Crumbling World* (Surviving the End Book One) from
www.GraceHamiltonBooks.com

EXCERPT

Chapter One

Violet must have sensed the furious crowd gathered in front of the gate. In the rearview mirror, Shane saw her sit up straighter and cock her head to one side. Ruby, her black lab guide dog, responded to the sudden change in her body language and looked at her with concern. Roughly two dozen people had gathered in a grassy area alongside the entry road to the Sequoyah Nuclear Plant, some of them carrying neatly stenciled signs as they marched back and forth. On the other side of the road two police officers stood watching in front of their patrol car.

"Dad, what's going on?" Violet said. "I can hear a crowd of people. It sounds like they're chanting."

He hadn't intended to tell her about the protestors. He had been hoping to avoid having to explain to his daughter why people were protesting his place of work on Take Your Child to Work Day. She was fourteen, but she was also somewhat naïve. Shane had perhaps sheltered her too much as a child, waiting to protect her from danger, from bullies, from so many possible problems, particularly because of her disability. This had only recently become difficult, as she began to push back, growing into a questioning teen who would no longer accept easy answers.

"Just some people," he said. "Don't worry."

As the car drew up alongside the protestors, the words of their chant became clear.

"Shut it down! Shut it down! Shut it down!"

Ruby had been sprawled across the back seat, but she rose now and placed her head on Violet's lap. Some would have mistaken this for a gesture of affection. Shane recognized it as a protective move.

"Why are they saying that?" Violet asked, pushing her sunglasses up the bridge of her nose. "Is something wrong? They sound angry."

Trying to ignore the hateful stares of the protestors, Shane slowed as he approached the guard station next to the front gate. He fumbled in his shirt pocket for his work ID, trying to think of the best way to explain the situation to his daughter. Violet tended to think the best of people, and he didn't want her to lose that optimism.

"They're just exercising their first amendment rights," he said. "Freedom of speech is a beautiful thing, even if the things being said are questionable."

"So they're protesting the power plant?" she asked.

"Well…yes," he replied, hoping she would leave it at that.

"That happens a lot here, huh?" she said. "A lot of people protest?"

"No, only occasionally. Generally, when we make the news for some reason or another."

"Why are they so mad this time? Did your company do something wrong?"

"They're upset because of the talk about adding a third reactor to the plant. Our service area is growing, and we could use another reactor, but as soon as it hit the news, people in the community started complaining. I imagine they organized some kind of protest gathering on social media, and here they are. It's fine. People are entitled to voice their concerns." He flashed his ID to the guard, who gave him an anxious smile and waved him through the open gate. The parking lot beyond was emptier than usual. At two minutes to four in the afternoon, they were smack-dab in the middle of a shift change. Had the protestors planned it that way, hoping to catch the bulk of the second shift workers as they pulled into the gate? It seemed likely. "If you ask me, they're being rather alarmist. People like this, I don't think they get it."

"They don't get what, Dad?" Violet asked.

He carefully considered his words before answering. Would his daughter think less of him if she understood the controversial nature of his chosen industry? "Well, Violet, sweetheart, nuclear energy is the cleanest and safest form of energy in the world—hands down, no question—but the word *nuclear* makes some people nervous. They assume radiation is seeping into the environment and creating three-eyed fish in the river."

Violet laughed at that. "Is it?"

"No, of course not. The radiation is fully contained."

Ahead, the vast gray cooling towers rose on either side of a domed containment building, billowing steam into a crisp late-April sky. Shane could see the curve of the Tennessee River where it slipped behind the plant in a broad arc. It was a sight that never failed to impress him, even after these many years, and he wished his daughter could enjoy it. As he pulled into the closest row of parking spaces, he considered ways he might convey the majesty of this place to her.

"Dad," she said, "we talked about nuclear power in our science class at school. Our teacher said nuclear power plants are dangerous because if they overheat, they can go into a meltdown. She said meltdowns have happened before, and they hurt a lot of people, even poisoned whole cities. Is that true? Could it happen here?"

"It's true. But did your teacher mention that more people die in coal mines *every year* than have ever died from nuclear meltdowns?" Shane said.

Violet persisted. "But a meltdown could happen here?"

Shane grunted unhappily. "That would require a very severe accident."

"But they've happened before," Violet said. "At Chernobyl in the Ukraine, and somewhere in Japan. One even happened in America, she said, at a place called Three Mile Island."

"Don't worry," he said. "Something like that is not going to happen here. The Chernobyl accident was mostly caused by the poor design of RBMK nuclear power reactors. We don't have that problem here. And Fukushima in Japan was caused by a tsunami, which probably isn't going to happen in the mountains of Tennessee. We're safe."

"But how do you know for sure?" Violet asked.

"Because I'm a nuclear engineer," he replied. "It's my job to know. It's my job to keep everyone safe, and I will. I will keep us safe."

"Promise?" Violet said.

"Promise."

The hallways were emptier than usual because of the shift change, but they met Landon just outside the control room. He was coming from the direction of the break room, his sleek black wheelchair making its gentle *whirring* sound. It had wheels with fat spokes that were slanted inward, a heavily padded seat and backrest, and a sturdy frame. As Landon had explained in the past, it was technically an athletic wheelchair, but he'd gained an affinity for them during his years of playing wheelchair basketball. He was broad-shouldered and strong, a former athlete with a well-built upper body. His legs had atrophied from spina bifida, but this had rarely been an issue on the job.

"Hey there, buddy," Landon said, when he spotted Shane rounding the corner. "I don't usually beat you to the office. What's the holdup?"

"I brought a guest with me this morning," Shane said, "so watch your salty language today."

"What are you talking about?" Landon replied. "I haven't even said my first four letter word of the day."

Shane shuffled slowly down the hall, holding his daughter's hand and guiding her. She came somewhat reluctantly, her other hand sliding along the wall. Passing through security had made her nervous—the great hum and hiss of the metal detector, x-ray machine, and radiation monitor—and she kept fiddling with the small radiation monitoring device hanging around her neck. Like the workers, she had been given an orange hardhat, and it was slightly too big for her head, pushing against the rims of her sunglasses.

To make matters far worse, security had insisted she leave Ruby behind. They'd made a place for her beloved black lab in the security office, but Violet had balked at the idea. It was Shane's fault. He'd pulled strings to get approval for Violet to come to work with him—no easy feat—but he'd forgotten to get clearance for Ruby.

That'll put a damper on the day, he thought.

Fortunately, Violet knew Landon well—he was practically family—so when she heard his voice, she relaxed a bit.

"Hey there, Vivi," Landon said. Only Landon could get away with calling her Vivi. "Where's your furry sidekick? I've never seen the two of you apart." He was particularly fond of the dog.

"They wouldn't let me bring her into the building," Violet said. "Even though she's a trained guide dog, they said it's not safe to bring an animal—any animal—into the plant, so she's sitting back there by herself."

"Not by herself," Shane said gently. "The security team will take good care of her, and we can check on her from time to time. We'll bring her something to eat during my lunch break."

"I don't know what they're afraid of," Violet said. "She never bites, and she doesn't get into anything. She doesn't even bark unless I'm in trouble. If we brought her inside, she would sit quietly and mind her own business all day long, except for pee breaks."

"It's just company protocol," Shane said. "Sorry, I should have tried to clear it first. I didn't realize it would be a problem."

"Don't you worry about it, Violet," Landon said. "I won't let this injustice stand. I'll file a formal complaint. It's not nice separating a kid from her loyal sidekick. If we have to take this all the way to the board of directors, so be it. Policy must be rewritten."

Shane shook his head at Landon. "It's fine. It's only for a few hours. Ruby will be okay. We'll check on her at lunchtime, get her something to eat, take her potty, and everything will be okay."

"She doesn't know that," Violet said. "She doesn't know we're coming back at lunchtime." Finally, Violet shrugged and rolled her head back on her shoulders. When she did, the orange hardhat almost fell off, and she had to grab it. "Oh well, nothing we can do about it, I guess. I'll give her an extra treat after we get home tonight."

"There you go," Shane said. "Great idea."

"I don't know why you wanted to come here anyway, kid," Landon said. "Should've gone to work with your mom at the CDC. You know your dad's job is incredibly boring, right?"

"Dad says his job is to keep everyone safe," Violet said.

"He's not wrong." Landon turned and wheeled toward the control room door, beckoning for them to follow. "But you'd be surprised how boring it is keeping everyone safe."

"Now, now," Shane said, laying a hand lightly on his daughter's shoulder. "Don't undersell the experience, Landon. She's been looking forward to this."

"All I'm saying is you should have gone with your mom," Landon said. "She works with diseases. She's battling deadly viruses on the daily, keeping world-devouring pandemics at bay with nothing but grit and determination."

"That's not exactly true," Shane said. "She does have a lot of grit and determination, though, I'll give you that."

"Centers for Disease Control. That's her place of employment, right? Disease *control*, man. They're protecting us from mutating Ebola and bio-engineered smallpox. Those are the real dangers right there, not some silly old nuclear power plant. Nothing exciting happens here."

"Dad said yes first," Violet said.

"I did," Shane said. "Plus, your mom is technically a statistician for the CDC. She's not battling bio-engineered smallpox, but they do work to prevent diseases. He's right about that."

"It's fine," Violet said. "Except for poor Ruby, I don't mind coming here. I can visit Mom's place next time."

The curve of a long green console took up most of the center of the control room, its surface covered in a complex array of gauges, screens, buttons, and knobs. A low hum filled the room. Violet reacted upon entering the room, perking up and turning her head first one way and then the other.

"The air is different in here," she said. "Feels kind of weird. Sort of electric, if that makes sense."

"Lots and lots of warm electronics," Landon said, wheeling himself up to the console and leaning in close to one of the monitors. "That's what you feel. It kind of smells plasticky, doesn't it?"

"Yeah," Violet replied.

Landon's elbow crutches were leaning against the end of the console. He kept them close, but he preferred using the wheelchair. When Shane took a seat, they started to slide so he caught them and set them on the floor. As Landon began cycling through system menus, Shane called his daughter over, took her right hand, and laid it on the console beside his keyboard.

"You feel that?" he asked. "That's my computer. I spend a whole lot of time at this computer."

"I can almost see it," she said. "The screen is bright right now, isn't it?"

"That's right. The starting screen is a light blue color."

Though Violet was visually impaired, Shane knew she could perceive light. She described bright lights as vague, distant blobs. She could also tell when she was in a completely dark room. Beyond that, she was incapable of perceiving shapes or colors.

"We monitor every system in the station from this room." Shane turned to Landon. "In fact, we can pretty much determine everything that's happening from right here, and we can call other departments if we need to talk to them."

"On rare occasions, we even leave the room," Landon said.

"That's true," Shane said. "In fact, I was thinking about giving her a tour of the facility when the rest of the staff get here. She could meet some of the department heads and hear what they do. What do you think?"

"Sorry, pal," Landon replied. "After the software upgrade, we've got to run through the rest of those scenarios this morning. The tour will have to wait until after lunch."

"Oh, man, I thought we finished those yesterday."

"Not even close," Landon said. "They're being especially comprehensive this time."

Shane guided his daughter's hand to the next seat, and she sat down.

"Sorry, sweetheart, I'll take you on a tour a little later," Shane said. "Just hang out here for a bit while we get some work done. Do you need a drink or anything? I could run to the break room and get you something."

"I'm fine, Dad," Violet replied, feeling the edge of the console and resting her forearms against a spot that was clear of buttons, gauges, or knobs. "Don't worry about me. Just do your work. I don't want to be a bother."

"You're never a bother," he said.

"Brace yourself, Vivi," Landon said. "Running through end-of-the-world scenarios while pretending they can never happen gets dull after a few hours."

Shane almost shushed his friend, but it was too late. The words were out. Violet pushed her sunglasses up the bridge of her nose and frowned.

"End of the world?" she said. "What do you mean by that?"

"Just scenarios," Shane said. "Not real life. We're testing a recent software upgrade by seeing how it responds to theoretical situations."

"What kind of situations?" Violet asked.

But at that moment, a harsh squawk came out of one of the tiny speakers beside Shane's computer console as a window popped up on his screen. A red message flashed brightly: CORONAL MASS EJECTION EVENT IMMINENT TWO MINUTES. It flashed a few times before he registered what he was reading.

"Coronal mass ejection," he said. "Landon, did you start the simulation already?"

Landon leaned back in his chair to get a look at Shane's screen. "I haven't done anything," he said. "I haven't pressed a single button yet." A two-way radio sat near the edge of the console, and he grabbed it. "Let me see if I can find out what's going on. Maybe they're running some kind of remote drill. Is that possible? I mean, it can't be real."

"If it was real they would have given us a lot more than two minutes warning," Shane said, feeling a flutter of anxiety despite his words. "It has to be some kind of test."

"Okay, let me see if I can get hold of someone," Landon said. "If it's an unplanned simulation from on high, I'm going to pitch a fit. We have enough scenarios to run through without the higher-ups messing around. Sometimes, they're too clever for their own good."

"Dad?"

Violet managed one plaintive word before the power went out. Every light and screen went dark, and Shane heard cooling fans winding down.

"Well, that's not good," Landon said. "We just lost everything."

Shane had been trained to handle this kind of scenario—he knew the steps—but having his daughter present changed everything. He could hear her panicked breathing, the squeak of her chair as she fidgeted. It was distracting. He wanted to comfort her, but he also knew they had to act fast.

"Dad, what's happening? What's a coronal...whatever?"

"Coronal mass ejection," Landon said. "A massive burst of plasma from the sun. Causes an electromagnetic pulse which can knock out the power grid, fry electronics, and do all sorts of bad, bad stuff. I'm going to take a wild guess here and say it's not a simulation."

The control room was quiet, too quiet, but Shane heard shouting in the hallway—panic throughout the building just as the second shift was arriving. Terrible timing.

"Backup power's not coming on," he said. "Could the CME have taken out the generators?"

"Doubt it," Landon said in the darkness. He sounded breathless. "If it's a CME, the backup generators might be fine. They're just old-fashioned diesel engines. No electronics in them to be fried. We'll have to start them manually though."

Shane was still half-convinced it was a test, but he didn't like the nervous edge in Landon's voice. The man was usually so calm and collected.

"I'll take care of it," Shane said. He started to rise from his chair, but Violet's hand clamped down on his arm.

"No, Dad. Don't leave. I'm scared."

"It's okay, honey. I just need—"

He heard the whir of Landon's wheelchair. "I've got it. You two stay here. I know the way, and I can move faster than either of you. We need to act quickly."

"No, I'll come with you," Shane said. "It might require two of us to get the generators working. Violet, you can come, too. I won't leave you here by yourself."

"Are we in trouble?" she said. "What happens if you don't get them working?"

"If the main power is knocked out, the control rods drop into the core, and the reactor is flooded with water to drive the temperature down," Shane said. "That can't happen until we get the backup generators on, but we will. It'll just take a minute."

"You're talking about a meltdown," Violet said, her voice quavering, her hand squeezing his arm tighter. "That's it, isn't it?"

"No, no, we have…plenty of time to get things under control." He had to force the words out. *But it's a test, right? It has to be? If it's a real CME, they would have warned us a lot sooner.*

Shane heard the hiss of the control room door as Landon heaved it open and wheeled into the hallway. Shane rose and grabbed Violet's hand. Then he followed after Landon.

He wanted to believe they had plenty of time. He almost did believe it, but he'd never heard Landon sound so scared.

Grab your copy of *Crumbling World* (Surviving the End Book One) from www.GraceHamiltonBooks.com

WANT MORE?

WWW.GRACEHAMILTONBOOKS.COM

Made in the USA
Las Vegas, NV
01 November 2023

80049640R10193